**"And that is what you want?" he asked softly.
"A stranger in your bed?"**

Somehow he managed to make this act of rebellion sound incredibly pathetic. It was infuriating.

"It is," she insisted, with as much pride as she could muster.

"Then may I make a suggestion?"

Her breath caught at the unexpected question. Oh, how she longed to deny him, but the fact was she was far too curious. "If you must," she answered with studied coolness.

Captain Harris stared at her for an endless moment as the scant air between them warmed. Until the furious beating of her heart filled her ears. Georgiana inhaled the rich scent of his skin, unmasked by cologne. As she leaned forward a little, his breathing quickened. "Take me instead."

Praise for Emily Sullivan and the League of Scoundrels

A Rogue to Remember

"The literary charms of Sullivan's superbly written debut are many, including a full cast of deftly nuanced characters, an exquisitely evoked Italian setting that would impress E. M. Forster, love scenes that deliver both emotional intensity and lush sensuality, and vivacious writing enhanced by ample measures of wit." —*Booklist*, Starred Review

The Rebel and the Rake

"One particular gem of a new voice is Emily Sullivan, whose nineteenth-century tales of romance and intrigue are designed to keep a reader on the edge of their seat....*The Rebel and the Rake* will steal a reader's heart before they even realize it's gone, entangling them in the storytelling with much the same stealth as Rafe's investigations." —*Entertainment Weekly*

"After wowing readers with her superb debut, rising historical romance star Sullivan returns with another entrancing addition to her League of Scoundrels series that brilliantly showcases her mastery of deep characterization as well as her gift for crafting a wit-infused plot that effectively threads the needle between desire and danger without dropping a single stitch." —*Booklist*, Starred Review

"The subterfuge provides an intense backdrop that only enhances the complex romance between Sullivan's intelligent, progressive protagonists. Readers will be taken by independent Sylvia's quest for love and companionship." —*Publishers Weekly*

THE HELLION

AND THE HERO

THE **HELLION**
AND THE **HERO**

A LEAGUE OF SCOUNDRELS NOVEL

EMILY SULLIVAN

FOREVER
New York Boston

Forever
Hachette Book Group
1290 Avenue of the Americas, New York, NY 10104
read-forever.com
twitter.com/readforeverpub

First Edition: August 2022

Forever is an imprint of Grand Central Publishing. The Forever name and logo are trademarks of Hachette Book Group, Inc.

The publisher is not responsible for websites (or their content) that are not owned by the publisher.

The Hachette Speakers Bureau provides a wide range of authors for speaking events. To find out more, go to www.hachettespeakersbureau.com or call (866) 376-6591.

ISBNs: 978-1-5387-5357-6 (mass market), 978-1-5387-5358-3 (ebook)

Printed in the United States of America

OPM

10 9 8 7 6 5 4 3 2 1

For the hellions.

Acknowledgments

There is writing a book, and then there is writing a book during a pandemic with a baby. I have now done both of these things, and the latter certainly could not have happened without the help of my parents, my in-laws, and my husband, who cared for our little hellion so I could lock myself away and hang out with made-up people for hours at a time. Thank you all so much. Many thanks to Junessa Viloria for still believing in me even after reading the initial draft of this story. Thank you to Amanda Jain for her continued support. Thanks also to Elizabeth Sampson for reading an early draft, repeatedly assuring me it wasn't terrible, and for always responding to my angsty texts. Thanks to Rebelle Island and the Slogging thread in particular for keeping me motivated. Writing is a lot less lonely with you ladies! Thank you to everyone who has blogged, tweeted, or posted about their love for this series. Your enthusiasm for my books has kept me going this last year. Thanks again to my friends and family for their enduring and enthusiastic support. And thank you to my brain for sticking with me. I'm so sorry I put you through this. You can rest now.

THE HELLION

AND THE HERO

CHAPTER ONE

———◆———

Y ou simply *had* to have the office with a view of the river, no matter how distant," Captain Henry Harris muttered to himself as he slowly mounted the stairs to the top floor of a building in a quiet corner off the Strand. It had been a more fanciful indulgence to be sure, but after spending so much of his adult life at sea, Henry found even the most fleeting glimpse of water comforting. That combined with an enticingly low monthly rent had made him dismiss the four flights of stairs. It wasn't much of an inconvenience—usually. But today he wasn't so lucky.

Henry paused to massage his knee before entering his office. If his secretary, Miss Delia Swanson, caught him doing so, she would only make a fuss. It was being particularly bothersome after he had spent most of the last week tailing a woman suspected of being unfaithful to her husband. Henry hadn't uncovered any evidence that suggested the lady in question had a lover, only that she appeared to have an excessive amount of time to spend in department stores. Privately, Henry concluded that his client would be better off actually talking with his wife rather than hiring a private investigator. But in his experience, clients rarely wanted his advice. Just results.

He released a breath as the ache subsided and opened the door marked HARRIS INVESTIGATIONS.

As usual, Miss Swanson was already at her desk, typing away. She looked up at his entrance and flashed him a bright smile. "Good morning, Captain Harris! How are you today?"

"Fine. Thank you," Henry grumbled as he leaned his cane against her desk to hand her his coat and hat. No one should be that chipper at half past eight in the morning, but the young lady's incessant cheerfulness had been one of the reasons Henry hired her, even though it never failed to make him feel like an old curmudgeon by comparison.

"I've left the morning's post on your desk. Will you be wanting coffee?"

"God, yes."

Henry retrieved his cane and made his way to his office. No doubt Miss Swanson's sharp eyes had already noticed he was favoring his right leg more than usual. Her attention to detail was an admirable trait in a secretary, but one that caused him a considerable amount of grief. It had been nearly two years since he had injured his leg during a mission gone awry while serving the Crown abroad, and though he had initially balked at using a cane, Henry had grown quite attached to it—not to mention that it came in rather handy when he found himself in a rough part of town.

Henry sat down heavily in his chair and glanced up as

Miss Swanson breezed into the room with a tray bearing a shiny coffee pot, a cup, and a plate of something that promised to be delicious.

"Maude made a batch of her famous scones last night specially for you, sir, after I told her how much you enjoyed the last ones," she explained unprompted. Maude Covington was Delia's flatmate, among other things.

He frowned as she set down the tray and began pouring the first of the many cups of coffee he needed to get through the day. "She shouldn't have done that."

"Oh, come now," she said with a wink. "Everyone likes to be spoiled a little." Her hazel eyes sparkled as she passed him his cup.

Henry took it and began riffling through the pile of mail on his desk. "Not me."

Miss Swanson laughed a little and returned to her desk. She was an attractive girl, and more than one client had assumed she was his wife, which Henry was always quick to correct. Besides, even if he had been interested, Delia was perfectly content to keep company with Maude. Together, the two women practically tortured Henry with their considerateness and constant stream of invitations to Friday evening gatherings with their eclectic group of friends, Sunday roasts, and holiday fetes.

One of these days he would have to put a stop to it. But until then he would suffer with a competent secretary and a stream of baked goods.

Henry set down the mail and took a sip of coffee before biting into a buttery scone. He couldn't help the little moan of delight that rumbled through him.

"I heard that!" Miss Swanson called out from her desk.

He responded by picking up his cane and using it to push the door shut. It was time for a little morning privacy. The muffled sound of Miss Swanson diligently typing up his reports wafted through the door, but Henry had come to find that comforting. A busy secretary meant business was good. He resumed his perusal of the mail: several bills, a letter of thanks from a satisfied client, and something with a postmark from Brighton. Henry didn't need to see the return address. He recognized the handwriting immediately. As he ripped open the envelope and scanned the short note, his chest grew tighter and tighter. Then he set it down and stared out the window.

The contents of the note were much the same as the one he received two months ago, and the one that came three months before that. It began with giving thanks for his previous generosity and extolling his virtue as a man of honor before getting to the point: His cousin Dale had lost yet another job, and his wife, Deborah, the writer, was again appealing to him for a loan. They both knew Henry would never get his money back, yet they kept up the pretense in their correspondence to save her the embarrassment that came from asking for help. The trouble was that Henry had already lent Cousin Dale nearly twenty pounds this year alone, a not insignificant sum, especially given that he had opened his business only a little more than a year ago. All in all, things were going well. Though clients had initially been attracted by his status as a naval hero, Henry had quickly earned a reputation as a thorough and discreet investigator. But he wasn't exactly rolling in excess funds, and this could be a precarious business. He needed to be careful. Conservative.

And yet, despite all these perfectly salient points, Henry still heard his mother's voice chastising him. Though she had been gone for nearly half a decade, her remonstrations were still very much alive in his mind: *But my dear, you must help your cousin Dale. It isn't his fault he drinks. His father was the same way, bless him. Think of his poor wife and all those children.*

Henry bit back a sigh and picked up the note. Deborah had added a postscript asking for twice the amount he sent last time, as their youngest child needed an operation. It had been years since Henry had visited the Brighton branch of his late father's family. Back then Dale had a decent job at a tire factory nearby and three boisterous children, with a fourth on the way. In truth, Henry had been a little envious of their obvious happiness, both with life and each other. But then the factory had closed without warning, as the owners discovered they could triple their profits if they moved operations abroad. Dale had never found a comparable position and thus began his slow descent into drink. Henry wasn't even sure Dale knew that his wife wrote to him. He glanced at the unopened bills on the desk and rubbed his eyes. There was never any doubt that he would send them the money. Henry just didn't know how he would scrape it together this time.

The comforting tap-tap-tapping of Delia's typewriter suddenly ceased, and he heard her speaking. Someone must have entered the office. Henry quickly set aside the mail and moved his cane to a more covert spot.

Delia entered the office. "A Mr. Fox is here to see you, sir," she said as she handed him a card. "He doesn't have an appointment."

Henry frowned as he took it, noting that it was made of heavy cardstock and embossed in glossy ink. Fox was a common enough last name; perhaps this man wasn't—

But Henry hadn't time to convince himself, as Reginald Fox trailed behind Delia.

"Hello there! Do you remember me? We met at Lady Harrington's house once. I was there visiting my sister during her season."

Georgiana Fox.

Henry was caught off guard, both by the man's sudden appearance in his office and the unwelcome reminder of that long ago afternoon. He rarely thought of his failed attempt on the London marriage mart eight years before. Had not allowed himself to. He exchanged a subtle look with Delia, who did a decent job of holding back a smile at his undoubtedly shocked expression, and she quickly excused herself.

He glanced at the young man before straightening a stack of blank envelopes that most certainly didn't need it. "Of course. How are you?"

"Quite well, actually," he said with a chuckle and took the seat on the other side of the desk. "It's been ages, and I was barely out of short pants when last we met."

Henry met Reginald's gaze. Along with similar shades of dark blond hair, the Fox siblings all had sapphire-blue eyes. The effect was momentarily unsettling. The young man who sat before him had once been a gangly youth Henry had played several games of chess with. But he had grown into his height and acquired an air of confidence that was usually accompanied by financial success.

"I know you are a busy man, so I won't keep you too

long this morning," he began before turning sheepish. "It's just that I'm in a bit of...a pickle."

Henry's shoulders relaxed a little at Reginald's visible discomfort. This was personal for him, then. Good.

"What sort of pickle?" Henry silently ran through the usual: an unhappy mistress, an unpaid gambling debt, a wayward wife. But Reginald wore no ring...

"It's my sister," he burst out. "I think she's in trouble."

Reginald Fox had three sisters. That didn't necessarily mean—

"It's Georgiana. Lady Arlington," he added unnecessarily.

Henry pulled his hands back from the envelopes and placed them on his lap, where Reginald couldn't see them tighten into fists. "What makes you think that?"

"I heard from her secretary that she has gotten a few upsetting messages recently. After the death of her husband about a year and a half ago, she inherited two garment factories my father once owned. They had been part of her dowry, you see."

Henry recalled that the late Mr. Fox had been a stock-broker but invested in a number of different businesses around London.

"My sister decided they needed to be improved. She's become something of a reformist," Reginald said with a little laugh. "At first we all thought it was a splendid idea. It kept her busy. Happy, even. Especially since she and her husband never did have any children."

Henry shifted in his seat. Though he had taken great pains to ignore any information about the Arlingtons over the years, it had been nearly impossible since returning to London. It seemed that everyone knew the viscount had died without an heir, leaving his beautiful younger wife a wealthy widow.

"Anyway," Reginald continued, "she's made a name for herself with all the changes she's implemented. And her workers love her for it. She pays them the highest wages in the business and enforces safe conditions. I suspect she aims to build a little empire."

"That's impressive," Henry said reluctantly.

Reginald flashed him a smile. "Don't let her beauty and perfect manners fool you. My sister is quite industrious."

Henry grunted. He would *not* comment on that.

"In any case, not everyone has welcomed her reforms."

"Her competitors," Henry guessed.

Reginald nodded. "They complain that her changes will put them out of business, but it's all nonsense. They want to be able to continue exploiting people without consequence, and my sister is making that increasingly difficult. She's planning to expand her operations, and it's caused talk. Plain old gossip I can abide by, but I've been informed that some of it is far more nefarious. These men are growing more disgruntled by the day."

"Has she been threatened directly? Aside from the messages?"

"Not that I know of," Reginald admitted. "But I think she's holding things back, so as not to worry any of us."

"You mean, your other siblings?"

Reginald nodded. From what Henry remembered, the five boisterous Fox siblings had been uncommonly close. One might even be tempted to call them *meddling*. Their father was usually tied up in his work, so when their mother died a few years after Ollie, the eldest, was born, Georgiana had stepped in as a de facto parent, though she had been little more than a child herself. But that had been years ago.

And she is no longer Georgiana to you.

Henry felt a slight tremor in his hand and refocused his attention on Reginald.

"Louisa, our youngest sister, has been particularly anxious. Her husband is related to one of Georgie's rivals and says there's good reason for caution, but she won't back down. Georgie's convinced she can pressure these men into changing their businesses for the better, but she doesn't understand that they don't share the same motivations."

Henry tilted his head. "What do you mean? For success? Power?"

Reginald turned serious. "Greed. Her improvements have come at a personal cost. One the other factory owners will never willingly make." He let out a breath. "It could all be nothing, of course. Idle threats from men railing against a swiftly changing world. But I'd sleep a hell of a lot better if I knew. And I've heard from a few other fellows that you are discreet," he added with a sheepish look.

"She doesn't know you're here, then," Henry supplied.

Reginald shook his head. "Georgie thinks I'm overreacting. Ever since her husband died, she's changed. I'm glad she's found something to do of course, but... well, she's become a bit reckless."

Henry ignored the voice in his head loudly demanding to know the details and instead maintained his impassive expression. "It will be difficult for me to uncover all the necessary information without Lady Arlington's cooperation."

"But not impossible," Reginald pointed out. "I'll pay you

twice your usual daily rate. And a ten-pound bonus if you uncover any actual threats."

"You're joking."

"Hardly." Reginald grinned. "My sister isn't the only one in the family that inherited our father's business acumen, God rest him. The past few years have been very good to me."

Henry pursed his lips as his gaze drifted to Deborah's letter. That would certainly help solve his financial issues...

Absolutely not.

He was not nearly in so desperate a state to consider taking on this case. "Why me?" he asked after a long moment. "Surely I don't need to explain to you why this might be rather awkward, for both myself and your sister."

Reginald hadn't been *that* young during their chess games. He must have known Henry had called on Georgiana, along with scores of others. And that she had chosen someone else.

The young man gave him a considering look. "I anticipated that, and I won't bother you for any of the particulars. Whatever occurred between the two of you is none of my business, but..." Reginald, the bastard, hesitated. "You should know that she always spoke highly of you." Henry realized he had been holding his breath. "And you have a reputation as a man of honor," he continued before the moment could turn awkward. "Why, you're a national *hero*."

Henry waved a hand. "That was nothing. And completely irrelevant here."

Reginald raised an eyebrow. "I'd hardly call coming to the aid of two innocent countrymen and then escaping from a Turkish prison nothing."

Only because you don't know the truth.

But Henry kept that thought to himself. It was part of his agreement with the Crown: He would dutifully play the role of the noble hero in public in return for being released from naval intelligence service. Forever.

It was times like these that he questioned whether he got the raw end of the deal.

"You don't need to give me an answer right now," Reginald went on. "In fact, I'd rather you didn't. Take some time to think it over and let me know by tomorrow evening."

Henry had already made up his mind, but he nodded anyway. If he said no now, Reginald would only try his damnedest to convince him otherwise. The two men then rose and shook hands before Reginald left.

Once he was alone again, Henry sank back in his chair and looked out the window.

She always spoke highly of you.

That had to be a misunderstanding on Reginald's part. Or perhaps a lie to further cajole him into taking the case. Well, it wouldn't work. There was absolutely no reason why she would have *ever* discussed him with her brother. With anyone.

But what if...

"No." The sharp, single word echoed in the silence of his office.

And that was to be the end of it.

* * *

The next morning Henry arrived at his office slightly later than usual. He had wasted long hours alone in his bed staring at the ceiling and recalling that fateful night he had met Georgiana Fox at Lady Harrington's ball.

Henry had been hiding out on the terrace, nervous as hell and second-guessing his decision to come to London for the season. A lieutenant in the Royal Navy didn't earn much, especially since he supported both his mother and his sister. His mother had come down in the world when she married Henry's father, and it irked Henry to no end that they were considered someone else's poor relations. Now he hoped to do something about it. Namely, marry the wealthiest woman he could find and elevate his family's social status permanently. It made him no better than a scoundrel, but it meant his sister would be saved from the dull horrors of spinsterhood and Henry would never have to worry again about his mother spending the rent money on ribbons. He also hoped to get the increasingly persistent and wildly intimidating Commodore Perry from Naval Intelligence off his back, as he didn't like recruiting family men. But that meant Henry needed to go back into that ballroom and be charming. And Henry had never been very good at that.

It was in the midst of these thoughts that Georgiana Fox burst onto the terrace, golden-haired and swathed in fine silk, like one of his sister's fancy dolls brought to life—aside from her distressed expression, though she had quickly recovered once she noticed his presence. And that was all it took for Henry to begin to fall. And deeper still once she actually spoke. For unlike him, Georgiana Fox was quite good at being charming. Enough for Henry to mistake her interest as genuine when it hadn't been more than a silly flirtation that had gotten out of hand until she put a stop to it. Permanently.

Delia was already at her desk, of course, busily tapping away when he entered. She looked up and arched a dark eyebrow.

"My goodness, I was starting to think you wouldn't show," she teased.

"It's barely a quarter after nine, Delia," Henry groused.

"You've a visitor," she said brightly, not at all put off by his foul mood. "I stuck her in your office."

Henry glanced toward the closed door. He could just make out the shadow of a figure through the frosted window. "I thought I didn't have any morning appointments," he murmured, so the woman wouldn't overhear.

"You didn't. She was pacing outside when I arrived. In a right mood, too."

It was probably some disgruntled wife who had learned her husband had hired him to follow her. "What is her name?"

"She refused to give one. Just demanded to see you."

Henry sighed and removed his coat and hat. That was never a good sign.

"I don't suppose Maude made any more scones last night?"

Delia smiled and shook her head. "Sorry, sir. I'm afraid you'll just have to use your charm to placate this one."

God help him, then.

Henry plastered a smile on his face and made his way to the office. "I'm so sorry to keep you waiting," he began smoothly as he opened the door. If he was the first one to talk, he found it was easier to gain control of the conversation. The woman stood before the window, her profile illuminated by the morning light. At his entrance she turned toward him, and Henry stopped in his tracks. He blinked a few times and very nearly pinched his arm, but this was not a dream.

It was *her*.

All the air seemed to be wrenched from his lungs, and for a moment he worried he would fall dead away right there before Georgiana Fox.

No. *Lady Arlington.*

He had last seen her more than a year ago in Scotland, moments after she had learned of her beloved husband's death. As with everything else about her, he had been unable to forget the image of her sobbing in the arms of Sylvia Sparrow, who had gone on to marry his good friend Rafe Davies. But now there was no trace of the heartbreak that had been etched so clearly on her face that day. Lady Arlington faced him fully, her posture ramrod straight, and lifted her chin. She was dressed in half mourning: a deep purple coat trimmed in black velvet that hugged the enticing curves Henry was trying very hard not to linger on and an outrageously large matching hat with a gauzy black veil pulled back to reveal her luminous face. Henry guessed the ensemble was the height of fashion—and expense.

She looked marvelous, commanding, and mad as hell.

Her sapphire eyes, so like her brother's, fixed on him, and her frown deepened considerably.

Henry failed to ignore the significant twitch of interest below his waist. He had yet to move away from the door and still gripped the knob. For a very brief moment he considered leaving the room entirely. He, who had served on an active warship for over a decade, had gone undercover on countless occasions, and had survived an imprisonment, was nearly undone by the glare of a lady.

No. Not *just* a lady. The woman who had torn out his heart before tossing it aside to bleed out on the ground.

Henry gripped the knob even tighter before he drew the door closed, his gaze never leaving hers. *That was ages ago*, he reminded himself. Henry had been an idiotic young man then. One who had mistaken deep infatuation, heady lust, and unsated desire for the beginnings of love. And, most damning of all, had believed she felt the same.

The click of the lock echoed in the silent room, and he gave a low bow.

"Lady Arlington. To what do I owe the pleasure?"

"Spare me the empty pleasantries, Captain," she said crisply. "I am not a jilted wife who needs mollycoddling. You know why I'm here."

Henry swallowed hard, both loving and hating the sound of his elevated rank on her lips. He gestured to the chair before his desk. "Please. Sit."

She let out a huff before gliding over. Henry's eyes were riveted to her every movement. The woman turned crossing a room into a veritable art form. Only when she was safely seated did he leave his spot by the door. As he walked around his desk, he saw that she noticed his cane, but the usual look of exaggerated pity did not follow. Well, that was a welcome surprise. Henry had endured enough shallow condolences from people to last him several lifetimes.

He took his seat across from her and met her eyes again, while a not insignificant part of him enjoyed the blistering feel of her gaze. How long had it been since anyone inspired such a visceral reaction in him? Of course it would be her.

He suddenly wished for a desk twice as wide.

As if that would make a difference.

There should always be miles and miles between them, at the very least.

"Your brother told you of our meeting yesterday," he began.

"Not willingly, but yes. Reggie has always been wildly transparent. It didn't take long for him to admit that he had hired you to spy on me."

"I wouldn't quite put it that way," Henry demurred, but this was entirely the wrong approach.

She raised a bronze eyebrow. "Oh? How *exactly* would you put it then?" she asked with deadly sarcasm.

He could have told her then and there that he hadn't accepted the case. And had no intention of doing so. But he didn't.

"Well, I wouldn't call it spying. Your brother expressed worry over your safety and asked me to investigate any threats. Your anger is unfounded."

Unfortunately, this did not have the desired effect of placating her. "How dare you," she hissed. "You have no *right* to dictate how I should feel. And my brother should have come to me first. Not gone behind my back and hired you without my explicit consent."

Again, the voice in his head urged Henry to clarify that he had not taken the case. And again, Henry ignored it. "My apologies. I...I can see why that would be upsetting," he admitted.

Lady Arlington's expression softened ever so slightly before the frown returned even deeper than before. "Good. Then we understand each other." She began to rise. "I will tell Reggie that this was all a misunderstanding. Send any bill his visit and mine have incurred to my office," she said airily with a flick of her wrist, as if she were brushing off a piece of lint. Something worthless and insignificant. "I will leave the address with your secretary."

Perhaps if she hadn't been so high-handed Henry could have controlled himself, but like hell would he sit there and be roundly dismissed by her. The woman who had breezed through his life once before and left a trail of smoldering ash in her wake.

"I don't think so, my lady," he called out as she moved toward the door. Lady Arlington paused and glanced back at him over her shoulder. Though her eyes spoke only of distaste, Henry could not look away.

"Excuse me?"

He placed his palms on his desktop and rose. "I was hired by Reginald Fox, and I answer only to him. If you want this investigation called off, you will need to take that up with your brother."

Her mouth dropped open for a brief moment, and Henry felt a surge of delight. He had surprised her. It was pathetic how good it made him feel. "In any case, your cooperation won't be necessary. But if you want your life disrupted as little as possible, I suggest you stay at home for the next few days while I begin."

Lady Arlington's lush mouth tightened ever so slightly before she continued. "And why would I need to stay home?"

"Because then I won't have to follow you."

She shot him a cool glare before sweeping out of the room without another word, her exit punctuated by the slam of the door. Henry smiled as he took his seat and leaned back in his chair.

Lady Georgiana Arlington. Still as beautiful as ever. And still full of damnable pride.

Henry would take this case. He would investigate any threats made and ensure her safety for a pretty penny.

All while making it perfectly clear that her decision to marry for a title had not devastated him.

Not one bit.

CHAPTER TWO

———◆———

As Georgiana charged out of Captain Harris's office, her anger grew with every step until it threatened to split her right down the middle. It wasn't until she was safely ensconced in her carriage and had snapped the curtains shut that she had been able to focus on anything other than the bewildering mixture of heat and fury coursing through her. Since last evening when Reggie admitted his ridiculous scheme during a family supper with their sister Louisa and her husband, Georgiana had been consumed by hurt and embarrassment. No one understood why she was so upset by the mere mention of Captain Harris, and Georgiana had no desire to explain her past humiliation to them. How the man she had once fallen for so readily, so easily, had turned out to be nothing more than a callous fortune hunter. And now he actually planned to *pursue this case*.

Georgiana slumped against the velvet cushions. She had gone to his office that morning hoping to appeal to his sense of honor. And, all right, to indulge her curiosity. Like nearly everyone else in the country, she had read the scores of articles that had been published lauding his heroic actions in Turkey: how he had been on leave in Constantinople and intervened when a pair of innocent British architecture students mistakenly entered a military building and were accused of spying. Captain Harris had tried to explain the misunderstanding, but one was shot and killed in the struggle, while he and the other man were thrown in prison. Eventually Captain Harris mounted an escape to save his fellow countryman, who had fallen ill. They made it back to his ship, but the young man didn't survive. There was no doubt that he had acted bravely and deserved every inch of newsprint dedicated to praising his actions.

Her dear friend Sylvia had also spent some time with the captain, as he was a good friend of her husband, and spoke highly of him. Surely he could be reasoned with. And perhaps, in a very tiny corner of her heart, Georgiana wondered if that long ago spark could be revived once more. If perhaps she hadn't been deceived. If there really *had* been something between them. Something rare and precious.

When he had first stepped into his office, it was as if all the air had gone out of the room. He moved more slowly than she remembered but with a subtle, stately confidence that was undeniably attractive, and Georgiana could have sworn his amber eyes heated with an aching familiarity as they swept over her. But then he opened his mouth and acted as if *she* had inserted herself back into his life in the most invasive way possible. Where was the winsome young man she had met on her godmother's terrace all those years ago? The one who had so tempted her to turn her back on the expectations of her family?

She had come to London from Kent on a mission: secure a proposal from the most desirable bachelor she could find. It was her duty as the eldest daughter in her family. While other young ladies might have been appalled by such a prospect, Georgiana wasn't a romantic. Her father was a successful stockbroker, but he had five children, including three girls. And though Georgiana's mother had come from an old family with aristocratic roots, at the time of her parents' meeting they were living in genteel poverty. Mr. Fox had, unfortunately, married his wife for love, not money. That had led to a blissful home life for over a decade before she passed, but it meant that there wasn't much for the girls' dowries.

So it was up to Georgiana to pave the way for her younger sisters. If she made an advantageous marriage to a wealthy man, she could secure all their futures. Rather than consider what she might be giving up by participating in such a cynical scheme, Georgiana did what she had been doing all her life: She put her family first. And there was no better accomplice than her godmother, Lady Harrington, or Aunt Paloma, as she insisted on being called. She had come out the same season as Georgiana's mother and landed herself a fabulously wealthy, much older earl. The late Lord Harrington had been gone for many years now, but his legacy lived on in the two strapping sons that Aunt Paloma treated like princes. Since Peregrine, the eldest, was already engaged to a duke's daughter, Georgiana had initially thought she would be paired with Tobias, the younger son, but Aunt Paloma subtly hinted that she was saving him for a girl with much bluer blood than her own.

A more sensitive girl might have been upset, but Georgiana understood. To aristocrats marriage was a kind of game, one that required strategy and a fair bit of ruthlessness. Georgiana didn't consider herself particularly mercenary, but if it helped her family, she had no qualms about doing whatever it took to win.

And that had meant dancing with Viscount Arlington, who was nearly twenty years her senior. He was a handsome but dark and forbidding man who had barely looked at her until just before their waltz ended, when he leaned over and whispered in her ear. "Your godmother was right. Your fleshly charms more than make up for such a middling bloodline. I will call on you this week."

Georgiana had been too mortified to offer a reply other than a curtsy. Then she had blindly moved through the crush of bodies until she reached the terrace doors, which had been opened to let in the faint May breeze. Once outside she found a secluded corner and let out a heaving gasp of breath that wracked her entire body. She placed her palms against the stone balustrade that ringed the terrace and leaned forward, waiting for her blood to settle as the viscount's coarse words echoed in her ears.

And she was supposed to *rejoice* that such a beastly man wished to court her?

Never.

Never.

Georgiana inhaled a few deep breaths until the anger slowly subsided. It was true that her family was neither as old nor as illustrious as the viscount's, but she would not listen to such drivel. No man was worth that, no matter his wealth and social status. Even she had her limits. Tomorrow she would explain everything to Aunt Paloma and tell her how rude the viscount had been. Surely the woman would be just as offended as Georgiana. And then that would be the end of the man's courtship.

It *had* to be.

"Glad to see I'm not the only one who hates crowds," someone quipped.

Georgiana whipped her head to the side, where the darkened figure of a man stood in the corner. Her heart thundered in her chest. She hadn't even noticed him.

"You are all right, aren't you?" he asked. "Shall I get someone for you?"

Georgiana relaxed at the clear concern in his voice. He stepped into a sliver of light from the ballroom. His face was still mostly in shadow, but she could see that he was smartly dressed in a naval uniform.

She shook her head. "No, thank you. I'm fine." It sounded silly, but she felt safe in this man's presence. Safer than she had all evening.

"I'm Lieutenant Harris," he said, extending a hand. "Henry Harris."

Georgiana paused and stared at his gloved hand. It wasn't the done thing, shaking hands, especially at a ball. Especially with a stranger. But she found it charming. He seemed to realize his faux pas and began to pull back just as she had reached out.

Lieutenant Harris huffed a laugh and bowed instead. "Sorry. I don't know what I was thinking. I suppose I've spent too much time at sea."

"Yes, I'd imagine that is quite different from a London ballroom."

"You've no idea," he murmured. None of the other men she had met in London would have allowed such a slip. Or even admit to having ever experienced such a feeling. They were far too proud.

"Is this your first time at one?"

He laughed again. "Is it that obvious?"

Georgiana shrugged. "Not necessarily. I've been to five now and here I am."

"Only five," he teased. "This is your first season, then?"

"Yes."

"Well, I'm sure by the end you'll be a master."

Georgiana couldn't help the sigh that escaped her.

"I take it you aren't filled with excitement at the prospect?" Henry guessed.

She hesitated a moment. It should feel odd, discussing such things with a stranger, and yet she wanted to keep talking with him. "Not really," she admitted. "I was when I first came to London, but now..."

"You'd rather it was all over with?"

"In a way." But certainly not if it ended in an engagement to a man like the viscount. She let the cryptic comment hang in the air, as there were still some things she couldn't speak aloud.

Lieutenant Harris seemed to sense her reticence and changed the subject. "You still haven't told me your name. Or should we find your chaperone to introduce us? Isn't that how these things are done?"

"They are, but no. That won't be necessary." She suspected

Aunt Paloma would not approve of this untitled young man, no matter how solicitous he was. "I'm Miss Fox."

"Miss Fox," he repeated as a delicious shiver slid down her spine. "I suppose I'll have to wait for a formal introduction to learn your first name?"

Georgiana smiled and was just about to answer when someone came bustling onto the terrace.

"Georgie! There you are." Tobias hurried over and stopped short when he noticed she wasn't alone. "Oh, you're out here with Henry? That's a relief. Mother was worried."

He held out his arm, and Georgiana had no choice but to take it. "I'm sorry. I felt a little lightheaded and came to get some air."

"That's all right. I told her I would fetch you. I believe we've a dance coming up. Thanks for watching over her, old chap," he said to the lieutenant. "We'll catch up later."

As Tobias led Georgiana away, she turned back. The lieutenant watched them in silence. He had taken a few steps forward and was now fully illuminated by the ballroom's light. He was rather handsome, with sandy blond hair and a sharp chin with a touch of boyishness to his features, but it was his amber gaze that struck her the most. He stared back with a directness that should have made her uncomfortable, but unlike with the viscount, there was nothing salacious there. It was determined. Noble. And unexpectedly mesmerizing. Georgiana didn't want to look away. Didn't want him to ever stop.

It wasn't until much later, after everything between them had been torn apart and ground to dust, that she realized he had begun to break her heart even then.

* * *

The carriage came to a sudden stop that wrenched Georgiana back to the present. Overhead she heard Jack the coachman yelling at the offending driver of a milk cart blocking the road. She let out a sigh and stared out the window at the traffic as Captain Harris's stern gaze flashed through her mind. She had wanted him to look at her the way he had that first night, as if she was the answer to a question he hadn't even thought to ask. His amber eyes were still distressingly familiar and still alight with the same sharpness, but he had grown thinner in the intervening years, with a rangy build that emphasized his broad shoulders and long limbs, while his sandy hair was now long enough to cover his ears. He had never been the most attractive man of her acquaintance, as his features were too angular to be considered conventionally handsome, but there was a magnetic quality about him that had always drawn her notice. Unfortunately, *that* remained intact. And now it was accompanied by a raw-boned intensity that was undeniably captivating, bubbling up through the hairline cracks of her battered heart—until he flat out refused to give up the case.

If you want this investigation called off, you will need to take that up with your brother.

Georgiana let out a loud huff in the silent carriage and crossed her arms. Impudent man. Lord knew Reggie had plenty of money to waste on ridiculous things like private investigators. But there was little she could do. Despite her protests last night, Reggie had insisted that Captain Harris's services were necessary, and he was backed up by Louisa. It was useless to try to convince them.

There is no harm in seeing what he uncovers, Georgie, Louisa had implored.

Georgiana appreciated the love and support of her siblings, but by God they were making the grumblings of a few competitors into some kind of nefarious plot to do her bodily harm. Captain Harris could uncover whatever he wanted. Georgiana would not alter her course. Come hell or high water, she would continue with her plans to expand Fox and Sons Fine Fabrics, which manufactured trimmings for gowns, by the end of the year.

Her father had purchased the factories nearly two decades ago, when he had an excess of disposable income. But despite the eponymous name, neither he nor his sons had ever been involved in the running of either factory. That had been left up to a management company. A majority stake in the two factories along with a board seat had been passed on to the viscount when he married Georgiana. But unlike Mr. Fox, the viscount was a much more involved owner—and solely motivated by increasing profits at any cost.

When Georgiana had learned there was a clause in the original agreement that ensured the factories would pass on to her in the event that she outlived her husband, it was assumed she would sell. But after taking a tour of her new properties, Georgiana had shocked everyone by declaring her intention to remain the owner.

Since then, she had discovered a new sense of purpose that had been missing from her life. Men like Reggie and Captain Harris couldn't understand the responsibility she felt for the scores of women her factories employed. By retaining ownership, Georgiana was able to ensure they were well compensated and offered childcare services on site for those who needed it. She also demanded that a set of stringent operating standards be followed at all times, so her workers were safe from both the machines and the foremen who oversaw the floor. Any foreman who attempted to deviate from the protocol was immediately dismissed.

Georgiana had heard enough horror stories from her employees about the foremen in other factories who thought it a benefit of their position to demand sexual favors from their subordinates in exchange for keeping their jobs. And if the women weren't willing, the men forced themselves on them anyway before dismissing them. There was little if any recourse for their victims.

The thought still made her stomach turn. Georgiana would hire every woman she could just to stop that from happening to anyone ever again. Word had quickly spread that Fox and Sons was one of the best places to work at in London, and there was a waiting list nearly a hundred names long. Though some of the company's board members had initially balked at Georgiana's changes, production rates had nearly doubled in less than a year. Now was the ideal time to expand operations, while she had the full support of the board, and she would not let this opportunity pass her by.

She glanced out the window. The carriage had already turned onto her street. Though a woman of her social position and means could live in any number of grand London mansions in Mayfair or Belgravia, Georgiana had preferred Pimlico. It was an easy route to her factories near the Thames, and she preferred this quieter corner of London, away from wagging tongues and prying eyes. As her driver pulled up in front of her home, Charles, her energetic young footman, bounded down the steps and opened her carriage door. Georgiana greeted him before ascending the stairs to her small but stately terrace house, where she was met at the door by Mossdown, the butler who had been with her since her marriage.

"Good morning, my lady," he said with a grand bow before taking her coat and hat. "I hope your visit to Mrs. Fernsby's was a pleasant one."

Only Jack the coachman knew where she had really gone, and he was a man of few words and greater loyalty.

"It was. I'd like a pot of tea brought to my study, as I will be working there for the rest of the morning. And I won't be home to any callers. I plan to return to Fox and Sons this afternoon."

Mossdown bowed again before disappearing in the direction of the kitchen. Georgiana preferred to keep her staff small, both to ensure her privacy and because as a lone woman she had no need of a dozen servants.

She made her way down the hall toward the room where she spent most of her time when at home. It was her sanctuary, a much-needed escape from the demands of her work and society. The study had been used by the former owner as a respite from his boisterous family, but Georgiana had removed the dark wallpaper and heavy curtains in favor of calming shades of pale green and silver. A writing desk was positioned by the large window, which overlooked the small back garden, and a pair of comfortable chairs upholstered in gray velvet sat before the hearth. Books Georgiana had collected over the years lined the shelves filling one entire wall from top to bottom, while an eclectic mix of both classic and modern art decorated the space. With no one to please now except herself, everything was just the way she wished. There were times she was lonely, especially in the evenings, but it was worth it to remain in control of her own life.

Barnaby, her faithful elderly terrier, dozed on the matching chaise longue in the corner. At the sound of her entrance he cracked open one liquid brown eye before deciding to go back to sleep. Georgiana gave him a couple of strokes before she sat at her desk and leafed through the mail that had arrived while she was gone. It was mostly invitations to events she had little interest in attending. But since she had entered half mourning, the pressure was mounting from her friends and family to move about more in society. Their ultimate goal was to see her married while she was still on the right side of thirty. While there was still time to have a family. But Georgiana had kept her plan to become a sophisticated old spinster to herself.

It would take a man of uncommon character to change her mind, and Georgiana had never been one for fairy tales. Captain Harris's golden-brown eyes flashed through her mind yet again, and she let out a scoff. A less likely candidate to restore her faith in love, she couldn't imagine.

Fine. Let him waste Reggie's money on his investigation. Georgiana had neither the interest nor the time to cooperate.

If you want your life disrupted as little as possible, I suggest you stay at home for the next few days.

Bollocks. Her life had already been disrupted. But for the first time since yesterday evening a smile crossed her face.

If he was so determined to go through with this "investigation," she would make it as difficult as possible—and enjoy every moment.

CHAPTER THREE

Henry hadn't really expected Lady Arlington to spend the next few days at home. He said that merely to needle her. What he hadn't planned for, though, was her schedule. Most ladies of leisure rose no earlier than ten in the morning and didn't begin making calls until afternoon. But when he arrived at Fox and Sons at nine a.m. sharp to interview her secretary, a young Anglo-Indian man named Mr. Khan, the viscountess was already in her office examining a document with an intense look of concentration that Henry reluctantly admitted was rather adorable.

Her only acknowledgment of Henry's presence was a slanted glance in his general direction before she returned to the document. "Give him whatever he asks for, Mr. Khan. Just see that I am not bothered while I'm meeting with the new accountants from Balfour and Company."

"Of course, my lady," the secretary practically genuflected

before closing her office door and showing Henry to a private room down the hall. The factory itself was large and well lit and already bustling with workers, the majority of whom were women. It took a moment for Henry to realize something else: They all appeared happy. Some were even *laughing*, both with one another and with the foremen who moved around the space.

"This appears to be a...spirited place to work."

"Oh yes, Captain," Mr. Khan said as he closed the door behind him. "Lady Arlington is the best employer I've ever had. That's why these threats have been so distressing."

Henry narrowed his eyes at this admission. It seemed rather overfamiliar. Was something going on between the viscountess and this man? He ignored the prickling in his chest.

"You care about her."

"Of course." Mr. Khan frowned in confusion. "Everyone here cares about her. I can't bear to think what would happen to all of us if she...if she..."

The man seemed unable to even *voice* the thought, and Henry felt a spike of annoyance at the distress on his face.

"Why don't you tell me how this started? Mr. Fox said there have been threats."

Mr. Khan seemed relieved to talk about something specific and stroked his thick black mustache in contemplation. "After Lady Arlington put a formal offer on an old factory on Tremont Street last month, letters began to arrive here. I'd say there have been six in total. They were never signed and had no return address. I'm still not sure how they got mixed in with the regular mail. I'd hate to think that someone hand-delivered them. There are a number of people who are in and out of these doors every day. It would be difficult to know who was behind it."

"What did the letters say?"

"That she should cancel her offer and sell her factories, if she knew what was good for her."

That was rather more direct than Reggie had said.

"Hmm. Who would you say are her biggest competitors?"

"DeLacey's, Moore and Co., and Rigby's. The list isn't nearly as long as it would have been a few years ago. Fox and Sons could potentially transform the industry, though sometimes I think that will come at a deep cost to Lady Arlington." Mr. Khan's worried expression then turned skeptical as he glanced at Henry's folded hands. "Shouldn't you be writing this down? I can fetch you some paper..."

"There's no need, I assure you," he said with a grim smile. "Now, was that the only demand made in the letters?"

"Yes." Mr. Khan then hesitated. "There was also an incident last Friday. After the announcement."

"What announcement?"

"Lady Arlington placed notices in several newspapers across the city about her plans for expansion and the benefits that would be offered to workers."

Henry couldn't help snorting at her brazenness. "This was in reaction to the letters, I take it?"

"Yes. The day after the notices appeared she was followed home."

All trace of amusement vanished, and Henry leaned forward. "Followed by *whom*?"

Mr. Khan shrugged. "All I know is that it was a man. You'll have to ask her for more details. She'll never admit this, but I think he scared her," he added.

Henry's lips pressed in a thin line. *That foolish woman.* She clearly hadn't told her brother about this. And if it turned out this incident was connected to the letters, she could be in real danger.

"I'll need to speak to Lady Arlington about this. Immediately."

Mr. Khan shot him an apologetic look. "I'm sorry, but she is booked all morning."

"Booked with *what*?" Henry made no attempt to hide his disbelief.

Mr. Khan chuckled. "Meetings. The viscountess is no mere figurehead, Captain. She really does oversee this operation."

"Fine. When is her next available appointment? *Today*."

The secretary looked through the leather appointment book he had kept by his side during the interview. "She should have a few minutes to meet with you at one o'clock."

He bit back a curse. "I will return then." The two men rose and shook hands. Henry then gave the secretary his card. "Thank you for your cooperation. Please let me know if anything else occurs."

"I will. And I hope it's not too forward, but may I just say it is a thrill to meet you. My wife in particular will be terribly jealous to know I met the gallant Captain Harris."

Henry had to look away from the man's smile as the blood rushed to his face. "Yes, well. Very good," he grumbled before leaving the room.

Henry still didn't know how to react to his admirers, as he couldn't very well say "Find someone else to fawn over. I deserve none of it."

As Henry moved toward the exit, two young men left Lady Arlington's office just a few steps ahead of him. They must be the accountants she had met with. They exchanged knowing smiles.

"Balfour wasn't exaggerating," said the first man. "She really is a beauty."

"And sharp. Bet nothing slips by her," the second one added in a suggestive tone.

"Only one way to find out."

"Like you'd ever have a chance with a viscountess."

The first man shrugged. "I'm not looking to marry the bird. Just have a night of fun. Lord knows she could probably use it after being with that crusty husband of hers for so long."

"Eh, maybe that's her type," teased the second.

"In that case, don't tell old man Balfour. Otherwise he might start coming here himself!" They both shared a loud laugh.

Henry bit the inside of his cheek as the blood pounded in his ears and he cut into a doorway. If he had to listen to their drivel for a second longer, he wouldn't be responsible for his actions. He pressed his forehead against the brick wall and closed his eyes to concentrate on his breathing. It took a minute before his heartbeat returned to normal. He couldn't believe they would speak about a lady—never mind a *client*—in such a degrading manner.

And are you *so very different from them?*

Henry pushed away from the wall at the bitter thought. Perhaps he hadn't voiced anything aloud, but he had broken one of the cardinal rules of a successful investigation: He had let his personal feelings influence his behavior. But regardless of their past, he had chosen to accept this case. At the very least he owed it to Reginald Fox to do his best to investigate these threats against his sister. It was time to do the job he was hired for. Henry straightened his shoulders and headed toward the exit. First stop: a visit to DeLacey's.

* * *

Henry returned to Fox and Sons shortly before one p.m. exasperated and irritable. He had visited each of the competitors Mr. Khan had named, but the owner of Rigby's refused to even meet with him, and Mr. DeLacey went so far as to welcome the threats against Lady Arlington: "That damned hellion is taking money out of my and my shareholders' pockets. I've also heard she's supporting efforts to unionize the workers. If that's true, then I *hope* someone puts a stop to her. We'll all be ruined otherwise."

Henry had politely but firmly pointed out that his words could be considered a threat, but Mr. DeLacey was unrepentant. "It isn't safe for her to be running that company. Everyone knows women lack the cognitive functioning to run large enterprises. It's a disgrace."

"Yet they seem to manage the work itself without issue. And at half the pay of men," Henry shot back, surprising himself.

Mr. DeLacey's thin mouth had twisted in disgust. "I didn't take you for a *reformer*, Captain."

Henry left shortly afterward without offering a response. In the end, he wasn't able to narrow down the list of potential suspects, as they *all* appeared suspect. Not one had even tried to hide their contempt for the viscountess, and once again Henry was left feeling dangerously naïve regarding the challenges Lady Arlington seemed to face on a daily basis.

Mr. Khan rose from his desk as Henry entered the room and shot him an apologetic look. "I'm so sorry, Captain. But Lady Arlington has left for the day."

"What? Didn't you tell her we had a meeting?"

"Yes, but I'm afraid she...she didn't—"

Henry held up a hand, saving the man from further embarrassment. "I understand. She didn't give a damn." Mr. Khan's eyes widened at the curse, but he nodded sheepishly. Henry sighed. "Will you at least tell me where she went?"

"Claridge's. She decided to have tea with a friend."

The hotel would be filled with toffs at this time of day. Apparently the viscountess did participate in *some* of the rituals of her class. Henry grimaced. He would have understood if something important had come up, but being passed over in favor of an impromptu visit with a friend stung. She knew exactly why he was here. Then again, her carelessness shouldn't come as a surprise.

He turned on his heel without another word, ignoring Mr. Khan's calls.

She would learn that she could not escape him so easily.

* * *

Nearly an hour later, Henry stalked through the lobby of Claridge's Hotel. The traffic had been an endless snarled mess, and his knee ached from the discomfort of standing in place on a crowded omnibus for so long. He half expected her to be gone when he finally arrived. Just as he had predicted, the place was mobbed with tourists and Londoners alike. Henry had to practically shove his way through the crowd to the Reading Room, where tea was held every afternoon. A bored-looking man he assumed was the maître d' greeted Henry, but he waved him away.

"I'm looking for someone," he snapped.

The room was filled with finely dressed people chattering away, but his sharp gaze immediately landed on Lady Arlington, seated at a prime table by a window with another woman. As she tilted her head back to laugh, Henry's traitorous heart beat just a little faster at the sight of her smooth, elegant neck. He imagined pressing his lips to the silken skin along the underside of her jaw. Would she still smell like a spring meadow? And would she tremble at the lightest touch, just as she once had—

Stop it.

Henry forced himself to focus on his throbbing knee and wove his way through the maze of tables, propelled by the sheer force of his irritation. Lady Arlington's companion took notice of his approach first, and her eyes widened in recognition.

Dolly Dutton had debuted the same season as the viscountess, though he guessed she had married by now. Henry came alongside them and addressed the top of Lady Arlington's hat, which, for reasons far beyond him, was decorated to resemble a forest scene with copious amounts of fake foliage and even a tiny bird's nest. He would never understand fashion.

"My lady," he said with unimpeachable politeness. "I

believe you forgot we had an appointment today. At one o'clock."

She slowly looked up at him and blinked, her expression perfectly tranquil. "I did not forget. I simply didn't see the need. Mr. Khan already told you everything of consequence." Then she narrowed her eyes in challenge. "Or are you *not* the brilliant investigator everyone makes you out to be?"

"I cannot speak to what others say about me, madam," he began, just as courteous as before. "But the fact remains that while Mr. Khan was incredibly helpful, only *you* can describe the man who followed you home last Friday."

Her companion let out a gasp, but Henry's gaze never left Lady Arlington's. Only a slight wrinkle between her brows betrayed her annoyance.

"Oh. That," she said.

"Georgiana, is this true?" Dolly asked.

Lady Arlington reluctantly turned to her. "Yes, but don't make a fuss, Dolly. You know how I hate it." Then she glanced back at Henry. "Don't worry. The intrepid Captain Harris is on the case, but I'm afraid I'll need to leave."

"Of course, of course!" Dolly said before giving Henry a warm smile. "It's so *nice* to see you again, Captain."

Henry grunted in response as Lady Arlington pushed her chair back and rose with her customary elegance. Without thinking he offered her his arm, and she paused for one barely perceptible moment before taking it.

It was a mistake.

He flinched at the feel of her gloved hand against him, even though it was the lightest of touches. If she noticed, she gave no indication. They then made their way toward the exit. With every step, he took in some new detail: the brush of her puffed sleeve against his shoulder, the involuntary flex of her fingers on his arm, the scent of her achingly familiar flowery perfume filling the scant space between them. Henry was so absorbed in cataloging these tiny details that they had nearly reached the exit before he became aware that the din of the room had lowered noticeably. The occupants of every table they passed shot them barely veiled looks of interest, and more than a few heads bent together to whisper. To his dawning horror, Henry realized he had made a spectacle of them both by storming in here and then leaving together. Lady Arlington was the kind of woman who made regular appearances in the gossip pages. The kind of woman whose movements were endlessly dissected and commented on. The kind of woman who could easily become the center of a scandal, even through no fault of her own.

"Thank you for the table, Paul," Lady Arlington said graciously to the maître d'. "Everything was perfect, as usual."

"A pleasure, my lady. I hope you come again soon." The man then shot Henry a knowing look. "And with Captain Harris next time."

Lady Arlington gave a charming laugh in response, but Henry had the urge to punch the man in his smug face.

"I'm sorry," Henry said once they were outside and waiting for her carriage. "I wasn't thinking."

Lady Arlington kept her gaze fixed ahead. "Whatever for?"

He wasn't fooled by her bored drawl. "I drew unnecessary attention to you. We'll be lucky if this isn't written about in the evening papers."

The carriage pulled up and a footman opened the door.

"How interesting," Lady Arlington began as she stepped out of Henry's hold and allowed the footman to help her into the carriage. He frowned at the loss of contact. "I didn't know you kept up with the gossip pages, Captain," she said and flashed him an all too familiar grin over her shoulder before turning away. Though her beauty had first caught his eye, it was her cheek that had ensnared his heart. Henry wasn't sure what that said about him. Surely nothing good. He scowled at her back and climbed in after her, taking the seat opposite. As the carriage pulled into traffic, she tucked her steel gray skirts neatly around her, and for a moment Henry was riveted to the smooth, precise movement of her hands.

Before he could stop himself the image of her in the Harringtons' music room came to him. He had been waiting for Tobias in a lavish upstairs parlor when the sound of piano music drifted into the room. The piece was infused with a melancholy that spoke to the deepest, most secret part of him, luring him away from the room and down the hall, where he paused in a doorway, dumbstruck by the sight of a young lady seated at a grand piano, her brow furrowed in concentration as her hands seemed to waltz across the keyboard.

Henry was so engrossed in the music that it took him a moment to realize who he was staring at.

Miss Fox.

"If you're going to hover like that, you might as well come help turn the pages," she teased before she looked over her shoulder and froze. "Oh! I'm sorry. I thought you were someone else."

"Please don't apologize," he began as a hot flush crept up his neck. "I shouldn't have intruded. I was waiting for Tobias when I heard the music." He then gave a short bow that must have looked as awkward as it felt. "You are incredibly talented."

It wasn't so much a compliment as the bare truth.

Even still, she dipped her head in a show of unexpected modesty that made his heart clench. "Thank you." Then she met his eyes and scooted over on the bench. "Well then. May I put you to work?" She patted the place beside her.

Henry inhaled sharply and struck the unbidden memory from his mind. He could not remember any more. *Would* not.

Lady Arlington looked up at the sound, and their eyes locked for a moment. Henry turned away first, but it still felt like she had caught him in the act. The act of remembering. Was it the same for her? He had wondered so many times. Surely she could not recall that afternoon in the same torturous detail, but did she remember playing while he sat beside her on that narrow piano bench? Or the way her hand had trembled ever so slightly as she smoothed the sheet music and explained when to turn the page?

She was full of confidence, certainly, but that slight tell of nerves had both charmed and intimidated him. This beautiful young woman could have any man she wanted. And yet there she was, indulging in the attentions of a lowly naval officer. It was a waste of both of their times: He had come to London to marry into the wealth his family needed, and she was supposed to bag a title. By the end of the season she had gotten one, while Henry...Henry had somehow ended up with even less than he began with. But for those few short weeks in the spring of 1891, Henry had hoped that perhaps things would turn out differently. That perhaps love really could conquer all.

"You wanted to know about the man?"

Lady Arlington's question cut through the silent carriage and drew Henry back from the past.

He nodded. "Please."

Lady Arlington cleared her throat. The unease Henry thought he saw in her eyes disappeared so quickly he must have imagined it. "Last Friday I left my office around seven thirty. Later than usual. It was a nice evening, so I decided to walk home—"

"From *Battersea*?"

"Yes," she said, frowning at his incredulousness. "When I am in my office all day, I enjoy the exercise. It helps clear my head."

Much good that will do when you've been robbed and left bleeding in an alley.

But he kept that particular thought to himself and merely gestured for her to continue.

Lady Arlington glanced out the window as Mayfair slowly passed by. "I didn't realize anyone was following me until I was almost home. He was taller than average and heavily built, with dark hair and a squashed nose. It was easy enough to determine that his presence on my street wasn't a coincidence." Lady Arlington met his eyes then, still as calm as ever. "Though I suppose that was rather the point, wasn't it? I was meant to notice him. And be frightened."

Henry felt himself lean forward. "What did you do?"

"I stood on the pavement and faced him," she said with

a shrug, as if the answer was obvious. "Then I asked if he was lost."

A laugh escaped his throat. "You didn't."

Lady Arlington's lips curved in a sly smile that was dangerously appealing. "I played dumb. That seemed the safest choice, as most men expect it of me." Henry begged to differ, but he kept his mouth shut as she continued. "That caught him by surprise, I think, for he took a few steps forward, then stopped and eyed my house. By then my footman had opened the door, and he left without a word."

Henry sat back as he reviewed everything she had just told him. "And you haven't seen him again?" She shook her head. "You would recognize him, though?"

"I believe so."

"Why didn't you go to the police?"

Her genial expression vanished at his scolding tone. "And say what? That I saw a suspicious man on my street?"

"Yes." Henry was emphatic. "That's *exactly* what you should have said, especially considering the letters you had been receiving."

Lady Arlington crossed her arms and shot him a mulish look. "Do you know how many times I have tried to get them to investigate the working conditions of my competitors? Or related my employees' absolutely *vile* stories about the abuses they or their friends or family have endured in any number of factories across this city? Even I have lost count, as my concerns were either dismissed outright or never followed through. They don't care, Captain. So do forgive me if I wasn't in a rush to be condescended to by yet *another* policeman."

"But this is different," Henry protested. "It isn't something you've heard secondhand. You experienced this personally."

She rolled her eyes. "Do you think *I* am the sort of woman men like that approve of? As far as the police are concerned, I've no business running my factories in the first place. I'm inviting harassment."

"You can't know that."

"Oh, but I do," she said through gritted teeth. "If I just stayed at home with my needlepoint, or if I found myself another husband and got with child, this would all go away. Problem *solved*." Her usually impassive expression melted away as color filled her cheeks and her blue eyes glittered. "They aren't interested in helping me, Captain. They are interested in maintaining the status quo, and I threaten that. God only knows what my rivals are paying them to look the other way while they continually break the paltry laws currently in existence."

Henry had never seen her in such a state, railing against the institutions that abused so many.

He had no idea she felt this way.

He had not thought it possible for a woman like her.

And he was thoroughly ashamed of himself.

Lady Arlington's chest rose and fell in quick breaths as she stared back at him in silence. Then she looked away. "I'm sorry. I shouldn't have said all that."

"No," he said sharply, drawing her startled gaze back to him. "You are right. I should be the one to apologize. I confess, I am used to having very different dealings with the police. It never occurred to me it wasn't a universal experience."

Her eyebrows rose in surprise at his admission, and a look of appreciation filled her gaze that Henry liked far too much.

He cleared his throat. Time to change the subject. "I spoke to some of your competitors today. I'm sorry to say I haven't narrowed the field of suspects. They're *all* threatened by you. Mr. DeLacey even called you a hellion."

The corner of her mouth tilted up. "Good." She looked quite pleased with herself.

Henry frowned and opened his mouth to point out that was *not* good, actually, when the carriage came to a stop. Lady Arlington glanced out the window.

"Here we are."

They were in front of a handsome brick terrace house on a quiet street. "*This* is where you live?" Once again, he was caught entirely by surprise.

She raised an eyebrow. "I suppose you were expecting a more upscale address?"

"Well, yes," he admitted.

"I left all that behind after…after…" Her voice thickened as she struggled to find the right words. Henry's hand tightened around the head of his cane. But the thought remained unfinished as her footman opened the door and her placid mask descended once again. "Is there anything else you need from me today, Captain?"

"No. Thank you for your cooperation," he said flatly. "This has been most enlightening."

She watched him for another excruciating moment and then moved toward the exit, pausing to look back at him over her shoulder. "Feel free to use my carriage. Jack will take you wherever you wish." Henry began to protest, but she held up a hand. "Please. It's the least I can do after forcing you to come to Mayfair this afternoon." Her eyes slid to his knee, which he had been absently rubbing.

Henry snatched his hand away. He could only nod in response. Then he watched her gracefully ascend the stairs of her home.

After the viscount died.

There had been no need for her to finish the sentence. Henry could well imagine the supreme grief that had driven her from whatever elegant mansion they had once called home.

Though the viscount had a reputation for being severe, he must have treated his wife far differently. For Henry had seen her devastation firsthand in Scotland. It should not be surprising that she had grown to love the man who had been her husband for so long. After all, she was no longer a careless young woman of eighteen. People could change. Lord knew he had.

And yet, there was no mistaking the deep pang that swam in his belly, though he had not felt that particular emotion in many years.

Henry was jealous of a dead man.

CHAPTER FOUR

Georgiana softly shut the door to her study and leaned against it, letting out the breath she had been holding as disparate thoughts whirled through her mind. It had been childish to leave her office earlier knowing that Captain Harris intended to return, but she had *never* expected him to come after her. Georgiana thought she had done a fairly good job of hiding her surprise, even in the face of the captain's commanding stare.

She pressed her hand to her cheek, recalling the way the heat of his arm had sank through her glove. Walking beside him for those few moments was like a form of time travel. He even *smelled* the same. Like starch and sun-warmed cotton. And how easily she remembered it all—the feeling of safety, of comfort, that had always come over her while in his presence. Because she could be herself around him, as there wasn't any pressure to play the coquettish debutante or appeal to his vanity. He was only Tobias's nice, quiet friend whom she enjoyed teasing. Wildly unsuitable, of course. But then how quickly he had become more. How quickly that belonging had turned to a kind of obsession. A madness she hadn't felt before or since.

A lie.

Georgiana pulled her hand from her cheek and made a fist as she pushed away from the door. No. She would *not* moon over this man once again. She stalked over to her desk and sat down, mindlessly shuffling the papers in front of her, including that morning's newspaper.

The captain was right. They would be lucky if their little display didn't make its way into the gossip columns. The Reading Room's maître d' was known as one of the city's most prolific sources, which was why Georgiana had always been unfailingly nice to him. In her experience, it had paid dividends. She had briefly thought about slipping him a few coins to ensure his silence, but it would have been fruitless. Dozens of people had seen them together, and Captain Harris striding through the Reading Room midday to escort Lady Arlington away in her carriage was simply too good of a scoop. The gossip columns had been absolutely ravenous for any tidbits about the captain, but the man was too reclusive. And on the rare occasion when he had attended a social event, he had always been alone. That Georgiana had both noted these entries in the first place and could now recall them with no effort was incredibly vexing. The last year and a half had been torturous enough without having Captain Harris's heroism breathlessly described in every newspaper and endlessly dissected in every drawing room. Georgiana had done an admirable job of ignoring the story at first—quite the feat considering how frequently he was brought up by the people around her—but few beyond her immediate family knew they had shared a very brief courtship before her marriage. And fewer still knew the truth of how it had ended.

But then she had seen him in the flesh at Castle Blackwood, mere moments after learning of her husband's death. It had been an absolutely horrid callback to years earlier, when she had made the worst mistake of her life. For one brief moment, his dark honey gaze had burned into hers again before he disappeared. When she had finally recovered from her shock, the captain had already left. Over the next few months, a very small, very foolish part of her had hoped that he would reach out in some way. But there was nothing from him among the piles of condolences she received. By the time she had learned of Reggie's ridiculous scheme, Georgiana had already effectively barred her heart once more—or so she thought.

Perhaps ducking out of their meeting that afternoon hadn't been an act of childishness after all, but one of self-preservation. A part of her must have known she should not be alone with him, of what it would do to her, and yet she had unknowingly created an even worse scenario. Her awareness of him while walking through Claridge's was nothing compared to the closed confines of her carriage. She had tried to make as little eye contact as possible, even though the man was like a living magnet. Did he have any idea of the strength of his pull? Of how much it took for her to stay separate from him? How she had pressed her back against the plush seat, fiddled with her dress, her hat, her gloves, anything to keep from reaching out to him?

And still, every time she had dared to meet his gaze, a bolt of pure heat, pure need shot straight to her core.

She recalled her conversation with Dolly shortly before the captain had arrived:

It's time you found another husband. But a young *one this time.*

I don't want another husband. Even a young one, Georgiana had said with a detachment she did not feel.

Dolly had then raised an eyebrow. *Well, if you don't want a husband, you should at least find someone who can satisfy your bedroom needs.*

Georgiana had nearly spit out her tea. Dolly was one of her more conservative friends. She married a pleasant, boring man a year after Georgiana had married, and they had gone on to have five healthy boys. Their conversations had always revolved around charity work, her children, or petty gossip. They never talked about anything remotely salacious, yet there she was, telling Georgiana to find herself a lover right in the middle of afternoon tea.

Dolly had then shot her a conspiratorial little smile. *Though in my experience it's best to have both. And better still if they don't know about each other.*

Georgiana threw her head back and let out a terribly unbecoming laugh at the wicked joke.

Captain Harris had arrived mere moments later, looking both extremely put out and undeniably handsome in a tan tweed suit that showcased his tall, lean figure. It was as if his appearance had been conjured by both Dolly's suggestion and her own untoward thoughts. His annoyed expression did nothing to quell the heat rising through her.

She had never argued with him during their courtship.

But then, there had been no undercurrent of antagonism coloring every conversation. No long-buried feelings of devastation that surfaced every time his eyes met her own. She had genuinely liked the young lieutenant, while he had been busy trying to charm her into looking past his unsuitability with kind words, thoughtful gestures, and seemingly endless patience, until desperation had won over for one heady, careless moment in a dark garden. Still, the ruse had very nearly worked.

Now she felt an overwhelming need to push him, to make him as uncomfortable as he made her until he lashed out. But though the captain made no attempt to hide his irritation with her, it never went beyond that. How she wished he would rage at her. It would be so much easier to manage her feelings if he was simply a brutish bully trying to force her under his thumb, or dismissing her every word with barely veiled contempt. She had *many* years of experience dealing with her husband's moods, not this confounding mixture of judgment coupled with occasional moments of understanding.

Georgiana sighed and did her best to push the confounding man from her mind. She would have no answers today. And in the meantime, she had work to do.

* * *

For the next two days Georgiana buried herself in a haze of activity. She arrived at her office each morning between seven thirty and eight, then worked until luncheon. Her afternoons were then filled with either additional duties or the social visits she hadn't quite brought herself to ignore entirely.

She had spent the first evening at home alone devouring the latest Inspector DuMonde mystery, but tonight she was supposed to attend the opera with her family, her first such outing since she had reentered society after the viscount's death. For weeks Louisa had been acting as if it was a second coming out, and her constant fussing was starting to grate on Georgiana's nerves.

When they met at Lady Gray's that afternoon, the very first thing Louisa said was "Is your gown ready?"

"Hello, dearest," Georgiana responded with all the poise she could muster. "And how are you?"

Louisa rolled her eyes before giving her a wide smile and a deep curtsy. "Good afternoon, my illustrious elder sister. I trust you are in excellent health?"

Georgiana had to roll her lips between her teeth to keep from laughing. Heaven deliver her the strength to deal with younger sisters. "You are an imp, Louisa," she said after regaining her composure.

Louisa shrugged one shoulder in blasé acknowledgment. "And you wouldn't have me any other way."

Now Georgiana couldn't hold back her chuckle. "I suppose not. Though I think your husband deserves the most blame for encouraging your behavior."

Louisa glanced down with a shy smile. "He is far too indulgent, I know." She had married her childhood sweetheart, David Pendrake, over the summer and was both deliriously happy and abominably spoiled. It had been a comfort to Georgiana to see her sister married to a man who truly loved her, but now, in the face of Louisa's obvious contentment, a sudden, vicious longing filled her chest.

Louisa, entirely unaware of the juvenile envy coursing through her, continued talking of the plans for that evening. For once, Georgiana was grateful for her sister's oblivious-ness. She spent the rest of the visit dutifully talking with every lady in the room, being introduced to fresh-faced debutantes eager for the season to commence and graciously accepting belated condolences from those she hadn't seen since the viscount's death.

Georgiana had been performing this social circuit since her own coming out eight years ago, and she enjoyed a particularly elevated status after her marriage. The late vis-count had come from a very old family, but his reputation as a rather reclusive bachelor had barred him from moving in the more exclusive circles of his class. Georgiana may not have had much money, but she was popular, and marrying her had opened a number of doors that had long been closed to him. And yet, he expected her to be forever grateful to *him* for making her a viscountess.

No one else would have married you, my dear. Not even that face of yours could make up for your father's debts.

He never missed the chance to remind her of this great personal sacrifice on his part, though they both knew he had fully expected to get an heir and had not handled his disappointment well.

After Georgiana had made the rounds, she kissed Louisa goodbye. "I'll see you at Reggie's for dinner."

"Do try to look a little happier when you arrive. It's only a bit of music, Georgie. Not an execution."

Georgiana shot her a chiding look before she left the drawing room. As she was descending the front steps of Lady Gray's Grosvenor Square mansion to her waiting carriage, she noticed a man standing across the street reading a newspaper in an apparent attempt to appear discreet.

Jack held open her carriage door, but Georgiana waved a hand. "Just a moment. I have something I need to take care of." She then marched across the road toward Captain Henry Harris.

He glanced up at her approach and folded the newspaper under his arm. "Lady Arlington," he said smoothly. "What a pleasant surprise."

Georgiana stopped a foot away from him and narrowed her eyes. "Yes. Quite. I can't imagine a better place to enjoy your afternoon paper than this particular stretch of pavement." She waited for his denial, but instead the corner of his mouth lifted.

"Touché."

"You'd do better to wear a disguise next time you follow me. I spotted you instantly."

Captain Harris's smile grew ever so slightly, and he shook his head. "I've never been able to stomach the idea of wearing a false mustache or a wig. It's simply too silly. Besides, I think I've done a fair job without such accoutrements. After all, you didn't notice me this morning. Or yesterday."

Now Georgiana couldn't hide her surprise. "You've been following me this *whole time*?"

"Not exclusively," he said with a shrug. "I do have other clients, my lady. But I thought it couldn't hurt to make sure that man you spoke of wasn't hanging about."

"Oh." Georgiana's anger faded. "Did…did you see him?" she added apprehensively.

He shook his head. "Thankfully, no. However, I took the liberty of discussing your encounter with a contact at

Scotland Yard. If you'd like, we can go down there this week and you can describe him. I'd say there's a fair chance he has an arrest record."

Georgiana's first instinct was to say no. But perhaps she would be treated with more respect if she went with Captain Harris. "I'll think about it."

This seemed to satisfy him. He then glanced past her. "I should go. I believe I'm drawing more unwanted attention."

She turned around to follow his gaze and noticed Louisa practically pressed up against the glass of one of Lady Gray's front windows. "Oh, for heaven's sake," she grumbled and gave an annoyed wave before turning back to Captain Harris. "That's my sister Louisa."

The captain was still watching the window with an amused expression. His eyes sparked with recognition. "Is it? Last time I saw her she demanded I hold her doll. I believe her name was Victoria Regina Copperpot."

A laugh escaped Georgiana. "I'd forgotten all about that."

He had once spent a long afternoon with her and her siblings, who were in town on a visit. In addition to allowing Louisa to accost him, he had also patiently taught Reggie chess, which Mr. Fox had always been too busy to do. But as Georgiana had watched the young lieutenant bent over the chessboard with her excited younger brother, an unfamiliar kind of ache came over her. A longing for something she hadn't ever thought to want. He must have sensed her gaze, for he had glanced up and given her a warm, familiar smile. It would always be like this with him, she had realized. This quiet happiness that seemed to blossom so easily between them. And it had been this revelation that had driven her to meet him the very next evening. Alone.

"Yes," she continued, suppressing the unwanted emotion welling in her throat. She felt so far removed from the naïve girl she had been that afternoon that the memory may as well have belonged to someone else.

"Victoria Regina Copperpot had a number of adventures before she was retired to the attic. Louisa married recently."

Captain Harris looked down at her, his stern expression so very different from the one in her memory. And yet, they were now standing closer than before. Georgiana couldn't say who had moved first. "She's quite young to be married, isn't she?"

Georgiana reared back a little. "Not much younger than I was," she answered, unable to keep the defensive note out of her voice. Louisa, willful as ever, had also threatened to go ahead and elope if they tried to dissuade her.

His eyes searched her own. "Is she happy?"

Georgiana's breath caught at the question. He was completely serious. "Yes. Very. Her husband adores her."

Captain Harris stared at her for another moment, then glanced away. "Good," he said as he began to adjust his gloves. "A girl like that should be adored."

Georgiana should have been pleased to hear him express such a sentiment. After all, it was true. Louisa had always been an odd duck, but she had found a man who appreciated her eccentricities instead of trying to bleed them out of her. And yet, Georgiana's mouth filled with the bitter taste of envy once again. She, too, wanted to be the kind of woman who deserved to be adored in his eyes. Georgiana wondered what he truly thought of her. Of what kind of woman she was to him now. Though she guessed she wouldn't much like the answer. Still, she burned with the sudden desire to ask such a ridiculous question, but before she could, Captain Harris touched the brim of his hat. "Good afternoon, my lady," he said without looking at her.

Georgiana stood on the pavement while both regret and relief warred within her. As he moved farther away, the decided click of his cane slowly melted into the street noise. When she finally returned to her carriage, she caught Louisa still standing there watching her from the window. Based on the pitying look on her sister's face, Georgiana guessed she hadn't done a very good job of hiding her feelings. She gave a slight shake of her head before turning away to let Jack help her inside.

CHAPTER FIVE

D inner with Georgiana's siblings had gone relatively smoothly, at least by their standards, but that was likely due to their reduced numbers. Franny was abroad acting as a companion for the viscount's aunt Mrs. Crawford after Sylvia had given up the position to marry, and Ollie was away at school getting into God knows what. Even still, Louisa heartily approved of her new silver evening gown, and Reggie only brought up Captain Harris once, asking if he had come by the factory. Georgiana's single nod in response seemed to suffice. Remarkably, Louisa said nothing of what she had witnessed that afternoon, though she did shoot Georgiana a telling look that was ignored. All in all, their prying had been kept to a minimum. David, Louisa's husband, usually offered his opinion only when asked, a trait Georgiana had come to appreciate more and more, but as they were preparing to leave for the opera, he gave her a conspiratorial wink.

"Good on you for standing up to Reggie," he whispered while Louisa was busy looking for her misplaced hat. "It was terribly overbearing on his part, the way he hired that man without even asking you. I said as much to him yesterday at our club."

Georgiana was touched, especially since David rarely interfered in Fox sibling dramatics. That likely explained Reggie's restraint during dinner.

She smiled and placed a hand on his arm. "David, have I ever told you that you are my favorite brother-in-law?"

He laughed good-naturedly. As of now, he was her *only* brother-in-law. "A designation I hope never to lose."

It looked quite promising, given that their other sister, Franny, seemed far more interested in books than men.

"What are you two giggling about?" Louisa asked as she secured her newly found hat to her head, a monstrously large creation resembling a garish floral display that she insisted was the height of fashion.

"I was just telling David how fond I am of him. You've truly done well in your choice of husband."

Louisa beamed as she slipped her arm through his. "Yes. Thank God I came to my senses and accepted his proposal before he could ask that horrid Kitty Webb."

"As I've told you many times, there was never *any* chance of that happening, my dear," David said with a blush.

"But you danced with her twice at Lady Bernby's ball the day after I turned you down! Her own mother was running around the room telling people it was only a matter of time."

Louisa's initial refusal, born out of nerves during her first season, had quickly turned into anxious regret, and she tearfully appealed to Georgiana for help. Little did she know that Georgiana had also been approached by an equally distraught David. She had been all too happy to help the thwarted young lovers, and their reunion had been near Shakespearean, complete with laughter, tears, and pledges of undying love.

"Well, I won't pretend to be above inspiring a little petty jealousy on your part," David said with a grin.

Louisa playfully batted him with her fan before giving him a sly look more suitable for the bedroom, which Georgiana pretended not to notice.

"Come along, children," she said as she headed toward the front door, where Reggie was already waiting in the carriage. "I won't miss the overture."

* * *

When Georgiana's husband was alive, attending the opera together had been one of the very few events she could fully enjoy. While many turned such outings into yet another opportunity to flaunt their wealth or seek connections, she had always come for the music. As the carriage pulled up alongside the Royal Opera House, Georgiana's stomach fluttered with excitement along with a thick sliver of dread. Reggie helped her down from the carriage and dutifully escorted her inside. Louisa and David lagged a few steps behind, mooning over each other like the newlyweds they still were.

Reggie cleared his throat a few times in an attempt to get their attention before he gave up. "I should have said so earlier, but you look wonderful tonight, Georgie. It's been so nice seeing you out of that awful black."

The opera would be the first major social event Georgiana

had attended since her full mourning period ended. She had dutifully donned plain black crepe and floor-length veils for the last year and a half, but with the encouragement of her closest friends and family, she had recently transitioned to half mourning. Nevertheless, her appearance would likely scandalize the more conservative members of society, for whom nothing less than two years of deep mourning for a widow would do.

But Georgiana simply couldn't do it. Between her marriage and mourning period, she had already given up eight years of her life to the viscount. She would not give him one minute more.

"Thank you, Reg," she said just as something caught her eye. Lady Phillips and Mrs. Elliott, two of the most esteemed society matrons, were noticeably glaring in their direction before they bowed their heads together. Georgiana's hold on Reggie's arm tightened. They weren't yet in the door and it was already happening.

Reggie looked down at her with concern. "What's wrong?"

"Nothing," Georgiana said quickly, tearing her gaze away from the gossips. She gave her brother a bright smile, but he wasn't fooled.

"Ignore them. They're nothing but a pair of petty old vultures who want nothing more than to feast on the misfortunes of others."

Georgiana raised an eyebrow, now thoroughly distracted by Reggie's turn of phrase. "My, that's an awfully poetic way to put it."

He shot her a grin. "Well, you aren't the only member of the family with some artistic talent."

Georgiana was an accomplished pianist, though she had largely abandoned the practice during her marriage. The viscount thought it vulgar for his wife to perform for anyone other than him, and eventually Georgiana decided she would rather never play at all. Taking it up again since his death had been a source of great comfort.

"Reggie, don't tell me you write!"

"It's only a bit of fun," he demurred, but Georgiana suspected it was far more than that. Her brother had always been an avid reader. It wouldn't be much of a leap to compose his own pieces.

"You must let me read some of your work."

The blood drained from his face. "Oh, please no, Georgie. I couldn't. What if you hated it?"

She smiled at his sudden gravity. "I could never. It is entirely at your discretion, of course. But if you need me, I am here."

By that time, Louisa and David had caught up and as they made their way through the well-heeled crowd, Georgiana was heartened to see that no other disapproving matrons were scandalized by her appearance, but she couldn't fully relax until they reached the safe confines of their private box. Reggie escorted her to a velvet-lined seat and then immediately excused himself. "I'll be just a moment," he said cryptically and was gone before Georgiana could say another word.

Louisa sat beside her. "Where's he off to?"

Georgiana shrugged and scanned the crowd that was slowly filling the theater. "He didn't say."

An attendant arrived bearing glasses of champagne, and Georgiana downed hers in just a few gulps. She couldn't seem to settle her nerves. Or shake the sensation that she was being watched.

"Steady on," Louisa murmured, but Georgiana pretended not to hear.

She closed her eyes and inhaled slowly, focusing on the crisp taste of bubbles bursting on her tongue. After a moment Louisa greeted someone, and Georgiana opened her eyes. She turned toward the entrance and was met by an all too familiar amber gaze.

Reggie had returned. With *Captain Harris*.

The champagne's heady effect was immediately deadened. She shot an accusatory glare at Louisa, but she was already rising from her seat, and David was pretending to be engrossed in the program. This had been the plan from the very start. And they all knew.

Georgiana stood. "Traitor," she growled at David as she passed him. He at least had the decency to look chagrinned.

Reggie, on the other hand was unrepentant. He stepped forward and blocked her path. "Don't be cross now. I thought only of your safety." Then he looked hurt. "You should have told me about that fellow following you home."

Georgiana let out a huff. "It was nothing."

"Captain Harris doesn't seem to think so."

"Of course he doesn't. You're paying him to think otherwise."

"Georgie," Reggie cautioned, but she ignored him and arched her neck, trying to catch a glimpse of the man himself. Louisa was busy chattering away, as if they were old friends, while the captain listened patiently. He looked terribly dashing in his black evening jacket, which emphasized his broad shoulders and lean waist. Georgiana's gaze lingered on his long white-gloved fingers, which were gripping his cane's handle. He happened to glance over at that moment and caught Georgiana staring. As their gazes locked together, the very air seemed to crackle before he quickly returned his focus to Louisa.

"That doesn't explain what he is doing *here*," she said, wishing she could stomp out the noticeable flutter in her chest.

"It's to send the message to the guilty party that we are taking these threats seriously, and we've taken steps to ensure your safety."

Georgiana was dumbfounded. "My God. You're serious."

"The only one who isn't taking this seriously is *you*," he said. "And I won't simply stand by and wait until something happens that can't be undone."

"You really are overreacting," she insisted, even as a chill ran through her. She glanced over her shoulder. "Look, it's about to start." Then she turned back to Reggie. "But don't think this is over," she said pointedly.

Her brother let out a little sigh and muttered something about *stubborn sisters* as she took the seat on the farthest end of the box.

David leaned over, his face the picture of contrition. "I wanted to tell you, but I was outvoted."

"I don't doubt it."

He glanced toward the entrance. "For what it's worth, he seems like a competent fellow."

Georgiana let out a very undignified snort and crossed her arms. "Oh yes. *Extremely.*" She then moved to the edge of her seat and faced the stage, where the conductor had just appeared. Georgiana clapped along with the rest of the audience, and after a moment she detected movement beside her. Louisa and Reggie must have taken their seats. She didn't give a damn where Captain Harris was. Perhaps Reggie had stationed him outside the box, to make sure that no agents of chaos attempted to burst inside and hand her another vaguely threatening note.

Honestly.

The lights dimmed and the orchestra started up. As the first notes of the overture rang out, Georgiana leaned back in her chair and let out a soft sigh. If nothing else, she would enjoy herself tonight. But just as she had begun to relax, someone cleared their throat.

"I'm sorry," a familiar deep voice murmured over her left shoulder. "I thought you knew."

The captain was directly behind her. She turned slightly toward him, close enough to detect his scent of clean linen. And feel the heat of his body. "You should have said something earlier."

"I hadn't received the invitation yet."

Then it had come after Louisa spotted them outside Lady Gray's.

Taking the threats seriously my foot.

Perhaps Reggie truly believed that, but Louisa was up to something else entirely. Georgiana worked her jaw and suppressed the urge to glare at her sister in front of the whole of London society. She had probably read the gossip item about her and the captain that appeared in the papers yesterday too. And now they were sharing a box together.

Georgiana tore her gaze from the stage, where a man was professing his undying love, and looked around the theater.

Her stomach sank as she noticed a fair number of pairs of opera glasses trained on her. On *them*. A few voyeurs had the decency to look away, but most did not. She should be used to this by now. For years her movements had drawn attention. Scrutiny. Judgment. And she had endured it all by assuming the mask of the viscountess. Of a woman entirely at peace with herself and the life she had chosen. It was her only defense.

Yet as more heads bowed together and bodies leaned to the side, her breath quickened and her heart began beating furiously in her chest. Georgiana stood as panic suddenly seized her. The men stood as well, and she mumbled some excuse and forced herself to exit the box as slowly as possible. Not that it mattered much now. She was already a spectacle.

Georgiana entered the hallway, still teeming with guests more interested in socializing than the performance, and headed for the powder room. It was nearly as crowded as the hall, but she took the opportunity to sit before one of the mirrors. By then she had calmed down considerably.

It was just the champagne, you goose, she silently reasoned to her reflection as she applied a bit of powder to her cheeks and checked her hairpins. *It always does this to you.*

And what he *does?*

Georgiana shook the intrusive thought away and left the room. She had taken only a few steps before someone appeared beside her.

"Lady Arlington."

She swallowed a curse. "You shouldn't be here."

If he were anyone else, she would have sworn hurt briefly

flashed in the captain's eyes before he assumed his usual expression of stern disapproval. "Your brother sent me."

No, she most certainly had imagined it. He would only come after her if ordered to do so. "Of course he did," she muttered.

He raised an eyebrow. "And I was also concerned."

She laughed at his stilted tone. "You don't even *like* me," she blurted out before pressing a hand to her mouth. Perhaps the champagne did still have a hold on her.

Captain Harris did not look amused. He quickly glanced around before he wrapped his hand on her upper arm and pulled her into a darkened alcove. It was slightly more private than the hallway, but not by much. As he loomed over her, his eyes took on an unnatural glow in the dim light. Like a wolf on the hunt.

Georgiana shivered again, but this time it wasn't from a chill. Quite the opposite. His hand still held her arm, his touch warm and sure. And distressingly familiar, as if he held her this way often. But then he had always felt unaccountably familiar to her.

The heat from his palm slowly sank into her skin and trailed down her arm. She leaned in a little closer, her senses drawn to the heat radiating off him, lapping at her edges. It had been so very long since she had been this close to a man. Even longer since it was a man she actually wanted.

Captain Harris must have read something in her expression that signaled her desire and quickly stepped back. Georgiana felt the loss of his heat immediately and her throat tightened. She was destined to be forever rejected by this man.

"I came tonight because I am concerned for your welfare."

"A concern that is paid for by my brother."

This appeared to catch him off guard. He opened his mouth, then promptly closed it. Georgiana's heart sank. He wouldn't even try to deny it.

But why would he?

She let out a sigh. "While you and Reggie may think you being here is sending a message, it is also creating gossip. About me."

Captain Harris lowered his head. "You're right," he admitted. "I hadn't considered that. Again. I suppose I'm not used to being the one who is watched."

"Really?" Georgiana raised an eyebrow. "You're one of the most talked about men in the country. You've become a regular fixture in the society pages."

"I never read that rubbish," he said dismissively.

"That hardly matters, as its existence is not contingent upon your attention. Many people do read them—and are interested in *you*."

His expression turned wary. "I can't imagine why," he demurred.

A smile tugged at her lips. This display of humility was unexpectedly charming.

"Some people find heroic actions a source of intrigue," she said dryly.

Captain Harris gave her an arch look. "Do they?" His voice noticeably deepened, and the words skated across her skin.

She cleared her throat and looked toward the hall, where plenty of people were still milling about. "I should return to my seat," she said, turning back to him. "I did actually come here for the music, you know."

"I do," he said softly.

She stiffened at his knowing tone. Georgiana had revealed that part of herself to him when she thought he was a different sort of person. One whose interest didn't hinge on the size of her dowry. It seemed crass to allude to it now.

"I suggest you stay here for a few minutes before returning to the box," she said as coolly as she could manage. "To prevent any further speculation."

Georgiana did not wait for his response and instead lifted her head and returned to the hall.

CHAPTER SIX

———◆———

L ong minutes passed as Henry stood in the shadowed
alcove, taking in slow breaths and waiting for her floral
scent to dissipate. He needed to stop touching her. Every
time he did, he was transported to that night in the Harringtons' back garden when he had put his entire heart in the
hands of a girl he had considered wildly out of reach only a
few weeks before.

Please say you'll at least consider me.

It had been the pathetic plea of a lovesick young
man. Henry knew there were far better men seeking
her hand, including that ancient viscount, but surely he
hadn't imagined this pull between them. And he liked her
family. Liked watching her take charge of her gang of
siblings with a firm yet fair hand. She was the kind of
woman he wanted in his life, and in any other setting,
any other time, he would have proposed already. But this

was a London season, and Henry was woefully out of place here.

She hadn't given him an answer, just a long, silent look edged in sadness. Then without a word she had stepped closer and drawn her arms around his neck. Her touch set off something within him. An electric jolt he had never felt before. She was both entirely new and achingly familiar.

All these years later, Henry could still feel the press of her divine body against his. The curve of her hips under his palms, the impossible softness of her skin as he ran greedy fingers along her cheek and jaw, and how her pillowy lips had grazed his ear as she invited his touch in gasping breaths.

Henry.

She had whispered that single word with a desperate urgency that unleashed something inside him. Something he had never known existed until this moment. Henry covered her mouth with his own in a deep, searching kiss that she answered with equal passion. As she gripped his shoulders and they both sank to their knees, a wild thought came to him:

She wants you. You could take her right now.

In a moonlit garden after midnight, like some beastly man in a twisted fairy tale.

And then she would be yours.

Even if she came to regret it later, it would be too late.

But somehow he had found the strength to pull away, to do this the honorable way. So he sent her back inside even while his body cried out in protest and watched her shadowy figure disappear into the grand mansion with her taste still on his lips and his trouser legs streaked with dew and dirt.

And then he hadn't seen her again for more than six years. Until that bright morning in Scotland when she learned of the viscount's death and fell apart before him.

Henry tightened his grip on his cane and emerged from the alcove. He shouldn't have let Reggie Fox talk him into coming here tonight—not that it had taken much prodding on his part. But it had been a damned foolish idea in the first place. Now Henry suspected Louisa Pendrake was behind the entire scheme. She was just as sharp—and charmingly devious—as she had been as a girl. Though she shared her older sister's honey-colored hair and sapphire eyes, Lady Arlington was careful and calm—one might even say calculating—whereas Louisa radiated the breezy nature of a protected younger sibling.

Henry had never before considered that perhaps that had been part of his initial attraction. Like him, Lady Arlington was the eldest. That came with responsibilities both spoken and assumed. Responsibilities that likely went unnoticed by the rest of her family.

You don't even like *me.*

The hurt in her eyes when she had proclaimed this was surprising, though Henry was in no position to deny it. Perhaps that was difficult for a lady who seemed to charm everyone she met to accept, but he *didn't* like her. What he felt now was only lust. It was primal. Illogical. But he would not become a fool over her once again. She had turned him down to marry for money and status. That made her spoiled. And shallow. Never mind that Henry's own intentions when he had first come to London were not so very different from hers. But he had been prepared to give it all up for her. And it was that unfulfilled hope that had cut the deepest in the end.

As he made his way down the hall, he fielded greetings from some people he recognized and many he didn't, including suggestive looks from more than a few ladies.

You're one of the most talked about men in the country.

He wasn't entirely unaware of this, but it embarrassed the hell out of him. Yet as an attractive brunette made eyes at him, Henry considered that perhaps it was time he reaped some benefits from this minor fame. He had spent these last years largely celibate. It had initially been a way to protect his shattered heart, but it felt more like a liability every moment he spent around Lady Arlington.

Then why don't you seduce her, if this is only lust?

But nothing good could come of that. It would be like touching a red-hot iron simply to feel the burn.

Henry forced himself to return the smile at the brunette as he passed by, but it felt more like a grimace. He was absurdly out of practice. The woman didn't seem to mind, though, as she dipped her head coyly and fluttered her eyelashes. He gave her a subtle nod and continued on his way. That was enough flirting for now. But as soon as he glanced up he locked eyes with another woman giving him a similar look of invitation. Henry again managed the same nod as he passed.

Lord, this might be appallingly easy. And a fair change from his disastrous attempt on the marriage mart. But then, finding a lover was an entirely different prospect. The neglected wife of an aristocrat or an experienced widow would not have the same expectations or requirements as a wife, while providing him with pleasure and a little companionship now and then to keep the worst of the loneliness at bay. That was all Henry wanted. He wasn't capable of more.

As he entered the box, his mind still turning over the possibilities, Henry noticed that another man had joined their party. One who had taken the seat closest to Lady Arlington. *And* draped his arm over the back of her chair. In plain sight of the entire opera house.

Henry narrowed his eyes. Surely this display was much more ripe for scandal than anything *he* had done, and yet Lady Arlington was all smiles for this man.

"That's Lord Pettigrew," Reggie said, startling Henry a little. He hadn't even noticed his approach, as he had been entirely fixated on Lady Arlington.

"Who?"

Reggie smirked but played along with his pathetic attempt to save face. "The man next to Georgiana. I mentioned him to you, didn't I?"

Lady Arlington let out a delighted laugh, and Henry couldn't stop himself from cutting a glance toward her. "No, you did not."

"Ah, well, he's a good lad. Inherited a barony last year." Reggie then leaned in closer. "To be frank, the family is hoping it turns into something more."

Henry's shoulders tensed. Lord Pettigrew was young and dark-haired, with boyish good looks. He couldn't have been more than twenty-two.

"I'd say it looks that way already," Henry said dryly.

Reggie chuckled. "Only in his mind. For now. He's one of the most eligible bachelors in London, but my sister is in no hurry to remarry at the moment, I'm afraid. Though I do hope she doesn't keep him waiting very long."

Henry swallowed hard, as if that could rid himself of the bedeviling mix of envy and jealousy that bubbled up inside him every time he was reminded of her devastation over the viscount's death. Lord Pettigrew found the strength to tear his attentions away from Lady Arlington for a moment and glanced back toward them. His eyes widened when he noticed Henry, and he immediately made his way over, making no attempt to hide his eagerness.

"Captain Harris?" He stuck out his hand and grinned. "I heard you were here. It is *such* a pleasure to meet you, sir. I read all about your exploits in Turkey. A simply marvelous adventure."

Henry stared at the young man's outstretched hand for an awkward moment before shaking it. "Is that so." He longed to point out that two men had died during the course of that *marvelous adventure* and that he didn't use this cane for fashion, but instead he merely attempted another bland smile.

The young man didn't appear to notice his dry tone as he pumped his hand vigorously. "I heard someone is writing a book as well?"

"That is just conjecture, I'm afraid," Henry replied. "There are no plans for a book written by anyone."

He had been approached by a few publishers but turned them all down. Henry would not relive that month. Not for all the sterling in the empire.

Lord Pettigrew's face fell in a near comic display of disappointment. Apparently he expressed every fleeting emotion that passed through his pretty head. "Oh, but they *must*. It would be a sensation, I'm sure." He then turned to Lady Arlington, who had joined them. "Don't you think so, Georgiana?"

Henry met her eyes with a sardonic look. *First names in public? Really?*

Her lips twitched slightly, but she maintained her veiled expression. "I'm sure there would be great interest in anything about the captain."

"Yes, absolutely!" Pettigrew said animatedly. "And if you need any introductions, I'd be happy to make them. I was at Cambridge with a chap whose father owns a publishing company."

Of course he was. It had been so long since Henry moved in these circles he had forgotten how these things worked for the privileged class.

"That isn't the issue," he responded as politely as he could manage. "But thank you for the offer."

Lord Pettigrew's brow lifted, but he accepted the rebuff like the gentleman he was. "Well, I'd better return to my box. I'm here with Mother and a country cousin she is launching this season. You're coming to her ball tomorrow, Georgiana?"

"Yes."

"Splendid, splendid." Then Lord Pettigrew turned to Henry. "You should come too, Captain! Oh, what a treat for all of us. And Mother would be *thrilled* if you danced with Cousin Lillian. I daresay it may well be the highlight of her season, poor girl. A bit awkward, that one." Henry began to demur, but the young man shook his head. "I simply won't take no for an answer. Convince him, will you, Georgiana?"

"I'm afraid the captain doesn't enjoy balls. He's likely to spend all evening on the terrace." Then she turned to him. "Isn't that right?"

Henry frowned at the reference to their long ago meeting and grumbled in response. Lord Pettigrew didn't appear to notice as he was too busy making a great show of kissing Lady Arlington's hand. "Until then, my lady."

Henry had to look away as a faint blush stained Lady Arlington's cheeks. Was she really taken by that dandy?

What do you care?

He silenced the voice in his head and managed to smile as Lord Pettigrew departed.

"Careful there, Captain," Lady Arlington teased. "Someone might mistakenly believe you're enjoying yourself."

"I didn't realize it was fashionable to bring children to the opera these days. That boy is barely out of short pants."

To his surprise, Lady Arlington muffled a snort of laughter into her handkerchief. "If I didn't know better, I'd say you were jealous."

Henry bristled at the accuracy of her comment, but he couldn't possibly admit to it. "Luckily, you do."

She stared back at him with that calm impenetrable mask, then turned around and took her seat without a word.

He spent the rest of the performance staring at the back of her head, memorizing every gleaming bronze curl and counting the number of pearl-topped pins. Nearly thirty. God knew how much it cost, never mind the rest of her outfit.

That is why she rejected you once before.

And would do so again, if given the chance.

Henry slipped away just before the final curtain call and

whispered his regrets to Reggie. Whatever message they had hoped to send tonight had been telegraphed to the entire room. He didn't need to see any more.

Later, he would lay awake for hours in his utilitarian bed in his rented flat staring at the water-stained ceiling. For every time he closed his eyes, all he could see was her wordless stare. His relentless mind combed the image, looking for the smallest flicker of hurt in that sapphire gaze, the slightest twitch of her rose petal lips, something, anything that gave some *hint* of what she had been thinking, been feeling in that brief moment. But for once his appalling memory was of no help. Try as he might, Henry could not see into her soul.

It was close to dawn when Henry finally drifted off to sleep. This time he dreamed of nothing. Nothing at all.

* * *

"You are looking a bit peaky, my dear. I hope you don't mind me saying so."

"Of course not, Aunt Paloma," Georgiana responded automatically before taking a sip of tea. She had come to Harrington House to pay her weekly visit to her godmother, who had effectively retired from society several years ago owing to poor health. But that did not absolve society from coming to her.

"It's those hours you keep," Aunt Paloma insisted, waggling a finger at her for emphasis. The afternoon light caught on the gold and ruby ring she wore on one swollen knuckle. A much-prized gift from her late husband. "You must give it up. You'll never win Lord Pettigrew looking like that. And heaven knows the young man won't tolerate a wife who *works*."

Georgiana set her teacup down with a delicate clink. "Well, then it's a good thing I'm not interested in winning him."

Aunt Paloma gave her a shrewd look. She had never been a celebrated beauty, as her nose was a touch too long and her forehead too wide, but she possessed a low, rich voice and commanding presence that could be mesmerizing when you were the sole focus of her attentions, even now. Aunt Paloma always knew exactly what she wanted, and she rarely didn't get it. "You say that now, but when you are my age you won't want to be all alone. A man like that will be snapped up by some enterprising young lady if you wait too long. I only speak from a place of concern. You know that."

Georgiana held back a sigh. "Yes, Aunt."

She was all too familiar with her godmother's *many* concerns about her. It was how she had ended up married to the viscount in the first place.

"And your dear mother would have wanted to see you settled again," she pronounced with the innate confidence of a woman rarely denied anything. "You know I made a promise to her to see you wed."

Aunt Paloma frequently claimed to know what the late Mrs. Fox would have wanted, as even the boundaries of the afterlife were no match for her.

Georgiana's fingers tightened on the teacup. "And you fulfilled that promise eight years ago. I'd like to think that now she would wish for my happiness above all else," she murmured.

Aunt Paloma's eyebrows rose. No one *ever* contradicted her. "Well, naturally," she allowed after a long moment. But Georgiana barely had time to enjoy this little triumph. "I understand you were at the opera last night," she continued. "With Captain Harris."

Her godmother made no attempt to hide the disapproval in her voice. Georgiana should have known this would come up. The older woman may barely leave her house these days, but she still had plenty of eyes to keep her abreast of the latest gossip.

"He was there, yes," Georgiana admitted. "But we were hardly alone. Lord Pettigrew even came by our box to meet him."

While Georgiana had made a pathetic attempt to act like the captain's presence hadn't bothered her at all and failed quite miserably.

If I didn't know better, I'd say you were jealous.

Luckily, you do.

That cool rejoinder had kept her up most of the night.

Aunt Paloma's faced screwed up in a frown. "Why? Because of that business *abroad*?" Then she made a dismissive noise. "I don't know why the papers have made such a fuss over him. It's hardly impressive. My Tobias would never have been foolish enough to be captured."

Georgiana bit her lip against the anger that had suddenly swelled inside her on the captain's behalf. While Peregrine Harrington, now the current Earl of Belmont, was the very picture of a studious, responsible oldest son, Tobias was his mother's pet. He was endlessly indulged and his bad behavior always excused. As far as Georgiana could tell, Tobias spent most of his time in gambling hells or at his club, and the only time he ever lifted a finger was to order another drink. The idea that he would ever risk his own life for someone else was patently absurd.

"But then his mother was a fool too," Aunt Paloma continued with a dismissive wave of her heavily bejeweled hand, oblivious to Georgiana's outrage. "Ran off with a naval officer of her own, and was never seen in London again."

This revelation caught her by surprise. "You knew Captain Harris's mother?"

Georgiana knew his late father had also been in the navy, and that his mother and sister lived in Glasgow, but they hadn't gotten the chance to share more.

Wariness briefly flashed in the older woman's eyes before it was supplanted by her usual loftiness. "Not very well, as she was merely the daughter of some country squire. But she made a spectacle of herself when she married such a man. And her friends always took pity on her, especially Lady Neville. That was why her son came for the season in the first place. He would never have been admitted into our circle without her connections."

Georgiana's shoulders tensed. She knew exactly his purpose in coming to London all those years ago. And exactly why she had not fit the bill in the end.

"You aren't renewing your acquaintance with him, are you? It would only make you even more a target of gossip."

It was not the first time Aunt Paloma had issued such a warning.

My dear, I hate to say this, but your little friendship with that naval officer is becoming a distraction. I'm certainly

*no stranger to the appeal of a man in uniform, but you must
know it can't go further. And I'd hate for the viscount to get
the wrong idea.*

Georgiana's heart suddenly ached with years of useless
regret. Captain Harris and his duplicitous motivations certainly hadn't been the answer to her problems back then, but
Georgiana could still have made better decisions for herself.
Decisions a woman like her godmother, who lived and died
by society's expectations, would never understand.

"Of course not," Georgiana responded dutifully before
changing the subject to the Pettigrews' ball.

* * *

"I can't believe I of all people have to say this again,
but will you please *stop* fidgeting? My goodness," Louisa
grumbled.

Georgiana immediately froze. She hadn't even noticed
she had been tapping her fan against her arm. "Sorry,
Louie."

"What are you so nervous about anyway?"

Georgiana kept her eyes fixed ahead and continued to
subtly scan the Pettigrews' ballroom. "Nothing." She could
feel her sister's sharp gaze upon her. "I'm not nervous."

Louisa let out a little huff of disbelief. "And yet, you've
been on edge since the moment we arrived. Though I can't
imagine why. You said yourself that Captain Harris hates
balls..."

Georgiana whipped her head toward her sister, who
wore a very self-satisfied smile. "This has nothing to do
with *him*."

"All right. Then is it about Lord Pettigrew?" Georgiana shook her head. "Well, that's a relief. I don't understand why you encourage him," Louisa added.

Georgiana shrugged and turned back to the crowded dance floor. She immediately spotted Tommy Pettigrew dancing with his cousin Lillian and smiling away as though he was having the time of his life.

He had insisted on claiming a waltz. Though Georgiana had told him she had no intention of dancing with anyone that evening, saying no to him always felt a bit like disappointing a puppy. And Georgiana found she hadn't the stomach for it tonight. "He's nice. Pleasant."

"Annoying," Louisa countered.

Georgiana remained silent. When she was younger, she too would have found Lord Pettigrew's constant enthusiasm exhausting. But she wouldn't tell her sister that there were far worse qualities to be found in a man. Lord Pettigrew could be grating at times, yes, but she had nothing to fear from him. He wore every single emotion on his sleeve. There was a kind of comfort in his complete transparency. His predictability.

Not that it would ever amount to anything.

For it did not matter how handsome or rich or charming Lord Pettigrew was. No man could tempt her back into the institution that had cost her so much. Between her family and her growing little empire, she had more than enough to occupy herself. And she would have her freedom. Always.

But that didn't account for the physical desires that had grown more pronounced, especially this last week. Georgiana could not open her heart to any man, but did she dare to take Dolly's advice and open her bed—at least for a night?

The hairs at her nape prickled with a sudden awareness, and she glanced back to find the gaze she had been searching for all evening upon her. She quickly turned away.

"Well, well, well," Louisa murmured by her ear and sounding quite proud of herself. "Look who showed up after all. And in a *very* dashing evening suit. What do you think?"

Georgiana hadn't realized she was holding her breath. "I don't care," she said in a slightly strangled voice.

"Then you might want to loosen your grip on your fan. It's in danger of snapping in two."

Georgiana immediately let her arm fall. "You really are being most irritating today."

"I'm sorry," Louisa said, though she didn't sound like it one bit. "I just don't understand why—"

"Don't." The word was out before Georgiana could think. "But I remember—"

"Louie, *no*." Georgiana met her sister's deep blue eyes, mirror images of her own.

Louisa pressed her lips into a hard line for a moment. "I was only going to say that he was nice to me."

Georgiana bowed her head. "He was," she said softly.

"It makes an impression on a child, when an adult treats you with respect."

She glanced up and found her sister looking at her with pity. "I know."

"Will you ever tell me what happened between you?"

As Georgiana pondered the question, her father's voice came to her, thick with unspent tears.

I've made a mess of things, Georgie. But there's hope for us yet, all thanks to you. The viscount has offered to help.

Could she tell her sister the truth? How she had nearly given in to Captain Harris during the most impetuous, passionate moment of her life, even though it meant breaking a promise to her father and throwing her family's future into disarray? And how she learned only the very next evening at Lady Wrenhew's ball that their entire courtship had been a sham? She had meant nothing to him. He had only been after her money. Money that hadn't actually existed.

"I don't know, Louie," she sighed.

There must have been something telling in her expression, because this time her sister offered no objection. Only a sympathetic gaze. "You wait here. I'll get us some lemonade."

Georgiana nodded absently. Once Louisa disappeared into the crowd, she moved to a nearby pillar and ducked behind a rather large fern. She leaned against the cool marble structure and closed her eyes, but it offered no respite. All she could think of was that awful moment eight years before when her illusions had been shattered and ground to dust under the heel of the captain's polished leather boot.

She had gone looking for him at the ball to reveal her impending engagement to the viscount. It had been a last, desperate attempt on her part to gain the courage she needed to defy her family. To confirm for herself that their embrace the previous night had truly meant the same to him as to her. Then she had noticed him in the card room, standing with his back to the doorway with another gentleman she didn't recognize. Before she could enter, he began to speak:

That was a close one, eh, Harris? The Fox girl is a pretty piece, but I hear she doesn't have two pennies to rub together.

Yes, Henry had replied in a bored tone Georgiana had never heard before. It was snide. Ugly. And made of all the qualities she thought he was too decent to possess. *I barely escaped without a scratch.*

Might have been worth it to get a few from her though!

As she slowly backed into the hallway unnoticed, her eyes had burned with unshed tears and shame. She waited there in the dim light a moment longer, hoping for something else—a kind word, an explanation, an admission of regret—but instead she learned there were other ladies he planned to propose to. Georgiana had not warranted more than a sentence.

She returned to the ballroom on leaden feet, where her soon to be announced fiancé would be waiting for her impatiently. She hadn't yet realized this was an ingrained personality trait. How incredibly stupid she had been, to think that her engagement would hurt the captain. That she could ever possess such power over him, even for a moment. But as powerless as she was, she had gotten her revenge in the end. Georgiana made sure the two other women he was pursuing knew he was only a callous fortune hunter. And he had left London shortly afterward. Alone.

"Hiding from someone?"

Georgiana opened her eyes and found the very same man invading her thoughts now peering down at her. She immediately straightened away from the pillar. Viscountesses did not slouch.

"Of course not."

A corner of his mouth lifted. "It rather looked that way." Then he leaned a little closer. "Don't worry. I won't tell anyone."

Was he actually *teasing* her? Oh, but that was dangerously appealing. "I was only feeling a little tired," she insisted. "So I was waiting here while Louisa fetched some lemonade."

"Ah, well, then she appears to have gotten distracted en route." He gestured with his chin.

Georgiana turned and spied Louisa in the middle of a small crowd, telling a story with her usual vigor while everyone laughed. Not a glass of lemonade was in sight.

"Oh, *honestly*," she grumbled.

He then held out his arm. Georgiana eyed it as if he was offering her a steel trap and not a common body part. Reggie or Louie must have sent him over here. That was the only explanation. And a thoroughly depressing one at that.

Just as the moment began to turn awkward, she took it with a resigned sigh. "Lead the way, Captain. Or should I say 'set sail'?"

He actually chuckled at her terrible joke. "Please don't."

She had never shown her sense of humor to the viscount, as the man didn't possess one. Now she bit the inside of her cheek to temper the spark of joy in her chest.

Remember, it means nothing.

They emerged from behind the pillar and joined the mingling crowd.

"There you are, Georgie!" Reggie cried out. "We sent the captain to find you."

Of course. Duty-bound, as usual.

They joined a small circle that included Georgiana's family along with a few friends.

"Did you," she said, meeting Louisa's eyes. "How fortunate I am to have such thoughtful relations."

"You disappeared," her sister insisted before her gaze fell to where Georgiana's arm was entwined with Captain Harris's. Georgiana resisted the urge to pull away. The man was only being gentlemanly. Surely she could endure it for a few more minutes.

Mrs. Dawson threw her head back with a throaty laugh. "I only wish *my* family would arrange for such a handsome escort." She then shot Captain Harris a saucy look that left absolutely nothing to the imagination. "Care to show me to the card room, Captain?"

Mrs. Dawson considered herself highly unconventional and made sure to participate in any activity that contributed to her reputation.

His arm stiffened beneath hers. "I'm afraid Lady Arlington needs a glass of lemonade."

"Oh no, don't let me keep you," Georgiana demurred.

He looked down at her with his usual sternness. "That's quite all right, my lady."

She couldn't hold back the shiver that ran through her as their gazes locked.

"Another time then, Captain. I insist on it," Mrs. Dawson simpered, still trying her hardest to capture his attention.

Captain Harris still stared at Georgiana with that unreadable expression, before he finally turned his head to acknowledge the comment. "Yes," he answered woodenly before directing Georgiana to the refreshment table.

"Well, now you've gone and done it," she began. "Mrs. Dawson will spend the rest of the evening in a hideous pout."

Captain Harris handed her a lemonade. "Does that bother you?"

"No," Georgiana admitted as she accepted the glass.

He held her gaze once again. "Good."

The single word shouldn't have pleased her so much.

His behavior was perfectly polite, and yet it felt like she was standing on shards of glass.

"Why are you even here?" she continued, unable to hide the bite in her words. "You hate these types of things."

He finally broke their gaze and took in the room. "I have my reasons."

That was certainly cryptic. Then he turned back to her, hesitant. "And your brother asked me to come."

"Oh," she said, unaware of the tiny bud of hope that had begun to unfurl in her chest until it was crushed by the disappointment that rushed through her. It felt like someone releasing air from a great balloon.

"Are you all right, my lady?"

Damn him for noticing. And damn him for not having the decency to ignore it.

"Of course." She stood a little straighter. "Why wouldn't I be? So then, have you uncovered a bloodthirsty plot to ensure my demise yet, or is my brother still wasting his money?"

There. That would get them back to their more familiar territory of mutual loathing.

A slight frown marred his brow before it vanished behind a blank expression. "No, I haven't. Which, may I remind you, is a good thing."

Georgiana managed not to scoff. "I suppose you expect me to be grateful, then."

"I harbor no expectations at all."

His even tone grated like nails against her skin.

That's certainly a change.

But before she could speak the words, someone came beside her. Through her haze of anger, she recognized Lord Pettigrew.

"I've come for a waltz," he said cheerily, while his eyes darted nervously between them.

Georgiana felt a twinge of guilt. Though she wasn't prepared to give Lord Pettigrew her heart, she could at least treat him with kindness. She knew how this must look to him, her standing here deep in conversation with another man. Her earlier reluctance to dance dissipated as she gladly took his arm.

"And a waltz you shall have." She gave him her most brilliant smile and pointedly ignored the captain entirely as they moved to the dance floor.

But though every step took her farther away, she still felt his gaze on her, dark and heavy.

"It's nice of you to keep the captain company," Lord Pettigrew began, giving her the perfect opportunity to dismiss his concerns.

She took it. Enthusiastically. "Yes. He is terribly uncomfortable at these things."

Lord Pettigrew nodded. "I understand you've known each other for quite some time?"

Georgiana made sure to smile even wider, to mask her surprise. "We first met years ago, but we haven't seen each other again until recently. He is nothing more than an old acquaintance. Practically a stranger."

Lord Pettigrew visibly relaxed. "Ah. I confess I had imagined something quite different. Especially with some of the insinuations the papers have been making. Been driving myself a little mad, actually." He then blushed and ducked his head. It was charming, how little he hid from her. "Star-crossed lovers reunited. That sort of thing."

Georgiana blanched. She hadn't seen anything like that. But then, she had been busier than usual recently. "No," she said just a tad forcefully. "It's nothing like that." She then patted his arm and looked ahead. "Nothing at all."

CHAPTER SEVEN

⸻◆⸻

H enry watched that damnable boy lead Lady Arlington through a waltz, but after a few moments, even he had to grudgingly admit that they fit well together. Pettigrew's dark hair contrasted pleasingly with her golden locks, and as they moved confidently around the dance floor, they drew the attention of a number of guests. Heads turned, knowing looks were exchanged, and bits of gossip were passed along in their wake.

As Lady Arlington smiled up at Lord Pettigrew, Henry couldn't ignore the sharp jab radiating in his chest.

So then, have you uncovered a bloodthirsty plot to ensure my demise yet, or is my brother still wasting his money?

He couldn't decide which he wanted more: to pull out that sharp tongue of hers or to demand she stick it down his throat.

The raw desire behind the thought jolted straight to his cock. Damn Reggie for insisting he come this evening. Henry had been honest with Lady Arlington. He hadn't uncovered anything of substance yet. But it was still early days, and, unlike some of his other wealthy clients, Reggie wasn't making any unreasonable demands of him.

I know it's probably silly, but I'd feel better if you were there, Reggie had admitted. *And, if nothing else, you can bask in the admiration of all the pretty young things who will be in attendance.*

Henry chose not to explain that he had absolutely no interest in attracting *any* kind of admiration, or that being in the same room as Lady Arlington was becoming its own unique form of torture. Instead, he had given his client a tight smile and asked what time he should arrive.

He almost hadn't recognized Lady Arlington at first when he found her slouching behind the pillar. Gone was the serene expression she usually wore. Instead, she had looked young and vulnerable and so much like the innocent debutante he had first fallen for that he had nearly lost his breath for a moment. Back then it had been all too easy to play the part of her rescuer, the knight in shining armor he had once imagined himself to be, saving her from a joyless future with a much older man for a quiet life built on love. With him.

Then she had gone and married the man without even bothering to say a word to Henry.

He had barely noticed the two older women tittering beside him until Lord Pettigrew swept Lady Arlington into a perfectly executed turn right in front of them.

"Oh, what a handsome pair they make," one sighed.

"You know, I've heard Lord Pettigrew has proposed *three times* already, but she insists on waiting out of respect to the late viscount. She must have been absolutely devastated to turn down a perfectly good match so many times. And at *her* age."

Henry had to hold back his snort, given that Lady Arlington couldn't be more than twenty-six.

"I heard the same," the second added. "Lady Pettigrew is certain she will accept him before the year is out. But mind you, his lordship is her only son, and she will demand grandchildren."

"Yes. I know it was a great disappointment to the late viscount to be without an heir. He had such high hopes for Lady Arlington, especially given her rather—er, prolific family."

The second lady nodded as if this was a perfectly reasonable comment to make in a ballroom. "One must make some allowances, of course, given the viscount's age, but if she still can't produce with a younger lad, then I'm afraid of what will happen to her."

Henry's grip tightened on his cane, and he pressed his lips together. Was this how the upper class talked about one another? All this fuss about bloodlines was nothing more than animal husbandry trussed up in silk and linen. If the names had been changed, this conversation could easily be had in a barnyard.

"If it does come to that, an annulment wouldn't surprise me," one of the women pronounced. "Not in the least. And then she would be an outcast. Poor girl."

"Oh, naturally."

Henry couldn't listen to another minute of this drivel. He

skirted his way through the crowd as nimbly as he could manage and kept going until he reached the terrace doors. The cool evening air was a relief on his overheated skin.

It wasn't that he had any illusions about the aristocracy. Henry knew very well that they were all horrible snobs, and that young women were often treated like little more than prized cattle, but it was still a shock to hear Lady Arlington discussed so casually and with such authority. Who were those women? How did they know such intimate details about her? And to then speculate about her *breeding* potential with another man...

Not once in all these years had he ever felt sorry for Lady Arlington, but the confounding mixture of jealousy and irritation that had been heating his blood just minutes earlier slowly seeped away. It was one thing for people to gossip about social calls or speculate on engagements, but Henry hadn't realized that *anything* was ripe for public dissection.

What a fool he had been. All he had ever seen—ever allowed himself to see—was the extreme privilege granted by her position. But of course it came at a price. And it was steeper than he had imagined. He turned around and looked back through the open terrace doors. The waltz had ended. He found her in the crowd just in time to see Lord Pettigrew place a chaste kiss on the back of her gloved hand. Lady Arlington gave him a close-lipped smile. Demure and polite, as usual. She had always known how to present herself in public. Henry had long thought it had been a mark of her class, but now he considered that it was her own suit of armor. A necessity when moving through these treacherous waters.

On those few occasions when they had been truly alone, she had given him such dazzling smiles. They had always made him feel like he could conquer the world. After everything between them had ended, he had assumed those smiles had meant nothing. Just the flirtations of a bored, spoiled girl trying to see how many hearts she could collect before the season ended.

But she still *did* smile that way. And only for trusted family and friends in more private moments. Not him, though. Never again.

Lady Arlington glanced over and caught him staring at her. As that close-lipped smile faded, Henry realized he had been glowering, but just before he could turn away, someone else came into view.

Tobias Harrington.

Lady Arlington and Lord Pettigrew greeted his old friend, though perhaps *former acquaintance* was a better term. They had met during Henry's London season, and Tobias had quickly taken him into the fold on account of his talent with cards. Together they had visited nearly every gambling hell in the city, where Henry had watched Tobias lose more money in an evening than he had ever possessed in his entire life. The excess had been sickening.

Henry instinctively stepped back into the near darkness of the terrace, but not before Tobias caught sight of him and approached. Tobias had once been strikingly handsome, but the years of indolence and late nights had taken a toll.

"I thought that was you," he said with that same old rakish smile, though his jawline was now soft from bloat and there was a sallow look to his face.

Henry nodded. "Harrington."

"It's been a long time. Too long."

"I've been busy."

"Yes, I heard all about your exploits. One could barely get through a dinner party last year without someone waxing on about the heroic Captain Harris," he said with a slight touch of disdain. Then he raised an eyebrow. "I saw you talking with Georgiana earlier." And before Henry had seen him. That didn't sit well. "Reggie Fox says he hired you to investigate these beastly threats."

Henry tempered his surprise. "He told you about that?"

"Of course." Tobias looked affronted. "I'm a trusted family friend. And it's a terrible shame, really. Poor girl has worked so hard."

Henry grunted in surprise. "I didn't think you'd approve of the viscountess running a factory."

"Well, I certainly wouldn't want *my* sister working. If I had one, that is. But then Georgiana has always been… different." Henry could agree with that. And it was good of Tobias to notice.

"I don't suppose you'll be renewing your suit?" he added.

Henry wasn't fooled by his light tone. Tobias had made it abundantly clear eight years ago that a lowly naval officer wasn't good enough for the likes of Georgiana Fox.

I know what you're after, but I suggest you valiantly step aside, old chap. She's intended for the viscount.

A pity for him he hadn't listened.

"No. I've decided I'm not the marrying kind."

Tobias stared at him for a long moment, then he broke into a grin. "That makes two of us. Say, I don't suppose you'd be interested in leaving here for a card game, like old times? It's very exclusive and the buy-in is highway robbery, but I can give you a loan. I know you'll be worth the investment."

Still up to his old tricks then. Henry wondered how much money he would lose tonight. Tobias was one of the worst gamblers he had ever seen. And the man never knew when to quit. "No, sorry. I don't gamble much these days."

Tobias pouted. "That's a shame. If I had your mind for cards, I'd be richer than the queen by now." Then he held out this hand. "Well, good luck with the search. If I hear anything, I'll let you know."

As Henry took it, he raised an eyebrow. "I can't imagine you would. Whoever's behind this is likely someone in business."

Which was a far cry from the libertines Tobias usually surrounded himself with. Henry had been tolerated merely for his adeptness at cards.

As if Tobias could read his thoughts, he leaned in a little closer. "Ah, but you've no idea what circles I run in thcsc days," he replied before releasing Henry's hand and striding back into the ballroom with the assurance of a man who had never felt out of place anywhere. Ever.

* * *

As Georgiana waited for the carriage outside the Pettigrew mansion with Reggie, she couldn't shake the uncertainty that had been hovering over her like a cloud for the last hour. It began when she caught Captain Harris staring at her from the doorway of the terrace, before Tobias went over to say hello. On first glance she thought he was simply frowning at her. Hardly unusual. But then she noticed a look in his eyes that she was tempted to describe as *longing*. Then he seemed to catch himself and assumed his usual stern expression, but the memory still lingered, even now. Daring her to consider the possibility that beneath the captain's stony exterior lay a heart as raw and ragged as her own.

Reggie kept looking back to the front door as more and more guests left. "Have you seen Captain Harris? I wanted to offer him a lift home."

Georgiana shook her head. "He was on the terrace with Tobias much earlier." But she hadn't seen either man since. "I think he was headed for the garden. Possibly an assignation under the cover of night."

Why on *earth* had she said that?

"I doubt it," Reggie said absently, still scanning the growing crowd. "Not really his sort of thing, I gather."

She tamped down the sudden urge to point out that her personal experience proved otherwise. Wildly inappropriate. And if she displayed any kind of interest in the captain, her brother wouldn't stop haranguing her about it.

"I thought all men were interested in that sort of thing," she said instead, then winced. Even she could hear the bitterness in her voice. Perhaps Reggie hadn't noticed...

But then he shot her an odd look. "I assure you, they aren't," he said stiffly.

Goodness. She had *offended* him. "I'm sorry, Reg. I didn't mean anything by it. I'm tired, is all. Not used to keeping these late hours, you see."

His eyes softened. "No. Don't mind me. I was only being silly."

Georgiana began to ask what, exactly, had bothered him, but Reggie then spotted the captain and waved his arm. "Ho, Captain Harris!"

As he came closer, Georgiana discreetly swept her gaze over him. Well, he certainly didn't *look* like he had been busy ravishing anyone in a hedge. If anything, he appeared to be just as tired as she felt.

Because you are both working people.

Georgiana's lips quirked. She rather liked that idea, even though the captain would likely strenuously object to her lumping herself together with him. It was true that she didn't need to work for a living. But she did need to work for a purpose.

Captain Harris forced his way through the crowd and reached them just as her brother's carriage was pulling up. "Hello there," he said rather breathlessly to Reggie as he cut a glance in her general direction.

"You're coming with us, and I won't take no for an answer."

Captain Harris still seemed on the verge of refusing, until something gave.

He really must be so tired.

Georgiana's eyes then drifted toward his cane. She had long since ceased to notice it, as he moved with that innate confidence. But he leaned more heavily on it now, and she found herself wondering what the nature of his injury was. None of the newspaper articles about him had ever mentioned the scars such an ordeal would leave behind, both visible and hidden.

When she was first married, she had volunteered at a home for military veterans. There she had seen that the true price of war went far beyond pounds sterling. It was found in the vacant expressions of the men she wheeled around the garden, in the sudden bursts of anger some displayed that seemed to erupt from nowhere, and in the lost limbs or powder burns that marked so many. She was still a patron of the home, but after a few months the viscount had demanded she stop, claiming it took too much time away from him. By then they had been married nearly a year and she was still without child. For a time she had wondered if he would seek an annulment, given his desire for an heir. But he must have concluded she was still a valuable asset even if she was possibly barren, and he chose another way to express his displeasure. It was to be the first in a long line of actions he took to punish her for this failure.

From now on I will choose your charitable endeavors, my dear. Your talents would be put to much better use elsewhere.

She quickly discovered that anything or anyone who brought her obvious enjoyment was banned, so she learned to barely show any emotion beyond serene contentment. It was simply easier—*safer*—that way.

When she gave her regrets to the home's matron, the older woman was surprisingly understanding. "To be honest, my lady, you lasted far longer than I expected. Most don't return after the first day. If you don't mind me saying so, I believe you've nerves of steel."

At the time Georgiana had shied away from the compliment. She had been in such a low place then, but the years had proved the matron right after all.

She was still here. Still standing. And still determined.

A footman opened the door and she climbed in. Reggie settled in beside her, while Captain Harris sat across from them, though he kept his gaze firmly on her brother. Georgiana took advantage of the darkened carriage to stare at him for a moment unobserved before turning her attention to the window while they talked about a mutual acquaintance who had been in attendance.

Between the gentle rocking motion of the carriage and the weariness that settled over her, Georgiana was close to nodding off when she felt a hand on her shoulder.

"Did you hear me, Georgie?"

She shook her head. "No, sorry. I think I was just about to fall asleep."

"I noticed." Reggie gave her an indulgent smile. "I was explaining that the carriage is taking me home first, as you're closer to the captain's quarters."

"Oh," Georgiana said softly, still in a daze.

"It's really not necessary. I can get out here," Captain Harris insisted.

"Don't be absurd. It will take you hours. Besides, at your age I trust you two can be unchaperoned for a few minutes," Reggie said with a wink, clearly joking, but even in the low light Georgiana could see the captain frown.

"Of course, Reggie. I will be on my best behavior," she chimed in lightly before the moment could turn awkward. As her brother let out a laugh, Captain Harris finally met her gaze. A hard pulse gathered between her thighs at the dark heat that flashed in his eyes. Her mouth suddenly went dry as the air thickened around them. Perhaps she had been right about him after all. The idea was unexpectedly thrilling—and just a little terrifying.

Reggie, bless him, noticed absolutely nothing as the carriage pulled alongside his townhouse. He simply said his goodbyes and climbed out, shutting the door behind him with a resounding thud that seemed to echo in the small space.

And then they were well and truly alone.

CHAPTER EIGHT

I'm sorry for this," Lady Arlington blurted out, cutting through the growing tension. "If I had known you were coming, I would have taken my own transport this evening."

"It is fine, my lady," Henry said. "I can endure a simple carriage ride."

She raised an eyebrow. "You just suggested getting out and walking home. From Mayfair."

Well, she had him there. "I was only thinking of you," he began. "And the possible implications of us being seen together again."

"Oh." Lady Arlington relaxed. "Well, don't worry about that. Anyone who cares about such things saw us with my brother. Hardly a scandalous combination."

"And Lord Pettigrew?" The question was out before he could stop himself.

She tilted her head and eyed him. "What about him?"

"Would he be among those who cared about such things?"

Lady Arlington gave him her profile and shrugged. "I suppose." Then she turned back to him with an arch look. "Luckily, he knows how easily gossip spreads. I assured him that he has nothing to worry about."

So they had discussed him. That shouldn't have interested Henry. At all. "Is that true?"

She blinked owlishly. "Is what true?"

Henry leaned forward ever so slightly. "Your response implies that there is something between you."

Her eyes widened as she gathered his meaning. "That is personal, Captain."

"Yes, it is. And it might be incredibly valuable. If you have an understanding with Lord Pettigrew, he could become a target too."

She scoffed and folded her arms beneath her breasts. Henry tried his best not to look directly at the soft swell of flesh that seemed in great danger of spilling over the low neckline peeking out from between the folds of her velvet cape. She was wearing a lavender evening gown. Henry liked it—he liked everything she wore—but he couldn't help wishing to see her in something more colorful. If those gossiping old ladies were right, it could be another year before she left mourning behind entirely.

"Really, that *is* a stretch," she sniffed. "Besides, nothing has happened in over a week."

Henry noted that she made no attempt to dismiss a connection to Pettigrew. "It is possible that those letters and the man who followed you will be the end of it. It hasn't stopped you from your plans, correct?"

Georgiana nodded. "I'm still waiting on the final

paperwork, but once I sign everything, it will be mine." She let out a heavy sigh. "This would never happen to a man. All my rivals own miles of properties around London and have their hands in all sorts of industries. Do you think *they* would ever consider backing down from a deal? Absolutely not."

"But you aren't just buying up property," Henry pointed out. "You're threatening the entire system they benefit from."

"*Exploit* is more like it," she said. "I took a pay cut to raise my workers' wages, which are well above my closest competitor's, I won't tell you what that translates to in pounds, but it's not exactly an obscene amount of money."

"But it means you can't live in Mayfair," he countered as he put the pieces together. "Or employ a full staff or host lavish events like the one we just attended."

"Well, no. I suppose not," she conceded. "But I never thought of it as a loss. For me, it was a relief to change house. And it isn't as though I live in a shack now."

Henry's lips quirked. "Hardly."

"If people like me did with just a little bit less, then the lower classes could be pulled out of poverty."

"Perhaps, but there are many who disagree. They would say they deserve their riches and that the poor would fritter away any handouts they received."

"I know that," she snapped. "*Believe* me. And it is the absolute height of hypocrisy. Most of the people in that ballroom have never worked a day in their lives. They either inherited their money or married into it or both."

"Like you." Henry didn't mean to say that aloud, but he hadn't yet mastered that old bitter impulse inside him.

She flinched, then went quiet for a moment. "Yes. Exactly like me," she finally said. "But at least I am trying to do something about it. If I didn't run this business, someone who didn't give a damn would have bought it. And then nothing would have changed at all. My employees want to work, Captain. Many of those women are the breadwinners for their families. They want to earn a fair living, and they deserve to be treated humanely."

Regret tore through him. Lady Arlington may have done him wrong years ago, but that didn't mean she was irredeemable. And she did seem to be making a genuine effort to improve the lives of people less fortunate than herself.

The carriage slowed as they turned onto her street, and she glanced out the window. "Nearly there." Her face was briefly illuminated by the streetlight, and Henry realized she had been blushing.

Christ. He really was an ass.

His arm shot out but stopped short of touching her. "Please allow me to apologize. I was unforgivably rude just now. And for no reason."

She met his gaze, and those sapphire eyes cut straight through to the heart of him, just as they had all those years ago.

"What you are doing is admirable. And you're right. If you were a man, this probably wouldn't be happening to you. It may all come to nothing, but for now you have people who care about you very much and are worried for your safety. I realize that might seem silly to you, and you think my work is unnecessary—and perhaps it is—but just know that I am doing everything I can to put them at ease. That must mean something."

She bowed her head and the blush deepened. "I hadn't considered how worried my siblings have been. I suppose I thought they were being foolish."

"It isn't foolish to worry about someone," Henry said softly. "It means you care. And it hasn't just been your siblings. Poor Mr. Khan seemed greatly distressed."

Her mouth curved as she looked up. "And Mr. Khan, of course. He really is quite the mother hen."

Henry laughed. "Is he, now?"

"Oh yes. He's forever fretting that I'm not eating or sleeping enough. Though I suppose that isn't a bad quality to have in a secretary."

"Mine is the same way."

"She seems nice," Lady Arlington offered, her eyes searching his own.

"Delia? She's very good. And are you?" Henry asked, now feeling rather like a mother hen himself. "Not eating or sleeping enough, I mean."

"Probably not. Mr. Khan thinks I need to go away for a few weeks. Somewhere warm," she added.

"It's not a bad idea."

"Maybe. Once the papers are signed."

She glanced out the window again. They had nearly reached her house.

Henry had been fully prepared to leap from the carriage just a few minutes ago to avoid her company. Now he didn't want her to leave, but he couldn't think of a damned thing to say. At least, nothing appropriate. She turned back to him with an expectant look, as his mouth was practically hanging open. "I . . . I hope you take that trip," he said lamely as the carriage came to a stop.

"I'll give it serious consideration," she replied with a soft smile.

A sudden desire to bottle it up and carry it with him swelled in his chest.

Henry did his best to strike the thought from his mind. He was not a maudlin man.

Except around her.

"Good night, my lady," he said as she moved to the door.

She had just begun to respond when an ear-splitting crash rocked the carriage.

* * *

Before Georgiana even had time to react, Captain Harris had pulled her to the floor and covered her with his body. Shattered glass surrounded them, and she could hear shouts from outside followed by pounding footsteps that faded into the night.

Captain Harris cradled her head to his chest. "It's all right, Georgie," he murmured against her hair. "I've got you. Breathe." He took a few deep inhalations to guide her, and she did the same.

"W-what happened?" she managed after a few moments.

He glanced around. "Someone threw a brick through the window."

"Oh." She couldn't keep the tremble out of her voice as her fingers curled into the fabric of his evening jacket. As he began to move away, her grip tightened. "Don't."

His face was not more than an inch from her own. She could make out the extraordinary color of each iris in the low carriage light, and his breath quickened as his lips parted.

All the air seemed to escape from her lungs. Apparently a brick through a window didn't rattle her *nearly* as much as Captain Henry Harris.

Either she was going to kiss him, or he was going to kiss her. And she wouldn't stop it.

Just as he began to lower his head, the carriage door was wrenched open. "My lady! Captain Harris! Are you all right?"

They both turned toward the speaker. It was Reggie's coachman. "I tried to catch the bastard, but he was too—oh, apologies," the lad said as he quickly averted his eyes.

As Captain Harris pushed off of her, she felt the loss of his heat. Did she look as dazed as he did?

"Mind the glass," he said softly as he pulled her into a sitting position before suddenly turning pale.

"Captain?"

He shook his head as he clutched a hand to his chest. Georgiana moved closer. "Henry?" But he didn't seem to hear her and began taking gulping breaths. She placed her hands on his arms and began smoothing them up and down. "There, there. It's over now. You're safe," she crooned softly. His eyelids began to flutter, but his breathing slowed a little.

She turned to the coachman. "Help me get him inside the house."

The lad nodded, and together they eased Captain Harris out of the carriage. By that time her footman Charles and Mossdown had arrived and took over.

"Put him in my study and bring a pot of tea. And some whisky," she added.

"Yes, my lady," Mossdown replied.

Georgiana watched as the two men helped Captain Harris up the stairs, and then she turned back to Reggie's coachman, who had begun clearing the broken glass. There was no way she could hide this.

She let out a sigh. "If my brother is still awake when you get back, please assure him that we are both fine and that he can call tomorrow morning." The last thing Georgiana needed was an overwrought Reggie showing up on her doorstep after midnight. She had just begun to ascend the stairs when the lad called to her. He held out a worn brick in his hands. "You should take this to show the police."

Georgiana forced herself to reach for it. The brick was heavier than she expected and looked like the kind used to construct large buildings. A piece of paper was wrapped around it and secured with twine. She glanced up, and the coachman gave her a sympathetic nod.

"Take care, my lady," he said softly. "I'm glad you're both all right."

A shiver jolted down her spine. If this had hit either of them, they could have been badly injured. Possibly even killed. And the perpetrator could very well still be near right now. Watching her. For the first time since the threats began, Georgiana felt true fear.

"Thank you," she murmured and hurried up the stairs into the house without looking back.

* * *

Henry couldn't say how long the attack lasted. Only that when he finally returned to himself, he was laid out on a chaise with a blanket over his feet like someone's invalid grandmama. The room was dark except for a blazing fire, and his heart began to pound again. As he pushed the blanket away and tried to sit up, a calm voice cut through the shadows.

"Easy, Captain," a woman murmured as a hand pressed against his shoulder and a familiar flowery scent filled the air. "Don't move so quickly."

Georgiana.

The last thing he clearly remembered was the feel of her soft, voluptuous figure beneath his own and how she tugged him closer until he grew ravenous with the need to once again taste the mouth that had haunted him for years. Henry shook his head in a futile attempt to rid himself of the memory.

God, he had almost *kissed* her mere moments after a violent attack. She must think him an absolute beast.

But as his eyes adjusted to the room's low light, she didn't look disgusted. Only concerned. "I had my footman and butler bring you to my study," she explained as she drew her hand away. "I hope that's all right."

Henry silently mourned the loss of her touch as he moved to a sitting position. "Yes. Thank you."

"Does that happen to you often?"

"Does what?"

She cocked her head at his obvious evasiveness, and he let out a breath. "No," he admitted. "Not anymore."

"I'm glad to hear it."

She rose and walked over to a tea cart, where she poured him a cup then held up a decanter of amber liquid with a questioning look. "Only if you join me," he said. She smiled a little as she poured a splash into his cup and one for herself.

"You don't seem very surprised by my episode," he said, accepting the warm beverage.

"I used to volunteer at a home for veterans," she said as she sat down beside him.

Henry raised an eyebrow. "Did you?" This was yet another unexpected revelation from Lady Arlington.

She nodded. "Some of the men still suffered from bouts of nerves. Even years later."

"Poor devils," he muttered before taking a sip. Then he leaned his head back against the chaise as the whisky burned through him. In some ways his return to England had been more difficult than his imprisonment.

"Would you like to talk about it?"

Henry rarely spoke about his experience, but she might understand. He wouldn't tell her everything, of course. There were some things he still couldn't speak of and some things he never would, like the exact scent of that dank, musty dungeon, the thick blackness of the isolated tower he had been thrown into after his failed escape attempt, and the haunting cries of fellow prisoners, men he had never seen whose fates had been far worse than his own.

"The first time it happened I had no idea what it was," he began. "I was staying with my sister and her husband. A pack of neighborhood boys ran past the window in the middle of Sunday dinner shouting bloody murder, and I thought I was going to expire with my face planted in a plate of pudding. Luckily my brother-in-law is an excellent doctor, and he made sure I got help. One of his mentors was a German who had been a medic during the Franco-Prussian War and went on to work with men who had similar issues after returning home. Thanks to him, I learned to recognize the signs and anticipate episodes. Things have been better since then. Mostly."

"That's wonderful." Her words sent a liquid heat through him that rivaled the whisky. "I read about what happened in Turkey," she continued. "How you helped those two students."

The gentleness in her voice settled over his shoulders like a warm blanket, but he shook it off. Henry took another bracing sip. "Considering they both ended up dead, I'd say my efforts fell rather short."

"You can't blame yourself for that," she murmured. "At least you tried. That's more than many would do in that situation. You were all strangers in a foreign country. Most people would probably have looked the other way, rather than offer help."

He turned toward the fire. What would she say if he told her the truth? That unlike the story she had read in the newspapers, those two young men weren't hapless architecture students at all, but fellow spies sent on a mission Henry had refused because it was too risky. He should have known the commodore would have found another way. Then perhaps those two wildly inexperienced young men might still be alive.

"Why did you stop volunteering?" he asked instead. What Henry would have given to be attended by someone like her in those first few harrowing months.

No. Not *someone*.

She stared at the fire as flickering light played on her face. "My husband."

Henry shoved down the jealousy rising in his throat at the despondence in her voice. He needed to be bigger than this.

Better. "I don't believe I've offered you my condolences yet. I am sorry for your loss."

She stared at him for a long moment before finally giving a single nod before standing. Henry couldn't quite read the expression in her gaze, but she certainly didn't seem appreciative. He felt like an ass for waiting so long to say something to her. And clearly his sentiments had fallen far short of the mark for her beloved husband.

She lit a lamp by her desk and the room grew a little brighter. Henry took in the pale green walls decorated with art. Much of it was the more modern sort he didn't really understand, but it looked nice here. A small brown terrier dozed in a bed near the fire, snoring softly.

"And who is that?" Henry asked.

"Barnaby," she said fondly. At the mention of his name on his mistress's lips, the dog shook himself awake and, noticing Henry, came trotting over for a pat.

"Hello there, Barnaby," Henry said as he leaned down to give the dog a scratch. His fur was soft and curly, and he gave a little groan of delight. "Well, aren't you a jolly old fellow."

"Yes, Barnaby is getting on in years, though I'm not sure his exact age. About six years ago, a maid found him in the alley outside my old house nosing around the trash, looking absolutely filthy and far too thin. I knew I had to keep him," the viscountess said fondly as she watched them. "He likes you." She sounded surprised. "Usually he barks at strangers, especially men."

Henry smiled as Barnaby pressed against his legs, so he could pet him even harder. "I always wanted a dog as a boy, but we weren't allowed."

She frowned in confusion. "Whyever not?"

"We moved around often when I was young. Mostly to flats. And my father was gone for long stretches at sea when he was still alive. A dog was one more thing to worry about, and it was too much for my mother."

"Of course," she said quietly. "How silly of me."

Henry glanced up. "It's not silly. How could you know that?"

Lady Arlington shrugged but didn't answer. "And how is your mother?"

"She died about four years ago."

"Oh, I'm so sorry, Captain."

Again Henry had to look away from the sympathy in her eyes, as even he could only endure so much compassion. "It's all right. Her health had been poor for some time. It was hardest on my sister, though, as she had to care for her while I was away. The only blessing is that she wasn't alive when I was imprisoned."

"Yes," she said roughly. "I imagine that would have been very difficult for a mother to bear." Then she retrieved something from her desk and set it beside him before pulling Barnaby onto her lap.

Henry's eyes widened. "Good Lord. I hadn't realized how large it was."

Lady Arlington hugged the dog as she stared at the brick. "I haven't read the note attached yet."

"Would you like me to?"

She nodded as she stroked Barnaby's fur. The vulnerability in her eyes tugged at his ragged heart. Henry pulled out his pocketknife and cut the string that held the note before opening it.

Next time I won't miss.

Henry swallowed hard as outrage began to swell inside him. Lady Arlington held out her hand.

"May I see it?" That familiar determination he had come to recognize over the last week now filled her gaze.

Henry passed the note to her, and she quickly scanned it. "It's the same handwriting as the others—not that there was any doubt."

"Do you still have them?"

"At my office."

"I'd like to bring them to my contact at Scotland Yard tomorrow, if that's all right. And submit a report on what happened here tonight."

"Yes, I think that's wise." She looked defeated for the first time since Henry had begun this investigation. He should have been pleased to see her finally taking this seriously, but all it did was reignite his anger. Whoever did this would pay. Dearly.

"Thank you for your hospitality," Henry said as he rose, giving Barnaby a farewell pat. "But I should be going."

"Oh, please stay, Captain. It's late, and you've had quite an or—"

"*No.*"

The word practically erupted from him, and her mouth clamped shut. If she were anyone else, he might have considered the offer. It was hardly salacious. But he simply could not spend the night here. Not with her so close. An image of her in a lacy nightgown spread out on a pristine white bed flashed in his mind.

Definitely not.

"That is, no thank you, my lady," he amended in a far gentler tone.

"Of course," she said with a tight smile, her serene mask firmly back in place. "I'll ring for Mossdown to bring your coat."

She set Barnaby down and glided over to the bell pull. Just as regret began to pump through his veins, Henry wrenched off the supply. It was imperative that he remain professional, and that required keeping a healthy distance between them at all times. It was safer for her this way.

And especially for him.

* * *

Georgiana sat up with a start. She glanced at the clock by her bedside and let out a gasp. She couldn't remember the last time she had slept past seven. Now it was nearly ten. It had been well past midnight when Jack the coachman finally took Captain Harris home.

Georgiana then let out a groan as she recalled their awkward parting and fell against the pillows. Barnaby had been sleeping at her feet and immediately climbed over her for his morning petting. As Georgiana obliged him, she tried to reason with herself. The captain had to have known she was offering a *spare* room, not her own. And yet he acted positively scandalized by the idea. It was mortifying.

After a few more moments spent indulging Barnaby, she threw back the covers, determined not to waste another minute thinking about Captain Harris, and rushed into the sitting room off her bedchamber. "Bea, why didn't you wake me?"

Her maid set down her sewing basket and came to her

feet. "Mr. Mossdown said no one was to disturb you after last night. He thought it was best that you rest."

"In this household we do what *I* think is best," she insisted, though the man had a point.

"Yes, my lady."

Georgiana immediately regretted speaking so sharply. "I'm sorry. My quarrel is not with you, but with Mossdown."

The girl nodded as she moved to prepare Georgiana's bath.

Afterward, Georgiana dressed and ate a simple breakfast of tea and toast in her room before hurrying downstairs. Luckily she had already cleared her morning's schedule ahead of the ball, but Mr. Khan would be worried if she didn't show soon.

As she reached the landing, she spotted her footman. "Charles, will you fetch my hat and coat?"

The lad gave her an apologetic look. "My lady, your brother has just arrived with Captain Harris. They are in the study."

Goodness, she would have to face him again already. Georgiana was not prepared.

"Very well," she said, trying to ignore the butterflies storming around her stomach. "Tell Cook to send in some tea."

She charged down the hall with Barnaby trotting behind her, hoping to release some of her nerves before she reached her study. Before he had practically fled her company, Captain Harris had been so open. How she had ached to respond in kind and tell him the truth about the viscount. Things she hadn't even yet revealed to those closest to her. But everything between them still seemed as fragile as a spider's web and as changeable as the weather.

Georgiana pushed open the door harder than she meant to and it banged against the wall.

Reggie and Captain Harris had been talking together before the fireplace and ceased their conversation at her noisy entrance.

"Georgie." Her brother looked like he hadn't slept a wink and immediately came over and grabbed her hands, while Barnaby made a beeline for the captain.

"I'm fine," she said. "Please don't worry."

Captain Harris greeted Barnaby like an old friend, but after giving him a few pats, he rose and put his hands behind his back, looking at Georgiana with a carefully blank expression. It felt like he was punishing her for last night. For having seen him at his most vulnerable. And that was infuriating.

She stuck her hands on her hips. "What did you tell him?"

Confusion flashed across his face. "I told him what happened, my lady."

"And now he's worried sick." She gestured to Reggie. "You should have waited for me."

Captain Harris and Reggie exchanged a subtle glance, while Barnaby scurried behind the desk. Georgiana felt a pang of regret for sounding so cross, as the dog was terribly sensitive.

"Why don't you sit down," Reggie said gently.

She bristled at his tone. "I need to go to work."

"Absolutely not," Captain Harris said.

She swung back to face him. "Excuse me? You do not make any demands of me, *sir*."

"Georgie, please," Reggie pleaded. "You can't possibly think that is a good idea. Not after last night."

Reggie really did look at his wit's end. Georgiana took in a deep breath, but the anger churning inside her didn't fade. "I'm sorry you were scared, but I will not hide away in my house. I refuse to give whoever did this the satisfaction," she managed to say in a relatively normal voice.

Reggie opened his mouth to protest, but the captain interrupted. "Give us a moment, Mr. Fox."

"I'll be in the parlor." Reggie actually looked relieved as he left, with Barnaby following at his heels.

Good. Now they could have it out.

As soon as the door closed behind him, Georgiana turned back to Captain Harris. "I wish you had let me speak to Reggie first. He needs to be told things in a certain way. Now you've put him in a state."

"A *state*?" Captain Harris raised an eyebrow. "He appears to be having a perfectly reasonable response to the situation. Why do you keep trying to protect him?" he then asked softly.

Georgiana blinked, blindsided by the question. "It's always been that way," she said, though it wasn't much of an explanation. That was just what Georgiana did. She managed things for everyone else. And no one ever questioned it.

"He's a grown man. And a highly capable one at that. Under the current circumstances, I suggest you let him help you rather than worry about his reaction to the basic facts of this case."

"Your concern is noted," she replied tightly. "Now shall we call him back in here?"

He cast a glance toward the door. "I wanted to apologize for last night first."

Oh.

"I acted unprofessionally. I should have left as soon as I knew you were safe." Georgiana's mouth dropped open. He was serious. "And my actions put your reputation at risk, as well as my own."

Oh.

"Captain," she began. "While I appreciate your thoughtfulness, I hardly think I was on the brink of ruination simply because you spent an hour on my chaise. One hopes it would take a bit more than that."

As color stained the captain's cheeks, Georgiana realized how suggestive this sounded.

"Yes, well," he said with a short cough. "I did appreciate your help, though. I don't usually talk about my... problems. Or my past."

Georgiana's heart melted as she watched him fumble for the right words. "I confess, I don't usually talk about mine, either," she added with a little laugh. What a pair they were.

He gave her a small smile. "I hope you understand why it's best if we keep our distance from each other whenever possible," he continued. "I don't want to create any more issues for you, or do anything that could further hamper this investigation."

Like spending more time with her. She bowed her head in disappointment. He was right, of course. So why did she feel so wretched?

"Yes, that's sensible," she said and glanced up.

Captain Harris was staring at her strangely. Like he wasn't quite sure what he was looking at, but he was determined to find out. Her skin prickled with awareness, but just as he began to say something the door opened. In came

Reggie followed by a maid with the tea tray. Somehow he looked even more anxious than before. "Well then? Have you told her yet?"

"I was just about to." Captain Harris replied with barely veiled irritation.

Georgiana looked between them. "Tell me what?"

Reggie sat down beside her. "The captain and I discussed it, and we think it's best if you leave London for a bit while we get to the bottom of this. Louie agrees, and so does Mr. Khan. I spoke with both of them this morning."

Georgiana ground her teeth. "Well, haven't you been busy." Putting distance between them indeed. "And am *I* to have a say in this?"

"You're well overdue for a break anyway," Reggie pointed out. "You've been promising to take one for months now."

"And I will," she insisted. "Once this deal is finished."

"You may not have the option," Captain Harris muttered.

Georgiana shot him a scowl as Reggie inhaled sharply. "You are *not* helping." Then she turned back to her brother. "Don't listen to him."

Reggie gave her a pained look. "It's hard not to, my dear. You must see that."

Georgiana sighed and closed her eyes against the frustration raging inside her. "It feels too much like admitting defeat. And after everything I've been working for..."

She couldn't muster the energy to finish the thought.

Reggie patted her hand. "I know," he said, his eyes filled with remorse. But he didn't. Not really. Neither of them could understand what they were asking of her. "Haven't you been meaning to visit Sylvia?" Her friend had moved to Berlin last winter after her husband accepted a position with the British ambassador.

"She's talked of us meeting in Monte Carlo, where her mother-in-law lives," Georgiana answered, resigned. Then she raised an eyebrow. "Is that acceptable, Captain?"

She had the distinct impression he would veto a location if he didn't approve of it.

"That depends on where you will stay."

"Well, considering Sylvia's mother-in-law lives at the Hotel Luna, I imagine we would stay there," she said dryly.

The dowager countess of Fairfield was the long-standing partner of the hotel's owner, Mr. Mahmood Previn.

Captain Harris gave a stiff nod. "We can arrange for several protection officers to guard you during your stay."

"No," Georgiana ground out. That was a bridge too far. "I will leave London, but I refuse to be surrounded by strange men. I won't be able to relax."

Captain Harris narrowed his eyes. "I suggest you reconsider, my lady."

Georgiana was just about to tell him where he could shove his suggestion when Reggie cut in.

"Why don't you go too, Captain?"

They both directed their ire at Reggie.

"What?"

"Are you *mad*?"

Reggie shrank back a little at their combined raised voices but then lifted his chin. "Well, doesn't that make the most sense? Georgiana doesn't want strangers protecting her, which I can certainly understand given the circumstances. And you're already familiar with the situation, Captain."

"But I need to be *here*."

Georgiana suppressed the urge to roll her eyes. The man was acting as if Reggie had suggested he travel across the Sahara with her on his back. Not take a trip to the Riviera and stay in a world-class hotel.

Reggie gave him a gentle smile. "I think we've moved beyond the services of a private investigator. If the danger is as great as you say, it's time to contact Scotland Yard again. Don't you agree?"

Captain Harris inhaled deeply, then gave a reluctant nod.

"But it will cause talk if we're seen together," Georgiana argued. If he insisted on acting supremely put out by all this, then by God, so would she.

"Things are different on the Continent," Reggie said. "You won't draw the same notice as you do in London, and you'll hardly be the most scandalous woman there, Georgie. Not when there are actresses and American millionaires flooding the gaming halls. And you can be discreet. Can't you, Captain?"

"Of course," he said curtly.

"Besides," Reggie continued. "If you really *are* worried about the gossip, there is something you could do before you left…"

She didn't like the suggestion in his tone one bit. His single raised eyebrow was even worse. "Don't you dare say it—"

"If you announce your engagement to Tommy Pettigrew, you will gain his protection. He has tremendous influence over the newspapers."

"Engagement!" Georgiana nearly choked on the word, but she didn't miss the way Captain Harris stiffened beside her.

"They won't print the same things about his fiancée," Reggie insisted.

"I will not *marry* in order to stay out of the gossip columns."

"Then just say that you are ready to seriously consider him. That should be enough. And you are, aren't you?"

Georgiana bit her lip. The hope in her brother's eyes tugged at her heart. She couldn't tell him what she truly had planned for her future. Not now. "I suppose I could invite him here this afternoon," she said after a moment.

Reggie broke into a wide grin. "Oh, that would be splendid!"

"Calm down, Reg," she grumbled. "Don't break out the champagne yet. I've no idea what he will say."

"Honestly, Georgie. You can be so dense sometimes." Reggie rolled his eyes. "The captain and I will head to Scotland Yard now."

"Fine. But I can't stay in Monte Carlo for more than a week. I'll need to return regardless of what they've found."

Captain Harris frowned. "How soon can you be ready to leave?"

"In a few days. I have some things at the factory that need to be taken care of."

"Make it two," he said.

Georgiana shot him a glare. "Giving orders already? I am not one of your petty officers, sir."

"No," he said, unamused. "This would be a fair sight easier if you were."

CHAPTER NINE

———

A few hours later, Henry parted ways with Reggie outside Scotland Yard. They had spoken at length with an
inspector Henry had never met before called Crenshaw. He
was new to the position and seemed hungry to prove himself. He was also terribly impressed by Henry, so for once,
he leaned into his hero status, even signing something for
the young man's mother. He felt like an absolute fraud, but
if it helped them solve the case, then so be it. He could play
the part of the hero for a bit.

"Well, that went far better than I expected," Reggie said.
"Look, I know this wasn't in your plans, and I am prepared
to double your price. In addition to covering your expenses,
of course."

Henry so wished he was in a position to reject the offer,
but he had received another, more urgent letter from his
cousin's wife that morning, as well as one from his sister.

His brother-in-law was opening a new clinic in one of the poorest neighborhoods in Glasgow, and one of the backers had fallen through. Agatha hated to ask, but she was wondering if he had anything to spare.

Of course Henry would do what he could. And that meant taking whatever Reginald Fox was offering, pride be damned. He felt like the worst kind of fool, nearly kissing Lady Arlington last night while she was practically engaged to a man like Tommy Pettigrew. He had gone and spouted all that self-important drivel about needing to keep his distance and remain professional, while she had a damned *baron* at her beck and call. Christ, she must think him an idiot.

Henry nodded. "That is more than generous. Thank you."

"No, thank *you*. You don't know what a relief this is for me. For the whole family. I can't even think of what might have happened last night if you hadn't been there with Georgie," he said, his voice growing thick with emotion.

Henry had shared his theory with the inspector that a different sort of attack might have been the original plan, but it changed once his presence was detected. Reggie had been absolutely horrified and made him swear that he would not tell Georgiana about it, but the viscountess seemed to be made of stronger stuff than her younger brother.

It's always been that way.

Now he understood what she meant. But why was she the one to take on the family's burdens? Henry had only his sister to look out for, so it had always made sense why he was the one to shoulder everything. But with so many siblings, surely things could be spread around a little. Or perhaps it didn't matter. Perhaps every family was alike in this way, each member locked in the roles they had occupied since childhood. But for now Henry was here. And he had a job to do.

* * *

"I've never seen someone so angry while packing for a trip to the *Riviera*," Louisa said as she draped herself across Georgiana's bed.

Georgiana glanced up from her spot on the floor before her steamer trunk and glared at her sister. She could have had Bea pack for her, but Georgiana needed to keep busy. So her maid had been tasked with gathering her toiletries instead.

"Yes, well, when someone is practically being forced to go, it is quite easy to access their anger."

"Oh, come on, Georgie. It will be *fun*. Lord knows you need a bit of that in your life. And I can think of much worse places to be banished to than Monte Carlo. David is terribly jealous, you know. He fancies himself something of an expert at roulette." She let out a fond chuckle. "Don't even try to tell him it requires absolutely no skill. You'll never hear the end of it."

Georgiana grunted her reply, something she seemed to have picked up from Captain Harris.

"You must be excited to see Sylvia," Louisa continued, not at all put off. "And isn't her husband friends with the captain?"

"Yes." Georgiana raised an eyebrow. "But how do you know that?"

"Gossip. You wouldn't *believe* the things people say

about Rafe Davies. If even half of it is true, Sylvia is a lucky woman."

Georgiana smiled to herself. "They're very happy and utterly devoted to each other. I know *that* is true." She had been there when the pair first met at Castle Blackwood and had watched them fall in love before either of them really knew what was happening. All in all, it was a very satisfying experience. And about as close to falling in love as she planned to come herself.

"What does she think of Captain Harris?"

Georgiana's shoulders tensed. "The same as everyone else."

That he was an exceptionally brave and honorable man.

Louisa tapped a finger against her chin in mock consideration. "And yet you seem to dislike him. In fact," she added slowly. "I'd say the sentiment is mutual."

Georgiana sighed and sat back on her heels. As much as she agreed with her sister, it still hurt to hear. And Georgiana *hated* that. She shouldn't be affected at all. Shouldn't care what Captain Harris thought of her. Why, she had just told Lord Pettigrew yesterday that she was coming around to the idea of being courted properly once she returned. Georgiana didn't like deceiving the man, but it seemed to put Reggie at ease. And she wasn't opposed to taking a few drives around Hyde Park or attending an exhibition or two with Tommy, after which she would make it perfectly clear to him that they simply didn't suit. No harm would be done.

"I'm sure he would much rather spend his time working on something more important."

Louisa snorted. "As I understand it, he spends most of his time trailing after straying partners. No, my dear sister.

I believe Captain Harris's particular brand of dislike is the remnants of a broken heart."

Now it was Georgiana's turn to snort, which she did quite loudly. "*That* is absurd."

"Is it? I can't imagine he spent all that time at Aunt Paloma's enjoying her company."

Georgiana huffed. "He was friends with Tobias. That was why he came to the house," she mumbled and looked down at her hands to avoid Louisa's too perceptive gaze. She had balled up a pair of stockings so terribly that Bea would have a fit.

"You know you can talk to me, Georgie. About anything," Louisa said quietly. "Sometimes I think you forget I'm not your annoying little sister anymore. I'm a properly married woman now."

Georgiana managed to give her a wry smile. "I certainly haven't forgotten. I spent enough time at the dressmaker's putting your trousseau together."

Louisa chuckled. "Yes. And thank you for having such excellent taste." Then she turned serious. "But I mean it. I've suffered my share of heartache, and I know marriage isn't all wine and roses. Goodness, David and I fight like cats and dogs sometimes."

"Do you?" That was surprising to hear.

Louisa lifted a shoulder. "Of course. But then we have an even better time making up."

Georgiana watched a dreamy smile take over her sister's face. She didn't know a thing about that. The viscount had never raised his voice to her, preferring instead to deliver subtle cutting remarks or demonstrate his control. He told her what to wear and where to go and who to talk to once she got there. And for years Georgiana endured it all with that serene smile of hers, dressed in the most fashionable gowns without a hair out of place, pretending like she wasn't at all bothered by his constant demands. Instead, she controlled the only thing she had left: her demeanor. Georgiana refused to become an object of pity, so she did her best to make sure no one suspected how unhappy she was.

"Well, I hardly think any of *that* applies to Captain Harris and myself."

Louisa turned thoughtful. "Perhaps not. But sometimes irritation can mask attraction. That's all."

Georgiana opened her mouth to violently deny this when Bea appeared with her train case, packed and ready. She gasped and nearly dropped it when she saw the state of Georgiana's stockings. By the time that was all sorted out, Louisa had to leave.

She rose and pressed a kiss to Georgiana's cheek. "Try to enjoy yourself. And remember, if the captain gets you riled up, just remind him he's supposed to keep you *relaxed*." Then she gave her a wink and slipped out of the room before Georgiana managed to respond.

* * *

Early the next morning Georgiana hid a most unladylike yawn behind her hand as she paced the platform of Victoria Station. Bea was waiting for her in the first-class lounge, but Georgiana couldn't sit still and decided to stretch her legs before they had to board the train for the ride down to Dover. Since yesterday afternoon her mind had been consumed with the same swirling thoughts. Could Louisa be right?

Did the captain's disdain really stem from heartache—and was *that* why he had never married? Her stomach had begun to prickle with guilt, but Georgiana was quick to dismiss it. After all, if he truly had been in love with her all those years ago, why did he say those vile things she had overheard? And why did he say nothing now?

Perhaps he was hurt when you chose the viscount. Because he really had *fallen for you.*

It was not the first time such a thought had occurred to Georgiana. That very evening she had told Tobias what she had overheard and demanded to know the truth about his friend. But he had set her straight.

Georgie, he came to London to marry a wealthy wife.

In other words, not a girl like her.

Then I suppose I saved both of us some trouble.

Questions tangled with long-buried memories, keeping her awake for hours. But this tiredness was not the result of just one night. It was a bone-deep exhaustion that had been accumulating for years from the great weight of regret pressing into her shoulders. The viscount's death had lightened her load a little, but it had all come rushing back the moment her gaze met Captain Harris's across his tiny, tidy office.

Just as her mouth began to twitch from another yawn, the train pulled into the station. She stepped back from the platform as the scent of oil and hot metal invaded her senses, and she closed her eyes for a moment against the heat rolling off the massive piece of machinery. She opened them just in time to see Captain Harris emerge through a burst of steam, his dark coat flaring out behind him. It was a most dramatic entrance, made even more so by the ever present scowl on his face. Georgiana saw the exact moment he spotted her because his frown immediately deepened.

Sometimes irritation can mask attraction.

She muffled a snort. If that were true, then the captain must be utterly *mad* for her. She did her best to ignore the answering pulse of interest. It was an unwelcome reminder of just how much she had once wanted him.

Once, she reminded herself. *Not anymore.*

And yet Georgiana couldn't help noticing the captain's long legs as they strode toward her, along with the sight of his gloved hand sheathed in black leather atop his cane. Her breath caught as he tightened his grip on the handle.

It was another moment before Captain Harris reached her, and another still before she realized she had been staring.

The captain raised an eyebrow. "You should be waiting in the lounge," he scolded. "It isn't safe out here."

"And good morning to you, Captain," she said briskly.

His lips twitched for a moment as he stared down at her, but Georgiana could swear there was the slightest glint in his eyes. "Good morning, my lady."

This felt like a small win, and Georgiana couldn't help smiling at him. "Ready for our journey?"

He let out a grunt and scanned the platform. "Surely I don't need to explain that this is a terrible idea."

It's best if we keep our distance from each other.

And this was the exact opposite.

But before she could respond, someone called her name. Georgiana and the captain both turned to the speaker. It was Tommy Pettigrew. *Here.*

"My Lord," Georgiana gasped, too surprised to hide it.

"Good morning, Captain. Lady Arlington," he said with a sweeping bow much too grand for a train station. When he straightened, Georgiana noticed the bouquet of flowers. "Forgive me, but I couldn't let you leave the country without seeing you off."

As he handed her the bouquet, he darted a nervous glance toward Captain Harris, who looked properly intimidating and very much like a mysterious duke in a Gothic novel. Georgiana couldn't help feeling a little sorry for Tommy in this moment.

She accepted the flowers and brought them to her nose. "Thank you. Ah, daisies. My favorite."

"A lady as lovely as you deserves roses, but you once mentioned that daisies reminded you of your family home in Kent."

"How thoughtful you are," she said, smiling with genuine pleasure.

Tommy grinned back. It put her in mind of the first time Barnaby successfully rolled over when she gave the command. How pleased they both looked to win her approval.

"Isn't it a bit early for you, Lord Pettigrew?" Captain Harris asked gruffly. "I thought gentlemen of leisure didn't rise before noon."

If his lordship picked up on the cut, he did not indicate it. "Oh, I'm quite the early riser, Captain," he said with his usual cheerfulness. "Always have been." Georgiana's smile grew as the captain's expression noticeably darkened. Perhaps this young man was exactly what she needed. Someone to draw her out from under the dark veil that had shrouded her all these years. Tommy Pettigrew may be many things, but Georgiana felt certain he would never intentionally hurt her or withhold his affection. No, one always knew exactly where they stood with him. And that was very, *very* appealing.

The train whistle went off, and passengers disembarked. It was nearly time to leave.

"Well then, enjoy your trip. I will call on you when you return," Tommy said to her before addressing the captain. "I trust you'll take good care of the lady."

Georgiana bristled a little. Regardless of what she had told Tommy yesterday, he was most definitely overstepping the mark here.

Captain Harris eyed his outstretched hand for a moment before shaking it. "As I understand it, the lady is quite capable of taking care of herself. I am merely here as a safeguard. But your concern is noted."

Pink stained Tommy's cheeks as his gaze flickered between them. "Of course," he mumbled, then gave them a wave before disappearing into the gathering crowd.

"Come. We should wait in the lounge until it's time to board," Captain Harris said.

Georgiana held back a sigh. Apparently her capabilities did not extend to waiting on train platforms. But as she had no desire to quibble with him so early into their trip, she held her tongue and allowed herself to be escorted inside. The captain seated her in a far corner of the room before standing guard at the doorway, though no one else entered except a kindly steward who looked old enough to be her grandfather.

Much to her relief, Captain Harris disappeared once she was settled in her private train cabin. Georgiana didn't think she could stand being trapped in the compartment with him glowering at her all the way to Dover. Bea claimed he was walking along the hallway, as his knee stiffened if he sat too long.

"Oh," Georgiana had replied, chagrined to learn that her maid knew more about the captain's injury than she did. "Has he said anything else to you about it?"

"No, my lady. But Charles said he goes to some kind of specialist on Harley Street who makes him do all sorts of exercises to keep up his strength. I even heard his cane hides a *sword*."

It was certainly a possibility, and a rather intriguing one that Georgiana did her best to put out of her mind for the length of the trip. He reappeared only once they were ready to depart, as dark and forbidding as ever.

As they waited at the harbor for their steamer, he kept his gaze faced toward the horizon. "There might be a storm tonight," he said.

It was a gorgeous day, though the sea churned with frothy waves.

Georgiana had to look away from the surf. "I hope not. I got sick the last time I went over."

The captain turned slightly toward her. "And when was that?"

Something in the tenor of his voice as he asked the question made it seem as though he already knew the answer, ridiculous as it sounded.

"I went to Egypt with my aunt last winter."

It had been her first time crossing the channel. The viscount hated leaving London and had rarely permitted Georgiana to travel without him. She had friends who spent most of the year going from house party to house party, but aside from a rare trip to Castle Blackwood, Georgiana's married life had been largely spent within a one-mile radius of her husband's Mayfair town house.

"You mean Mrs. Crawford. Your husband's aunt."

Captain Henry's statement brought her back to the moment. He was now looking at her curiously. She couldn't read his expression and raised an eyebrow. "Yes. But I still consider her family, of course."

He stared at her for another long moment. "Of course," he repeated.

"My sister Franny is acting as her companion now," she continued, attempting to break the tension gathering between them once more. "They're somewhere in the Holy Land."

The captain's response to this was little more than a grunt, and then he turned away once more to discuss something with the ticket agent.

Georgiana stared after him. She wasn't sure which was more surprising: that he knew of her trip with Mrs. Crawford or that he admitted to it. For so long she assumed she was little more than an afterthought to him, that the minor details of her life both before and after their brief courtship were entirely inconsequential. She frowned at his back, unable to keep from noticing the appealing set of his shoulders. Why couldn't he continue to keep his distance and behave as though she were just another client? But even more irritating was the small flicker of joy it brought her.

* * *

After a simple supper in the steamer's dining room, Henry made his way to his cabin. He had not seen Lady Arlington since they boarded and guessed that she had decided to take a tray in her room. It was a smart choice given the particularly beastly state of the channel this evening. Thanks to over a decade spent at sea, Henry wasn't much affected by the steamer's constant rocking, but the few passengers he had just dined with looked rather green around the gills. He paused outside his door and considered checking on Lady Arlington. But if she was absolutely fine, he would feel rather silly. Besides, she had Bea to look after her. And Lord knew how difficult it would be to keep his distance once they reached Monte Carlo.

That settled it.

Henry entered his cabin and began readying himself for bed. He had just finished washing up when there was an urgent knock on the door.

"Captain, it's Bea! Please open the door!"

He glanced down. He wore no coat or waistcoat, and his shirt was unbuttoned at the throat.

But in that brief pause, Bea knocked even harder. "Her ladyship has taken ill!"

Any reticence vanished, and Henry was at the door in two strides. He tore it open just as the maid was preparing to knock a third time.

"Oh my," she murmured as her wide brown eyes fell on his exposed throat.

"Bea," he prompted, and she immediately looked up. "Is it seasickness?"

"I believe so. But I've *never* seen her like this before."

Then he noticed the girl looked rather pale herself. "I'll be right there." He ducked back into his cabin to retrieve his coat and cane.

As they made their way down the hall, the steamer hit a particularly violent patch of sea and pitched forward, nearly knocking Bea to the floor.

"Hold on to the walls," Henry instructed as he eased her back on her feet.

"Yes, Captain," she gasped.

Their progress slowed significantly as Bea gingerly inched down the hallway. Henry pressed his lips together to keep his frustration in check, but when they reached Lady Arlington's cabin, he was beside himself.

It's only a bit of seasickness, you dolt. She isn't dying.

The lady herself confirmed this when she took one look at him and groaned.

"I told you not to bother him, Bea. I'm *fine*."

Henry begged to differ, given that she was currently lying facedown on the floor. When he asked what she was doing, Lady Arlington sighed as if he was terribly slow and turned her head toward him. "It feels better down here," she mumbled, then squeezed her eyes shut.

Impeccable logic, that.

He turned to Bea. "Fetch some water and towels."

"Yes, Captain," the girl said and disappeared into the en suite.

"I think you will be more comfortable in your bed, my lady." Her only response was another groan. "Come," Henry added as he gently wrapped a hand under her shoulder and eased her up.

Lady Arlington let out a little whine of protest, but

otherwise complied. He settled her on top of the bed just as Bea returned, looking worse than before.

"You should get some rest as well," Henry said as he took the supplies from her.

The girl began to protest, but Lady Georgiana waved her off. "It's all right, Bea. Goodness knows the captain doesn't have enough bedside manner for the both of us."

"Glad to see that sharp tongue of yours is still intact," Henry replied once Bea left for her sleeping chamber.

"Oh, it would take more than a bout of seasickness to get rid of it, I'm afraid."

Henry smiled to himself as he dampened two cloths with water. He slipped a hand behind her neck and tucked one against her nape. Then he placed the other on her forehead. As his finger brushed against her temple, he lingered there for a brief moment, unable to keep from stroking the golden silk of her hair just once.

"That feels nice," she said on a breathy sigh.

Henry snatched his hand away. Thank God her eyes were still closed so she couldn't see his cheeks ablaze.

He cleared his throat. "Are you feeling feverish?"

"No, only nauseous. Though it's much worse than last time."

"It's a particularly rough crossing." As if to demonstrate that point, the ship began to rise up another steep swell. Lady Arlington reached for his hand and squeezed it.

"There, now. Keep breathing," Henry said softly.

As they made their swift descent, the steamer creaked in protest and Lady Arlington reached for his other hand.

"It's all right," he continued. "Perfectly normal."

He wasn't actually sure about that, but better to stay calm.

"I *hate* this," she sputtered as her teeth chattered from nerves. "I'm never leaving England again after this trip."

"Perhaps you should take something. At least to help you sleep."

He expected her to put up a fight, but she cracked one sapphire eye open. "In my valise by the washstand."

Henry pushed to his feet and lurched over to her bag, from which he retrieved a small bottle of laudanum.

"Just a drop," Georgiana said.

Henry measured the dose, mixed it with water, and held the glass to her mouth. Her lips parted as she swallowed and Henry had to clear his throat again.

No man should be this aroused by a woman in the throes of nausea.

She leaned back against the pillows and Henry changed her cloths. "Tell me about your first time at sea."

He let out a chuckle. "You want to hear about that now?"

"I need to be reassured that I won't always feel this wretched. And I could use the distraction."

"Well, I'm afraid I can't help you much there," he said dryly and she cracked a smile. "I was ill a time or two in the beginning, though never bedridden. Then again, they don't really tolerate that in the navy."

"I can imagine. How old were you?"

"Sixteen."

"So young?"

"They take boys as young as twelve. I would have gone sooner, but my mother wanted me to have more schooling first. My father had been a captain too, and he was my hero all my life."

"You wanted to follow in his footsteps," she said sleepily.

The laudanum was taking effect. She didn't look quite so pale as before.

"I did. We also needed the money, as he had died a few years earlier."

She made a sympathetic sound. "That must have been hard. All that responsibility heaped on your shoulders."

"It was," he murmured. "But I made do."

"Yes. We always seem to find a way, don't we? When the situation demands it."

Henry suspected she was speaking from personal experience. That was interesting. He was dying to ask her more, but it felt wrong in her current state.

"I should go," he said and moved to stand, but she reached out.

"Please. Not yet." Her hand brushed down his arm, setting off a trail of sparks.

"I don't think Lord Pettigrew would approve," he said in a strangled voice, fighting the temptation to stay. But she didn't seem to notice his reticence.

"Him?" Based on her reaction, Henry might as well have suggested P. T. Barnum.

"I thought you had an...understanding."

"Oh, no," she said airily. "I won't be marrying again."

Henry blinked. She sounded quite certain.

She was quiet for so long that he thought she had fallen asleep. He watched the even rise and fall of her chest until his own eyes began to grow heavy. Then she spoke: "Do you regret going into the navy, considering all that happened?"

Henry had a feeling she never would have asked him that, if not for the laudanum. But given what she had just revealed, he owed her a little truth as well: "There are a great many things I regret, my lady, but no. Never that."

"I'm glad," she said. "I had wondered..." But before she could finish the thought, she drifted off to sleep.

* * *

The first thing Georgiana noticed when she awoke was that the steamer was no longer being tossed about like a thimble in a tub. The storm must have passed, thank God. The second thing she noticed was that she was no longer stretched out on the floor. Then she remembered being helped into bed by *Captain Harris*.

She sat up with a start and found the man himself asleep at her feet with his back up against the cabin's wall and his hands folded across his chest. She had never slept beside a man before, as her husband had always retreated to his own bedroom after their infrequent marital relations. Georgiana wasn't sure how the captain managed to sleep sitting up, but he must have gotten used to sleeping in all sorts of awkward places over the years. His face was softer in repose, and he looked younger, like he had when they first met. But she found that she preferred him as he was now, with lines around his eyes and mouth, and a sterner set to his features. There was an edge that hadn't been there before, when he had been on his best behavior. But now that artifice was gone entirely. He was not trying to charm her at all anymore. And she quite enjoyed it.

His shirt was unbuttoned at the throat, and Georgiana couldn't tear her gaze away from the triangle of exposed skin covered in a light dusting of golden brown hair. She also couldn't stop imagining what the rest of his chest looked like.

Sylvia had mentioned that Rafe had several tattoos from his years in the navy. Did Captain Harris as well?

While she was thinking about what lay beneath the captain's shirt, his eyes slanted open before widening in alarm.

"I fell asleep," he blurted out unnecessarily.

"Not a problem," Georgiana chirped, though it was most *definitely* a problem. Morning light streamed through the cabin's porthole. He needed to leave before anyone saw him.

Georgiana stood up too quickly, and black spots danced before her eyes. A warm, firm hand wrapped around her arm to help balance her.

"Careful, my lady," he said in a gravelly voice. "You had laudanum last night."

Georgiana tried not to tremble too obviously at his touch. "Right." She remembered now, along with his gentle touch. Her breath quickened at the hazy memory of his fingers brushing against her nape and temples. Of his care. "I rarely take it, but I was quite desperate."

He pulled his hand away and nodded, then glanced toward the porthole. "I should go." He straightened his jacket and retrieved his cane.

"Thank you for your help last night. I hope I wasn't too much trouble for you."

She also hoped she hadn't been sick in front of him.

The corner of his mouth lifted. "No, you were just enough. I'll see you at the port."

Then he turned and left the room. Georgiana slowly sat back down on the bed as his words sank in.

Just enough trouble.

Georgiana may have weathered the storm, but there was a far greater one awaiting her. She needed to get through this trip without losing her head to Captain Harris once again. And at the moment he was making it very difficult.

* * *

The next day Henry stared out the window of the carriage at the foothills of the French Alps stretching toward the heavens. He had traveled quite extensively during his naval career, but never to the Riviera.

He cut a glance toward Lady Arlington. Her complexion looked much improved. One would never know she had spent the evening of their cross-channel journey on the floor. They hadn't spoken beyond basic pleasantries since he slunk out of her cabin in the early morning light yesterday. Not that he had a clue what to say to her. *Please let me nurse you again* seemed a touch forward. And besides, Henry was here to work. He needed to remember that. Yet all he could think of was her soft sighs as she drifted off to sleep in the steamer's cabin, along with the words that had haunted him ever since:

I won't be marrying again.

He still wasn't sure if she had spoken the truth or if her mind was jumbled from the laudanum. Not that it mattered anyway. She was not for him.

"Here we are," the viscountess said as they turned up the drive to the hotel, but her cheerful tone couldn't hide the strained note in her voice. She must be exhausted. Lord knew he hadn't slept well aside for those few short hours in her cabin. It had been damned foolish of him, nodding off like that, but he had been worried about her. Henry didn't think of himself as the nurturing sort, but somehow this woman softened his edges in a way he hadn't ever experienced.

This woman.

They had passed by many impressive buildings, including the Prince's Palace, but the Hotel Luna still managed to be exceptional. Tucked away on a cliff above Monte Carlo, the brilliant white exterior sparkled in the sunlight, with rows of huge crystalline windows and an expansive upper terrace that looked out onto the sea, while the stairs leading up to the grand entrance were made of matching white marble. It reminded him of the palaces of the Roman emperors he had read about as a boy.

"Goodness," he burst out, then immediately regretted it as Lady Arlington flashed him a small smile. Lord knew all the stately residences she had visited over the years. She would think him a rube.

You are *a rube.*

The carriage had barely come to a stop when a uniformed employee opened the door and helped the ladies down, while two more swiftly unloaded their luggage and brought it up the stairs. The bellhops worked together in competent silence, like some sort of strange modern ballet. Henry gripped the handle of his cane a little tighter as he eyed the stairs while the employees raced up and down with ease.

A year and a half ago he would not have been able to make the ascent. Now, thanks to a hell of a lot of hard work, he could, but at a slower speed. Henry liked to think it stately, but that meant he would noticeably lag behind Lady

Arlington and her maid. The back of his neck prickled. It had been a long time since he felt so self-conscious. He swallowed hard and straightened his shoulders.

"Captain?"

He turned to find Lady Arlington by his left side. "I don't want to make any presumptions," she began in a low voice, "but I know carriage rides can be uncomfortable for you."

"Movement always helps."

"Well then, would you do me the honor of your escort? I'm afraid I'm still feeling a bit lightheaded," she added after a moment.

Henry realized he had been too surprised to reply. "Of course, my lady." He held out his arm and she took it. Together they ascended the stairs at a steady, if slower pace, but Lady Arlington didn't seem to mind. When they reached the top she pulled away and patted his arm.

"Thank you for your assistance." Then she stepped away to greet the concierge, not looking the least bit lightheaded.

Henry blinked. She must have noticed his reticence and tried to make him feel more comfortable. The concierge was giving her the now familiar look of interest that came over the faces of most men who encountered the viscountess. He had yet to determine if she was entirely aware of the effect she had on men. He had thought her guileless when they were younger, until she had chosen to marry the viscount. But she still seemed just as unaffected as before. Henry frowned. Such a deception would take an awful lot of effort on her part, but the alternative would mean he had been completely wrong about her all these years. Neither option was terribly appealing.

Before he could ruminate on that any further, a

sophisticated older man in an expertly tailored gray day suit approached him with a friendly smile. He had a full head of striking silver hair and a neatly trimmed beard that complemented his olive skin.

"Greetings. I am Mahmood Previn," he said, bowing slightly, his words tinged with a subtle French accent. "You must be Captain Harris."

"Yes, hello." Henry shook his proffered hand. "A pleasure to meet you. I understand Mr. Fox messaged you ahead of our arrival?"

Mr. Previn glanced to the viscountess, who was still conversing with the concierge, and gave Henry a subtle nod. "I have made arrangements with my most trusted staff to ensure the lady's safety. I have also taken the liberty of putting you in a suite of rooms on the top floor. It can only be accessed by private lift. We often use it when family or friends visit, as it is close to the countess's quarters."

"Thank you, Mr. Previn," Henry said. "That is very kind."

"I understand you have made the acquaintance of the countess?"

"Yes. But that was many years ago." Rafe had brought him around once for tea when they were on leave. "I was barely more than twenty. I doubt I made much of an impression."

The countess, on the other hand, had lived up to her reputation as a noted beauty.

Mr. Previn chuckled warmly. "On the contrary. She is very excited for your visit and has asked me to invite you to her suite for refreshments once you've settled."

Before Henry could give his regrets, Mr. Previn turned to address Lady Arlington as she approached them. "Welcome to the Hotel Luna, my lady," he said as he bowed and placed a kiss on her hand. "I am the owner, Mahmood Previn."

Lady Arlington gave him a genial smile. "Hello, Mr. Previn. What a beautiful hotel you have here. Your concierge was just telling me about the building's history. Thank you so much for accommodating us on such short notice."

He waved a hand. "It is nothing. Anything for the friends of our Rafe and Sylvie. And I know you English love your formalities, but please call me Mahmood."

"Happily, but only if you call me Georgiana," she said with a grin. Her immediate comradery with the handsome and sophisticated hotelier made Henry feel even more unrefined by comparison.

"I was just telling Captain Harris that the countess would love for you to join her for some refreshments in her suite once you have settled in."

"That sounds lovely. I'll be there."

Mr. Previn turned to him and raised a questioning brow.

"I was hoping to meet with your head of security and scout out the hotel. But I will try to come afterward," he added awkwardly.

Mr. Previn nodded. "Of course. I will arrange for a meeting right away. In the meantime, Michel will escort you to your rooms." He gestured to the concierge, who still hovered a few feet away. "If there is anything you need, please do not hesitate to ask." This was directed at the viscountess.

"Thank you, Mahmood."

He bowed to her once again and shook Henry's hand. "Enjoy your stay."

"Such a charming man," Lady Arlington said, watching as he walked over to warmly greet another group of guests.

"Yes. Rafe—er, Mr. Davies has always spoken quite highly of him."

She turned to him. "So *Mrs.* Davies has told me." It took Henry a moment to realize she was teasing him.

Before he could respond, the concierge had appeared to escort them to the private lift. The man was all too eager to have the viscountess's attention once again. Henry hung back a little so he could take in their surroundings. The lobby was open and airy, reminiscent of the Moorish buildings he had visited once in Spain, with brightly colored tiles, accent fountains, enormous potted ferns, and other vegetation. Impressionist art was featured prominently on the walls.

The concierge had begun discussing the hotel's history, most of which he already knew from Rafe: how Mr. Previn had been born into a family of well-respected hoteliers, but when he took over the property after his father's death, he began a massive renovation plan. Gone were the dark, heavy furnishings so popular with English tourists. Instead, Mr. Previn took inspiration from the airy and bright riads of Marrakesh, his mother's birthplace. When it had reopened, some declared that the hotel wouldn't last a year, that Mr. Previn had thrown away the reputation his father's family had worked decades to earn on a silly whim, but the naysayers had been wrong. The hotel was an immediate success and drew more guests than ever before. It had been well over a decade since the reopening, and the hotel still continued to be extremely popular, boasting all of the latest amenities and technological advances. It was one of the first in the area to feature electricity in common rooms, along with a heated outdoor pool open year round.

"How fabulous," Lady Arlington said, her neck craning to take in a blue and yellow stained glass dome above them that let in natural light. They reached the private lift around the corner from the public one.

"I'll wait," Henry said. He had little desire to be crammed into a small space, even less so with Lady Arlington.

Not if it were just the two of us.

He ignored the thought.

The concierge barely masked his joy as he ushered Lady Arlington into the compartment. "It is automatic. Only push this and it will engage," he explained in a thick French accent as he tapped a button.

Henry's eyes met Lady Arlington's as the man pulled the wrought iron door closed. "Easy enough," he replied. Their gazes remained locked together as the lift slowly rose until she disappeared into the floor above, far out of reach.

CHAPTER TEN

Georgiana was certainly no stranger to luxury, but the Empress Suite of the Hotel Luna still managed to take her breath away. Much like the downstairs lobby, it was filled with natural light, with a row of floor-to-ceiling windows along one wall that immediately drew the eye. A set of French doors opened out onto a spacious balcony, and beyond that, the blue-green of the Mediterranean Sea glittered like a precious stone freshly polished.

Monsieur Ormonde, the concierge, had barely paused for breath as he discussed the hotel's storied history and the many design elements that Mr. Previn—Mahmood—had incorporated, fusing Moorish and French style.

In Georgiana's opinion, her host was nothing short of a visionary. She would love the chance to talk with him about his inspiration, if he had the time.

The concierge opened the door that led to the master

bedroom, clearly wanting to take her on a tour of the entire suite. Two years ago Georgiana would have let him, too polite to put her own desires first. But no more. She had finally learned to prioritize herself. And right now what she wanted was a bit of quiet and something delicious to eat.

"Thank you very much, monsieur," she said sincerely as she pressed a very generous tip into his hand. "That will be all."

Ever the consummate professional, the man immediately bowed. "If there is anything you need, please do not hesitate to notify me directly."

Georgiana smiled. "I will."

Soon after he left, Bea appeared from the master bedroom. "I've unpacked your luggage, my lady. Would you like me to order something to eat?"

"You've read my mind. A plate of sandwiches, perhaps?"

Her maid nodded then hesitated for a moment. "Will Captain Harris be joining you?"

The concierge knew the captain was here acting as her protection officer and had explained that his room was on the other end of the suite, off the parlor. It made sense for him to share the suite with her—it was massive, after all—and yet it still felt dangerously close.

"No," she said quickly. Just as Bea began to turn away, Georgiana called her back. "But perhaps see if he needs anything."

It had only just dawned on her that every man of her acquaintance traveled with a valet, while Captain Harris had come alone. That was an appalling notion to most of the people Georgiana knew, but she only felt self-conscious. Guilty, even. After all, she didn't *need* a maid, though Bea certainly made her life much easier. And Georgiana paid her handsomely for her service.

Bea, unaware of the warring thoughts within her mistress's head, went to consult Captain Harris and order the food. Georgiana headed for the balcony, as the lure of the sea was too strong to ignore. She tried to focus on the beauty of the view and remembered how fortunate she was to be here, even though she had been thoroughly annoyed by both her brother and Captain Harris for all but forcing her to come in the first place. No, that wasn't quite true. She did want to see Sylvia, even though the timing wasn't exactly ideal.

She had been assured by her lawyers before she left London that everything was progressing just as it should. And Mr. Khan had gone so far as to suggest that her continued presence in the city could be detrimental. If anything else occurred, it could scare off potential investors. And Georgiana certainly didn't want that.

But now that she had made the journey, she would do her best to put aside thoughts of the business and focus on the present. A pity that had to include the most confounding man she knew. He had barely looked at her since that morning in her cabin. Georgiana couldn't tell if it was because she'd been a complete disgrace that evening or he was simply trying to remain as professional as possible. Either way, it hurt.

Soon enough the view did its magic and she was lost in the cliffs and the waves and the chattering sea birds. For a few precious minutes she was not the viscountess, or a lonely widow, or an unruly woman. But merely herself. Belatedly, Georgiana felt a presence beside her.

"Captain," she said, not needing to look at him. That was how familiar his scent had become to her once again.

"Please give my regrets to the countess," he murmured. "I will join you as soon as I can."

Georgiana finally dared to look at him. He was gazing out at the sea beyond with an inscrutable look on his face.

"What a fantastic view."

"Yes, indeed."

At least that was something they could agree on.

"I know things haven't turned out as you wished," he began softly as he turned to her, "but I do hope you are able to enjoy yourself while we're here."

Then before she could respond, Captain Harris gave her a nod and left.

She blinked and turned back to the view. The loneliness she always fought to keep at bay was now clawing at her tattered edges. Time for a distraction.

"My lady?" Bea asked, the note of worry cutting through her vicious thoughts. Georgiana realized she had been glowering down at the surf below, her hands gripping the balcony rail. This was not the posture of the elegant, almost perversely self-controlled viscountess. She inhaled deeply and schooled her expression before turning around. "Your food has arrived."

"Thank you." Georgiana gave her a serene smile. The one that had been practically frozen to her face during her marriage. The one that only a very select few ever bothered to look past.

Bea looked immediately at ease and returned her smile before stepping back into the room. Georgiana glanced back toward the view, beautiful and unchanged, as she was meant to be.

You should find yourself a lover.

Dolly's suggestion was now more appealing than ever. Georgiana decided in that moment that she would indeed do just that. Tonight.

* * *

Henry left the meeting with the Hotel Luna's head of security feeling more relieved than he had in days. Commandant DuBois was a short, bulky man in his late forties who had served a lengthy stint in the French military, primarily in Egypt. The years of exposure to the heat and sun of the desert shone in the heavy lines of his tanned face, which seemed cast in a permanent frown. But that was perfectly fine by Henry. Security was a serious business, after all.

We host many guests of importance, Captain. Ambassadors, heads of state, titans of business, many still with targets on their backs. I promise you, Lady Arlington will be safe here.

Henry believed him. The viscountess had agreed to be discreetly trailed by two protection officers for the duration of her stay at the hotel as long as they kept their distance. He checked his pocket watch. Lady Arlington should still be having tea with the countess. He picked up the pace as much as he dared and headed toward the private lift.

It was an unneeded reminder that despite his physical training, Henry was not a professional bodyguard, and even without his injury, she was far more distracting to him than he would ever admit. Therefore this was an ideal arrangement. Any immediate threats could be handled by the protection officers, while Henry . . . well . . . Henry would collect a handsome fee for acting like a glorified companion.

The thought made him grimace as he stepped into the lift. He certainly didn't intend to spend the next week lounging on a sun chair beside her, yet he couldn't shake the feeling that his presence wasn't really necessary. But then he recalled the look on Lady Arlington's face when he had found her on the balcony earlier.

Without an audience to perform for, she had been stripped completely of artifice, and all that was left was a woman who looked very much alone. And so, so lost. It was a feeling Henry had needed to overcome when he had first returned to civilian life. Though it had been difficult at times, remaining in the navy had not been possible for him. Not after what happened in Turkey.

It had taken considerable effort on his part not to reach out and fold her into his arms. Was this how she always felt in those moments of quiet since her husband's death? Was that why she had thrown herself into running a business and left her marital home? So that she did not have to face the evenings alone in an empty mansion in Mayfair?

I won't be marrying again.

When she had first uttered those words that night on the steamer, all he could think of was that annoying smile being wiped off Lord Pettigrew's face. But now something that felt dangerously close to disappointment throbbed in his chest.

Once he arrived at the top floor, he made his way toward the countess's suite, where her butler showed him to the terrace. It was much larger than their own suite's sizable balcony and decorated with a number of potted palm trees and other tropical plants, some in full bloom in shades ranging from blushing fuchsia to blazing yellow. The ladies were seated in the shade under an awning on a pair of wicker sofas, accompanied by a gleaming silver teacart laden with pastel confections. Lady Arlington's back was to him, but the countess noticed him immediately and waved.

"Hello there, Captain Harris!" She had been a celebrated actress earlier in life and could still project quite beautifully.

Henry waved back, suddenly feeling rather awkward. Lady Arlington's shoulders had visibly tightened, and she didn't bother to turn around. Instead, she simply glanced up once he stood before them.

"It is so lovely to see you again, my dear," the countess said as she embraced him. "And how well you look!"

Henry had forgotten how much Rafe favored his mother. They both shared the same dark brown hair, and though the countess's temples were now streaked with gray, she was still a strikingly attractive woman. It was little wonder that Rafe's father, the late Earl of Fairfield, had fallen in love with her on sight—and created the scandal of the decade by marrying the former actress.

"Sit, sit. Tell us about your meeting with Commandant DuBois. Isn't he a character?" Before Henry could answer either question, the countess continued: "He refuses to tell me how many men he's killed. Not even after I revealed my own history with espionage."

Lady Arlington choked on her sip of tea.

"And when was this?" Henry asked pleasantly, as if they were talking about summer travel plans and not state secrets.

The countess shrugged as she poured him a cup of tea. "Oh, when the earl was still alive and working for the government, we were involved in intelligence gathering now and then. Mostly it meant I flirted with dull men at dinner parties. It could be terribly tedious." She waved a hand as if it were nothing. "Do you take sugar or cream?"

"A little cream."

"Just like my son," she said, smiling warmly as she handed him the teacup and saucer. "You must eat something as well. The kitchen made enough for ten hungry men. I recommend the apple tart, while Georgie liked the éclair, didn't you?"

Georgie. Only an hour together and they had already progressed to nicknames.

"Everything is delicious," Lady Arlington agreed. She had resumed her usual mask of serenity, which seemed even more subdued when compared to the countess's vivacity.

Realizing resistance was futile, Henry submitted to the countess's fussing as she piled a plate with sandwiches and tarts. "I was just telling Georgie that there will be some musicians in the hotel garden tonight. It might be a nice thing to do this evening if you are still tired from traveling and wish to stay on the property. Do you gamble, Captain Harris?"

"Occasionally. Cards, mostly."

"Well, you can't come to Monte Carlo and not visit the casino. But we should save that for when Rafe arrives. He'll be *very* put out if we go without him. I'm sure you know how he can get."

Henry was too surprised to hide it. "I didn't realize he was coming here." He had only known Sylvia would join them tomorrow.

The countess nodded. "At first he didn't think he could

get away. The ambassador keeps him busy. But he cabled last night with the good news. Oh, I'm so glad to have you all here. And how nice for you both to see your dear friends again."

He managed a tight smile. "Yes. Splendid." He could feel the viscountess's eyes on him, but Henry kept his gaze ahead. Normally, Henry would have been delighted to see Rafe for the first time in nearly a year. But he knew all about Henry's past with Lady Arlington, and dammit, the man would insist on talking about it. And *meddling*. Henry couldn't allow that.

The butler appeared and whispered something to the countess, who shook her head in irritation. "Please excuse me. A friend is staying here at the hotel, and she is having an emergency with her evening gown that apparently only *I* can solve." She set her cup down and rose. "No, don't get up," she said to Henry. "Stay here as long as you wish. Have another sandwich, Captain. I hope to see you both this evening."

Before either of them could answer, the countess was already gliding down the terrace with purposeful grace.

Lady Arlington had also turned to watch her leave and shared an awkward smile before taking another sip of tea. Henry cleared this throat and fiddled with the handle of his delicate porcelain teacup as the silence stretched between them as tight as a wire.

"So then," she finally said. "Am I to be given any information regarding the plans for my protection? I do assume it came up during your meeting."

"Of course," he mumbled as his neck grew hot. "I'm sorry. I did mean to tell you. The countess distracted me."

Along with her. "You're to have two plainclothes protection officers, but they will be very discreet. You shouldn't even notice their presence."

"Unless I'm attacked," she added dryly.

"Well, yes," Henry answered, then realized she was teasing him again. The corner of his mouth turned up. "One does hope they'll pitch in if you need a hand."

The viscountess briefly returned his smile before looking away again. "What are your thoughts on this musical evening?"

Henry shrugged. "I'm sure it's perfectly safe. Go, if it interests you."

She watched him closely for a moment, an unfathomable expression on her beautiful face, then sat back on the sofa. "I think I will, rather."

He took a considering sip. Henry didn't much care for the gleam in her eyes. The viscountess was up to something, and protection officers or no, he did not intend to stand idly by this evening. But he kept that to himself.

* * *

Georgiana stepped out onto the terrace that led down to the garden and inhaled the warm evening air, slightly tinged with sea salt and night-blooming jasmine. She wore a new gown in a shade of brilliant topaz that nearly matched the Mediterranean Sea. The color and the cut would have caused a minor scandal in London, but here she looked almost matronly compared to some of the risqué gowns worn by other women.

She subtly scanned the elegant crowd, but there was

no sign of Captain Harris. The man had all but vanished after luncheon. Georgiana pursed her lips, trying her best to ignore the annoying little pang of disappointment in her chest. It was better this way. Having him glowering by her side wouldn't help attract would-be suitors.

Not suitors. Lovers.

Georgiana tilted her chin, unfolded her fan, and descended the wide stone stairs. The countess and Mr. Previn stood near a small fountain talking with several guests, two of whom were gentlemen. Georgiana smiled as the countess caught her eye and waved her over. One of the men, dark-haired and pleasingly tall, glanced in her direction and smiled.

Oh, he would do. He would do quite nicely indeed.

Georgiana pretended to ignore him as she approached, taking care to exaggerate the sway of her hips just a little bit more. It may have been many years since she properly flirted, but she hadn't forgotten a few of the tricks she had learned during that long ago season.

The more disinterested you are, the more determined the gentleman will become, Aunt Paloma had advised. *If there is one thing a man can't stand, it's being ignored.*

The countess gave her a subtle nod of approval. "Lady Arlington, I'm so glad you could join us this evening. What a beautiful shade of blue."

"Thank you," Georgiana nodded. "That is a lovely necklace."

The countess laughed lightly as she ran a finger over the outrageously large set of rubies nestled against her chest. "Oh, this? Mr. Previn got it for me years ago," she demurred, as if it were a child's gold locket and not an eye-popping piece of jewelry. "He has excellent taste, doesn't he?"

Mahmood turned away from the other couple he had been conversing with and bowed to Georgiana. "Good evening, my lady." He waved a waiter over and handed her a glass of champagne.

Then he took the countess's hand and kissed it. "Only the best, of course. In all things." A look of deep affection passed between them, making Georgiana feel like she had intruded on something quite intimate. But before the moment could become awkward, the countess looked to the dark-haired gentleman, who patiently waited beside them.

"Mr. Talbot, may I introduce Lady Arlington? She has just arrived today from London."

The man bowed over her hand, meeting her eyes. "A pleasure."

Georgiana smiled a little at his accent. "You're American?"

"Guilty," he said with a grin, displaying a set of strong white teeth. "But my father was an Englishman born in Manchester."

"Mr. Talbot is a business associate of mine," Mahmood explained.

"Oh? What sort of business?"

"Dishware."

Georgiana's coquettish smile widened in genuine interest.

"Lady Arlington is a business owner herself," the countess supplied.

There was a subtle change in Mr. Talbot's gaze. He was impressed. "Is that right? I didn't realize proper English ladies were interested in such activities. I thought it was all afternoon tea and fancy balls."

"Oh, but ladies can do all sorts of things, Mr. Talbot," she said teasingly. "If given the chance."

"I'll drink to that." He raised his glass as his eyes warmed, and Georgiana joined him.

This was going to be easier than she expected.

* * *

"Another, Lady Arlington?" Mr. Talbot asked as he handed Georgiana her third glass of champagne. Or was it her fourth? She couldn't quite remember.

"Thank you," Georgiana said graciously.

Once the string quartet began to play, the garden became considerably more crowded. The countess and Mahmood had gone off to mingle with more guests, and Mr. Talbot had suggested they move to a more secluded corner, where they could talk.

"As I was saying…" Mr. Talbot launched back into a monologue on shipping lines and raw materials. He was keen on convincing her to expand her business to America, despite Georgiana explicitly voicing her disinterest. Since then her mind had begun to drift. Mr. Talbot talked of business—and little else. But he was good-looking and interested in her. That was enough for her purposes. Better that she find him boring anyway. Anything more could lead to complications. And that was the last thing Georgiana wanted from a meaningless tryst.

"My lady?"

Georgiana turned back to Mr. Talbot. He was smiling at her, having obviously caught her not paying attention.

"Terribly sorry." Her cheeks heated. "I…I think I may

have had too much to drink," she admitted and set down the glass on a nearby table.

"Please, it is I who should be sorry." Mr. Talbot moved closer, and Georgiana's nose wrinkled as she caught the scent of his expensive sandalwood cologne. The viscount had worn something similar. She glanced down just as Mr. Talbot's hand moved to rest on her waist. "For boring such a lovely creature. How can I make amends?"

Georgiana raised an eyebrow. Well, that was a bit more forward than she had expected, but she couldn't deny that this was the perfect opportunity to proposition him. She opened her mouth to speak, and Mr. Talbot's expression filled with anticipation.

Say it. Say it now.

He would not deny her. She was certain. And yet, she couldn't make her lips move. Couldn't tell him to take her away from here. Somewhere much more private.

Mr. Talbot continued to watch her with a look that bordered on predatory. Georgiana inhaled, gathering her nerves—and buying herself another minute. Perhaps it would be easier with her eyes shut. But just as she closed them, a familiar deep voice joined them.

"Lady Arlington. Sorry to interrupt, but you are needed."

Georgiana blinked and turned to find Captain Harris at her side. The sight of his stern expression filled her with relief.

"Oh. Captain, this is Mr. Talbot," Georgiana explained, proud of how steady she kept her voice. "From America."

Mr. Talbot had tactfully removed his hand from her waist, but Captain Harris shot him a filthy glare that left no question what he had seen. "A pleasure," he grumbled, then he turned back to her with an expectant look on his face. "My lady, I'm afraid it is most urgent."

While Georgiana was grateful for the chance to leave, she would *not* be ordered about like a child. She held the captain's gaze until his eyes narrowed ever so slightly, as if daring her to deny him, then she let out a little huff and took his arm. "Thank you for keeping me company, Mr. Talbot."

Mr. Talbot made no effort to hide his disappointment. "Yes. Good evening," he said curtly before he bowed to her then stalked into the crowd.

As Captain Harris led her back toward the hotel, all she could focus on was her pounding heart and ringing ears. The terrace was filled with chattering guests, but they all blurred together until the music and conversation was replaced by the faint bubbling of the hotel's fountain and the clacking of her heels on marble. The lobby was nearly empty at this hour, as fellow guests were either outside on the terrace or enjoying Monte Carlo's many entertainments. She looked up at Captain Harris's stony profile. Was the man even *capable* of enjoying himself?

I'm afraid enjoyment of any kind isn't safe, my lady.

She let out a snort at the imagined admonition, and he slanted her a glance before wordlessly drawing her into a darkened alcove, where they would be hidden from view from any passersby.

"Just what the hell did you think you were doing back there anyway?"

The force of his words took her by surprise, but Georgiana hid it behind a sharp laugh. "My goodness, I was only *flirting*. You're acting as if you caught the man ravishing me in full view of the entire crowd. Don't worry, you won't have to defend my honor or call the vicar."

Captain Harris shot her a scowl and took a deep breath. "I'm not opposed to a little flirting," he said after a moment, more calmly than before. "And yes, perhaps I...I over-reacted a little—" She scoffed at this, but he continued. "Might I remind you what brought us here in the first place? You don't *know* that man."

Perhaps he had a point there, but like hell would Georgiana admit it. "I hardly think Mr. Talbot threw a brick through the carriage window, if that's what you're worried about."

He let out a huff and pinched the bridge of his nose. "Of course not—"

She leaned forward, her hands clenched in fists by her side. "I know my brother is paying you to be here, but if I want to spend the evening with a handsome man I will *damn well do it.*"

The words vibrated in the air between them as she stepped back. Georgiana couldn't believe she had spoken to him like that. If Captain Harris was offended by her little speech, he didn't show it. He merely stared at her in his usual way, like he was examining something that was both confusing and mildly unpleasant.

"And that is what you want?" he asked softly. "A stranger in your bed?"

Somehow he managed to make this act of rebellion sound incredibly pathetic. It was infuriating.

"It is," she insisted, with as much pride as she could muster.

"Then may I make a suggestion?"

Her breath caught at the unexpected question. Oh, how

she *longed* to deny him, but the fact was she was far too curious. "If you must," she answered with studied coolness.

Captain Harris stared at her for an endless moment as the scant air between them warmed. Until the furious beating of her heart filled her ears. Georgiana inhaled the rich scent of his skin, unmasked by cologne. As she leaned forward a little, his breathing quickened. "Take me instead."

She immediately reared back. No. She must have misunderstood. *Had* to. She eyed him with suspicion, but he only continued to stare at her, awaiting her answer. "If this is some horribly misguided attempt to protect me, you can take your pity elsewhere."

His brow furrowed. "What? No, I don't *pity* you. My God." He let out a harsh bark of laughter, and Georgiana realized he was nervous. And entirely serious. He let his gaze drag down her body, and her corset suddenly felt much too tight. She could practically feel him taking in every single inch of her, lingering on certain places, like the space where her neck met her shoulder, the hollow at the base of her throat, and where her cleavage disappeared into the bodice of her gown. By the time he reached her hem, Georgiana was embarrassingly breathless. Then his gaze returned to her face.

"You are a beautiful woman, Lady Arlington. Surely you know this."

"That still doesn't explain why you are offering yourself to me."

His lips quirked. "I'd like to think the attraction is mutual. Unless I imagined your reaction while underneath me in the carriage. Or... before."

Georgiana's breath caught at the reminder of that long

ago night—and the answering ache between her legs. "I should slap you for that remark."

The corner of his mouth lifted. "But you won't."

"No," she rasped after a moment.

His gaze heated as he watched her, as if he too was lost in the same memory. Though she remained silent, her eyes darted to his cane and he read the question there.

"As long as you don't object to a little creativity, that won't be a problem," he murmured. "I assure you."

Georgiana's chest tightened at the unmistakable confidence in his voice. God, she was *really* considering this.

She cleared her throat, which had become very dry. She couldn't possibly let him know what he was doing to her. That was the only way she could go through with this mad idea. But the thought of going back to her room, to that empty bed, was unbearable.

"Very well." She lifted her chin. "You've scared off all other available options anyway."

His eyes gleamed as he held out his arm. "Then shall we, my lady?"

CHAPTER ELEVEN

———◆———

As Henry led Lady Arlington toward the private lift, the silence between them grew charged enough to power the entire hotel. He must have finally lost his senses completely, beginning when that damnable American had put his hand on Lady Arlington's waist and ignored her obvious discomfort, which had been perfectly clear to Henry from his vantage point across the garden.

That was the only explanation for why Henry had actually *voiced* such a salacious offer. It seemed like a far better alternative than simply standing by while she went off into the night with a strange man. But the truly mad part was that as soon as the request left his mouth, he knew he would absolutely do it if she said yes.

Very well. You've scared off all other available options anyway.

He bit back a smile. Lady Arlington could claim to be

unaffected as much as she wanted, but she couldn't hide her dilated pupils nor the fluttering pulse at the base of her neck. She wanted him. Physically, at least. And that was enough for him.

Still, it would be best to harbor no expectations. Perhaps the entire scene had been nothing more than an impulsive reaction to the end of her mourning period, and she would have second thoughts as soon as they were upstairs. Either way, he would not judge what someone did to cure their loneliness. Henry had only just pulled the door closed and pushed the button when she was in his arms, her mouth locked on his. He could not say with any certainty who had made the first move, or if they had both come together at exactly the same instant. Only that it was a kiss of such force, such fierceness that he found his back up against the wall of the lift. His hands gripped her nimble waist as tightly has he dared, pulling her lush figure closer. She was even more delectably proportioned than he remembered, and as her generous curves pressed along his body, the rightness of it shook him to his core. Whatever this was, it was not supposed to be like *this*.

The lift came to a bobbing halt as it reached their floor and they broke apart. Lady Arlington stared up at him, breathless and wanting, just like that night in the carriage. And just like that all too brief encounter eight long years before in a darkened corner of the Harringtons' back garden. As Henry dipped his head to kiss her again, a single thought flashed in his mind:

You fool.

After several intoxicating moments, they managed to stumble into the hallway, only for Henry to go back to retrieve his cane. The blood fizzed in his ears as his heart pounded. He felt awkward and bumbling, like a man at sea for the first time. He took her hand and pulled her down the hall, but when they reached their suite, he stopped short. Lady Arlington shot him a questioning look.

"What about Bea?"

"I told her not to wait up," she murmured, her lips swollen from his kisses. Henry was much too pleased by the effect he had on her. Then he frowned as he grasped her meaning.

"You had this planned."

"Does it matter?"

"No," he answered truthfully. "I suppose I should be thankful for your foresight."

The corner of her mouth lifted, and she moved to open the door. Henry followed her into the darkened suite. A lamp had been left on, providing just enough light for them to find the door to Henry's room. They moved silently, even though there was little chance of them being seen together, as Bea resided on the other side of the suite in a room connected off of Lady Arlington's quarters.

Henry entered first and turned on a small bedside lamp. He had left the door to his balcony open, and a comforting breeze kept the room pleasantly cool. One could hear the faint sound of the endless surf churning in the near distance. He sat on the bed and placed his cane against the night table, then loosened his necktie.

"I've wanted to do that all evening," he groaned, then glanced up.

Lady Arlington hadn't moved from the doorway. She was watching him with a veiled expression he couldn't read.

"Having second thoughts already?" He forced the question out and braced himself.

She blinked at the sound of his voice and pushed away from the door. "No. Are you?"

Yes.

"Of course not," he answered as she came toward him. "Why would I?" His gaze fell on her gently swaying hips. How was it that she always seemed to glide across the room? He had never seen another woman move the way she did, as if she were floating.

"I don't know." She came to a stop just in from of him, her skirts kissing his shins. "Some people take physical intimacy seriously."

Henry's chest tightened in recognition, but he buried the feeling and merely raised an eyebrow. "And you don't?"

She placed a hand on his shoulder and smoothed her palm over the fabric of his evening jacket. Her eyes followed the movement of her hand, before meeting his gaze. "There are a few select things I take seriously, Captain." She leaned down until her lips brushed his ear. "But no, sex is not one of them."

Though a part of him wanted to challenge the accuracy of that statement, her bold words burned through him. Henry turned and captured her mouth with his own. He could take no more of this teasing. Every limb itched with the need to touch her. Let her use him then. He would beg her to, if it came to that. But that seemed unlikely as she pulled a hand through his hair and jerked him toward her.

* * *

Brazen was not a word Georgiana would ever have used to describe herself, but she could think of no other way to explain her behavior. First she practically mauled Captain Harris in the lift before admitting that she had planned on taking a lover that evening. But both paled in comparison to her insistence that *sex*—a word she had never even *said* before—did not warrant much significance in her life. And yet, Georgiana was positively delighted with herself. Everyone kept insisting that she was acting recklessly, so why not actually *do* something reckless? And sleeping with a man who had a dangerous hold over her seemed to absolutely fit the bill. She may regret it tomorrow, but that was a problem for her future self to contend with. In the meantime, she intended to unbutton this gentleman's shirt.

Captain Harris grunted as she stepped between his legs, and Georgiana quickly pulled back. "Did I hurt you?"

"Not at all," he said mildly, before pulling her down until they both fell onto the bed. Captain Harris kissed her again as he moved over her, demonstrating more control this time. Rather than an explosion of need, this was more exploratory. His lips parted her own as he sucked and tasted, while his hands encircled her waist, just as they had before in the lift. Georgiana moaned her encouragement, and he smoothed his palms over her bodice. He touched her softly, reverentially, like she was precious. Like it was a privilege granted to him, rather than something he was entitled to. The feeling was intoxicating. And terrifying. This was supposed to be meaningless. Hedonistic. In response, Georgiana pressed her mouth harder against his, searching for the velvet of his tongue. And with every stroke, she felt an answering pulse between her thighs.

It was embarrassing how wet she already was. She wanted him far more than she had even realized until they came together in the lift. And he would know the moment he touched her. As if he could read her very thoughts, his hand slid farther down her side, no doubt searching for the hem of her gown. Not for the first time Georgiana cursed the current fashion for more narrow skirts. At least massive bustles were out for the moment. How she longed for the simple lines and diaphanous gowns of, say, the Regency, an era practically *made* for clandestine assignations. But Captain Harris seemed undaunted as his hand moved competently beneath the topaz silk of her gown to the fine lawn of her petticoats. Her breath hitched as his long fingers stroked gently upward toward the slit in her drawers.

She tugged her hand through his thick hair once again in a vain effort to distract herself from the inevitable. He groaned against her mouth, breaking their kiss to drag his lips along the line of her jaw and press urgent kisses down her throat. She gasped as he slowly bit the soft flesh where her neck met her shoulder. It really was quite rewarding to her vanity to see Captain Harris driven out of his stoic shell with desire. For her.

"Georgie," he rumbled, his voice even deeper than usual. She met his eyes and was nearly undone by the intense gravity on his face. "May I?"

It took her a moment to realize he was asking to touch her. Intimately. She smiled, unwillingly charmed by his politeness and nodded her answer. He slowly parted the soft linen, his gaze never leaving hers.

"Will you show me what brings you the most pleasure?"

Georgiana's cheeks flushed even more than they already

were by the question. He looked at her with a mixture of heat and anticipation that gave her the courage to be that brazen woman. She slid her hand slowly down her front until she reached the place between her legs. He watched, riveted, as she pressed her fingers against the sensitive bud of her sex.

"Here," she said breathlessly, showing him exactly how she touched herself.

After a few moments, his hand skimmed up her inner thigh. "Allow me."

Her eyelids fluttered at the feel of his larger, stronger fingers, so different from her own. But he stroked her gently, slowly. She let out a sigh and opened her thighs a little more. The moment was disturbed when he brushed against her entrance and bit out a curse. Georgiana's eyes flew open.

"Sorry," he said a little breathlessly. "I—you're so—" Rather than finish the statement, he slowly pushed a finger into her channel while his thumb continued to stroke the bundle of nerves. Georgiana let out a bewildered cry at the sensation blooming within her. Dear Lord, Captain Harris was *good* at this. Georgiana threw back her head as he made a swirling motion with his thumb.

"Oh God," she moaned. "Do it again." Then she immediately stiffened, not sure how he would respond to being ordered about. But Captain Harris simply flashed her a smile and obeyed.

"Yes, my lady."

And that was all it took for Georgiana's slowly gathering release to suddenly thunder through her. A part of her was incredibly annoyed by how quickly she had been undone by this man, but at the moment she felt too good to care. She hadn't known it could be like this. Hadn't known she could feel this way. Her encounters with the viscount were always brief and perfunctory. They were designed to get her with child, not give her pleasure.

When the sensation finally faded and she opened her eyes, Captain Harris was staring down at her, an unmistakable look of triumph on his face. The reality of what she just did, and with whom wrenched through her. Georgiana sat up so quickly she nearly knocked right into Captain Harris.

He jerked back, his brow now furrowed in concern. "Are you all right?"

"This was a mistake," she blurted out.

Something dark flickered across his face, but it vanished so quickly Georgiana was sure it was just a shadow. She couldn't possibly have *hurt* this man. And certainly not the way he could hurt her.

He glanced away as she began to straighten her skirts and rise from the bed. "I see."

She stared at the rigid set of his shoulders in his dark tailcoat. Somehow the room had become stifling, filled with the scent of his shaving soap mixed with his heated skin. She bit her lip, trying in vain to distract herself from the ferocious desire beckoning her to stay, beguiling her with the maddening certainty that she would come again if he touched her. But she would be a fool to let him anywhere near her again.

Georgiana backed away toward the door, nearly stumbling on wobbly legs, and reached one hand out behind her until she grasped the cool brass knob. "Good night then, Captain." But he only grunted in response, not turning to look at her again before she stepped out into the darkened parlor and fled to her bedroom.

* * *

After Georgiana had her fill of him, Henry lay awake staring at the elaborately decorated plaster ceiling, listening to the wind rustle the palms below his window and, beyond that, the waves crashing at a distance. There were men who would have barred her exit and felt entitled to take their pleasure from her, while others would have been reduced to sobbing in the corner after being so coldly dismissed. But not Henry. Instead, he passed the long hours by going over the entire evening again and again in painstaking detail. First to uncover what had driven her from the room, and then, when that proved futile, to simply relive it. Every shudder, every labored breath, every soft moan that broke through her rose-colored lips. She had tried hard at first to hide her reaction to him, but she had been warm and slick from his touch. It had been so very gratifying to have the unmistakable evidence of her attraction right there on his fingertips. To know that when she cried out her pleasure, he had brought her to this release. Then it had been over all too quickly. For reasons Henry was still trying to uncover.

But then you have always *misread her. You have never once understood her motives.*

Henry's fist tightened over the bed linen. Whatever this was between them, it would not go beyond the physical. Lady Arlington clearly had no interest, and Henry would not allow his heart to become entangled again. And yet, if he turned his head to the side, her scent would still be on the sheets: a summer meadow baking in sunlight. The same as it had been eight years ago. Imprinted on him just as every word, every look, every touch that had ever passed between them. Surely that had to mean something. Surely it was not possible to feel this drawn to another person without some reciprocity on their part. At least something that went beyond mere attraction.

No. It is mindless lust. Do not mistake it for more. Do not delude yourself again.

Henry sat up with a sigh and stretched his aching neck. In a way it was a relief to admit what he had been fruitlessly trying to deny this last week and a half. He still wanted her just as he had the first time they met, if not more. And if she came to him again, Henry would not turn her away. He simply lacked the strength. He knew exactly what to expect from this woman, and yet he had still made a series of errors ever since he found her standing in his office. If he were a bit younger, or a bit stronger, then perhaps he could have found the will to expel her from his life once again, and without remorse. But the years had not been kind to Henry, and though he was a fool in many ways, he was wise enough to recognize that pleasure and happiness were fleeting gifts. Best to take them while on offer. And not think of what the future might hold.

Henry rose from the bed and walked toward the balcony. The sky had just begun to lighten. Soon enough the sun would rise, and he would have to face her: the beautiful mistake he seemed destined to make over and over again. He placed his hands on the balcony's elaborate wrought iron railing and watched the sun rise across the Mediterranean. Then he turned to meet his fate.

* * *

"I've tried my best," Bea sighed. "But I think we've done all we can, my lady."

Georgiana met her maid's distressed eyes in the dressing table's mirror. "Goodness, Bea. It's only some dark circles." She added a little laugh, hoping to reassure the poor girl, but Bea only frowned deeper and moved toward her, once again wielding the powder brush.

"No." Georgiana held up a hand and jerked back. "Really. Any more and I'll look like the undead."

Lord knew she certainly felt that way. She had slept terribly, and it showed in her wan complexion. But one poor night's sleep shouldn't have made such an impact.

The truth was that Captain Harris's presence in her life had been steadily weighing on her. A veritable lodestone around her neck, affecting her to a degree she had been reluctant to acknowledge. Last night should have definitely snuffed out the flame that had begun to grow between them. He had kissed her, had touched her, had *pleasured* her, and she had finally scratched the itch that had been nagging her for eight long years. That should have been the end of it. And yet, to her great regret, Georgiana was not the least bit satisfied. Somehow her desire had only grown. Until it was all she could think about. This...this *need* for him. And, based on her ghostly pallor, it seemed to be sucking the very life from her. A pity that she had effectively ruined any chance of sating it by fleeing his room.

This was a mistake.

Georgiana bit back a sigh and rose from her chair. "I'll wear the yellow silk. That should help, I think."

Bea shot her a skeptical look but went to fetch it. As Georgiana submitted to the lacing, tightening, and flouncing required to become Lady Arlington, she decided that the only thing worse than this pathetic wanting coursing through her would be if the captain learned of it.

"Please breathe, my lady," Bea said gently. "If I make this corset any tighter, you'll faint."

"Of course," Georgiana huffed and her chest noticeably loosened. Damn that man.

She would have to act as though she was perfectly fine. It shouldn't be hard. She had been doing so for years now. What was another week?

But as she entered the suite's sitting room, her heart lurched at the sight of his shut door.

Get a hold of yourself.

He wasn't even *in* there. Bea had told her the captain had been up and dressed when she went to fetch her breakfast, grumbling something about taking a morning constitutional.

Georgiana frowned at his closed door. Clearly she had been the only one who spent the night tossing and turning. Then she turned to her maid. "Thank you, Bea. Take the afternoon off and enjoy yourself. I won't need you until dinner."

Bea looked worried. "But shouldn't you wait for Captain Harris, my lady?"

Georgiana was due to have luncheon in the countess's suite with Sylvia and her husband. She assumed the captain had been invited too. Not just because he was a good friend of Rafe's but because the whole *point* of him coming on this trip was to watch over her. But he clearly wasn't here.

"I'm quite certain I can walk down the hallway without his assistance," she said more sharply than she meant to, and the girl's face fell. "I'm sorry, Bea. My quarrel isn't with you. But please don't worry yourself. I'll be fine."

"Yes, my lady," Bea said quietly, but she didn't look up before disappearing back into her room.

Georgiana felt a pang of guilt as she left the suite. Bea was a sensitive girl. And by far the best maid she had ever employed. She would need to make amends later. Georgiana paused before a large accent mirror in the hallway to collect herself. An elegant woman perfectly coiffed, if a bit pale, in a gown of sunflower yellow stared back. But that glum expression would never do. Lady Arlington was serene, not sad. The very picture of aristocratic refinement. Untouched by the trivial annoyances of daily life. She forced her mouth into a smile, but it looked more like a grimace.

"Ridiculous," she muttered to herself before walking over to the door. She had barely begun to knock when it was swiftly opened by the countess's butler.

"Oh, hello," she said awkwardly. The man must have been watching from the peephole. And had likely witnessed her little display in the hall. Luckily, he was too well trained to give any indication and had merely bowed and swept his arm aside to welcome her. Georgiana attempted to regain her fragile confidence as she entered the suite, but it was quickly smashed to pieces when the very first person she saw was Captain Harris properly glowering down at her like a gentleman in an Austen novel.

Someone should tell him the act was far less appealing off the page.

"I thought you had gone for a walk," she accused.

He raised one imperious eyebrow. "That was hours ago."

It was his composure that rankled most, she realized. As

if he hadn't had his hand up her skirts last night. As if he hadn't kissed her with such bruising force, she could still feel the phantom pressure on her lips.

Georgiana's cheeks flushed as Captain Harris continued to stare at her. "Are you all right?"

"Of course," she lied and lifted her chin as chaos whirled inside her. "Why wouldn't I be?" she asked before her eyes widened. Why, why, *why* had she said that?

The man then actually opened his mouth. As if he intended to *answer* her asinine question. But Georgiana quickly turned away and found Sylvia standing at the entrance to the terrace, watching their exchange with avid interest. Georgiana had been so distracted by Captain Harris that she hadn't even noticed her dearest friend.

"Sylvia! There you are!" She opened her arms and immediately went to her. But as they exchanged a hug, Georgiana could feel the captain's heavy gaze on her back. Sylvia said something, but as she was several inches shorter than Georgiana, it was muffled by the fabric of her sleeve. Georgiana pulled back. "Sorry, my dear. What was that?"

Sylvia gave her an amused smile. "I said it is lovely to see you." Then she looked past her. "And you as well, Captain Harris."

"The pleasure is all mine, Mrs. Davies," he said with a short bow.

Georgiana was a bit miffed that Sylvia was accorded an actual response, rather than his usual grunt.

Sylvia grinned at him. Though she had been married for over a year, she still had the glow of a newly—and happily—wed woman. "Please come outside," she said to them both as she linked her arm through Georgiana's. "The food has just arrived."

Georgiana wished they had a moment to speak privately. There was so much she needed to tell Sylvia, as she hadn't been able to bring herself to mention anything about Captain Harris in her latest letter.

"I'm so glad this worked out," Sylvia said as they stepped out onto the sun-soaked terrace. "I've missed you terribly." Rafe and his mother were up ahead in the seating area where they had tea yesterday. "What do you think of the countess?" Sylvia murmured.

Georgiana swallowed her feelings with a smile. "She is delightful. Thank you very much for arranging all this."

"Of course! I only wish I could have done more. I'd have invited you to Berlin, but Monte Carlo is much nicer, isn't it?"

Georgiana laughed. "I suspect it is."

Ever the gentleman, Rafe rose as they approached, but he had eyes only for his wife. One would never know that he was once considered a rather notorious rake. Sylvia returned his coy smile. They were one of those rare couples who seemed able to communicate without words.

A hollow spot in Georgiana's chest began to ache. Sylvia had undergone quite an ordeal before finding happiness with Rafe Davies, and while Georgiana was happy for both of them, she was also incredibly aware of what she lacked in comparison. For when had a man ever looked at her that way and meant it?

"Lady Arlington," Rafe said warmly as he kissed her hand.

"Please, I think we can refer to each other by first names now, don't you?"

He smiled. "Of course. Georgiana, always a pleasure to see you."

"I'm so glad you were able to make the trip. I understand the ambassador keeps you busy."

Though the smile never left Rafe's face, his jaw tightened slightly. "Quite so." Then his gaze shifted behind her to Captain Harris, and he broke into a wide grin. "You are looking well, Captain. I'd say the Riviera agrees with you."

"Hard for it not to with this weather," Captain Harris replied as they shook hands.

"And the company," Rafe added in a low voice, giving Georgiana a subtle glance. Captain Harris shot him a frown, and she immediately turned away so he could not see her shock. Had they discussed her? But when? And *why*?

Georgiana sat down by the countess and tried to compose herself.

"Did you have an enjoyable evening, my dear? I observed Mr. Talbot talking your ear off about business matters. Luckily, he's pleasant enough to look at," the countess said with a laugh.

Georgiana returned her smile. "Yes," she said absently as her traitorous eyes drifted toward Captain Harris, who sat down diagonally across from her. "He was trying to convince me to open a factory in America."

Then she turned back to the countess. The woman eyed her with great interest. She must have noticed the object of her distraction. "And? Was he successful?"

Georgiana shook her head. "I'd have to cut wages significantly to make it profitable, and I have no interest in doing that."

The countess nodded her approval. "Sylvia told me what you've done for your employees. It's quite admirable."

"I don't know that it should be considered admirable simply to pay people a living wage. It should be the norm," Georgiana said with a shrug. She found it difficult to accept praise for doing something that was so clearly right.

"Yes, but as you very well know, it isn't." The countess's gaze narrowed. "My mother was an East End laundry woman."

Georgiana stared at the elegant, bejeweled woman before her. "I had no idea."

She knew the countess had been an actress in her youth, and that her marriage to Rafe's father had sparked a scandal, but nothing beyond that.

"She worked herself into an early grave, like her mother before her and so on and so on," she said matter-of-factly, with an idle wave of her hand. But though she spoke of this generational suffering in a clinical manner, there was a flash of anger in her gaze that could only come from someone who had experienced extreme loss firsthand. "It still takes courage to challenge the status quo. Do not discount yourself. You are making your mark on the world the best way you can. And don't forget that there are many others with far more power than you who do much less," she said before patting Georgiana's hand. "Now then, who is hungry?"

The countess began making idle chatter about the weather as she poured everyone's tea, while Georgiana sat there dumbfounded. She had become so used to hearing people disapprove of her that listening to the countess's spirited defense had rendered her speechless.

As she accepted her teacup, her gaze landed on Captain

Harris. She held her breath, bracing herself in anticipation of his familiar glower, but when their eyes met she saw none of the usual contempt. Only thoughtfulness. He slowly brought the teacup to his lips, still watching her with that penetrating amber gaze. Georgiana was the first to look away as she felt a flush crawling up her neck.

"Are we off to the casino tonight?" Rafe asked, breaking the charged silence. "I know you must be itching to hit the tables, Captain."

His lips twitched, as if he was holding back a smile. "Perhaps."

Georgiana leaned forward. The captain was a *gambler*? She could hardly picture it.

Rafe took notice of her reaction and chuckled. "Don't let his monkish ways fool you, Lady Arlington. This man is an absolute shark at cards. He takes no prisoners."

"You're mixing metaphors," the captain replied.

"So I am," Rafe said happily.

"I was thinking we could go to the casino tomorrow, my dear," the countess said. "Since you've both traveled so far today. Why don't I arrange for all of us to eat at the hotel restaurant this evening, say around eight? The new chef Mahmood hired is said to be one of the best in Europe."

Rafe flashed his mother a smile. "I can hardly say no to that. Is that all right with you, darling?" he asked Sylvia.

"Yes," she replied. "I don't feel much up for the casino tonight anyway."

Georgiana noticed that Sylvia looked a bit pale herself. Perhaps she had trouble sleeping last night too on the train over.

"Then it's settled," Rafe announced. "Dinner at eight. All of us together."

Georgiana didn't miss the glance he gave Captain Harris, who continued sipping his tea as if he hadn't heard a word. Then she caught Sylvia's eye, who gave her a knowing look. They would speak about this later. And she would finally know at least one of the captain's secrets.

CHAPTER TWELVE

———◆———

After nearly an hour of enduring the most excruciating luncheon Henry had ever attended, it finally came to an end. The ladies planned to take a late afternoon walk around the hotel grounds, but the guards would keep watch over Lady Arlington, so Henry planned to bury himself in work until dinner and avoid Rafe as much as possible. Otherwise, he would insist on *talking*, and that was the last thing Henry wanted to do right now. She had made it very clear that last night was a mistake not to be repeated. Now he just needed to figure out how to be in her presence without picturing how enticing she looked when she came.

It was proving to be damned difficult.

He made his goodbyes and headed for the doorway as briskly as his leg would allow. Henry had just stepped into the hall when Rafe called after him. He briefly considered trying to make a run for it, but that would just be embarrassing for both of them. Instead, he made sure his expression was perfectly blank before turning around.

"Yes?"

"I wanted to make sure you're all right."

"Why wouldn't I be?"

Rafe let out a huff. "In Scotland you could barely say Lady Arlington's name. Now you're sharing a suite with her in Monte Carlo. How did this even happen?"

"Her brother hired me to investigate the threats against her. That's all."

Rafe merely raised one dark brow in response.

"It's just business. She's a *client*," Henry ground out.

He hated being under inspection, especially by someone like Rafe. Before joining the ambassador's staff, he had been one of the Crown's most dedicated spies. And one of Henry's oldest friends. One of his *only* friends, actually. That meant he knew all his weaknesses, including Lady Arlington.

"Then I hope you're being careful," he eventually murmured.

"Of course I am," Henry sniffed, ignoring the sympathy in Rafe's gaze. He wanted none of it. "She also has two protection officers watching over her."

"That isn't what I meant, and you know it. Henry—"

"*Leave* it. Please," he added, softening his tone.

Rafe watched him for a moment, then nodded. "If that's what you want."

There were a great many things Henry wanted, but he had learned to make do with far, far less over the years. And this would be no different.

"Thank you," he murmured. "And I'm sorry I didn't tell

you beforehand, but I didn't think you would be able to come here. I know how busy you are."

The ever present gleam in Rafe's eyes suddenly vanished, and he dragged a hand over his face. "Yes, well. I don't have much to do at the moment."

The hairs on the back of Henry's neck prickled. He had never seen Rafe look so morose before, aside from the week he spent wallowing in self-pity before he confessed his feelings to Sylvia. "What do you mean? Is it the ambassador?"

But Rafe only glanced back to the suite and lowered his voice. "We'll talk later. I can't explain it all now. You understand."

Henry nodded as a sense of unease rippled through him. There was something afoot in Germany. Something big enough to affect the unflappable Rafe Davies. And as curious as he was, Henry also dreaded the answer.

* * *

Later that afternoon Georgiana met Sylvia at the edge of the hotel's back garden, where a winding path that ran along the scenic coastline began. They chatted happily about Sylvia's new life in Berlin, her work chronicling the suffrage movement abroad, and her transition from a scandalous New Woman to the upstanding wife of an aristocrat.

"When we first arrived, some of the other embassy wives completely ignored me until the ambassador's wife invited me to tea," Sylvia explained. "She's quite civic-minded herself, so we get along very well."

"I'm glad to hear it," Georgiana said, though secretly she wished Sylvia wasn't so far away.

"Perhaps you could come for a visit soon? Germany is lovely during Christmastime. And you did mention how you wanted to travel more, now that you could."

That had been when the viscount first died. When Georgiana had been horrified to find herself feeling incredibly lost without her overbearing husband. Before she threw herself into her work reimagining Fox and Sons. Her smile tightened at the hopeful note in Sylvia's voice. "I'm not sure I'll be able to slip away then. If all goes according to plan, the new factory will have just opened."

But with her siblings away in the countryside, that would mean spending the holiday in London, alone. Georgiana brushed away the regretful ache before it could grow roots. She would be fine on her own.

"Of course." Sylvia glanced away, but not before disappointment flashed in her eyes. "I know you didn't want to come on this trip at first, but it's good to have a little break now, isn't it?"

"Everyone seems to think so," Georgiana grumbled before giving Sylvia an encouraging smile. "But being able to see *you* makes it worth the hassle. And it is very beautiful here."

"It certainly is," she paused, then changed the subject. "I tried to induce Rafe to tell me about Captain Harris, but my usual methods weren't very effective." Sylvia then flashed her a saucy smile.

"Please spare me the details," Georgiana groaned and pressed her hands to her ears in mock horror.

"Very well." Sylvia laughed. "I won't say *how* I extracted the information. But he would only admit that he was surprised to see Captain Harris with you. Then by that point I got rather distracted myself."

Now it was Georgiana's turn to laugh. "He used your own methods against you, didn't he?"

"I don't know why I was surprised," Sylvia admitted with a happy shrug. "But I can certainly vouch for its effectiveness."

They walked a little farther, basking in the warmth from the late afternoon sun. "Has it been awkward seeing the captain again?"

Georgiana hadn't told Sylvia about her courtship with the captain until after the viscount died, and even then she only related the basic details. As far as her friend was concerned, Georgiana had willingly married the viscount to ensure her family's future, though many young gentlemen had called on her, the captain included. Sylvia didn't know about the night in the garden, or what Georgiana had overheard the next evening, nor what she had done with the information afterward. And Georgiana had no intention of telling the full, humiliating truth to anyone. Ever.

"It was at first," Georgiana admitted. "But mostly I was angry that Reggie hadn't consulted with me beforehand. I am quite capable of managing my own affairs without my younger brother's help."

"No one is suggesting you aren't, but everyone could benefit from some assistance now and then. Even you." Sylvia's eyes softened. "He's only worried about you."

"I know," Georgiana sighed. "And I'm here, aren't I?"

"Yes, you've made everyone very happy, coming here on holiday and avoiding possible threats to *your life*. And Captain Harris barely lets you out of his sight. Though that might be more than just business," she added with a suggestive glance.

"I assure you, it is not."

Sylvia arched a brow. "You don't have to tell me any-thing if you don't want to, but you have never been a good liar, Georgie."

Georgiana stared out at the turquoise sea, glittering in the late afternoon light. "It's difficult for me to talk about."

When she dared to look back at Sylvia, she was met with sympathy.

"It can be terrifying to voice your feelings for someone. Believe me."

Georgiana let out a dismissive huff. "I wasn't speaking of anything romantic. That is hardly the issue here."

"Darling, I admit that don't know Captain Harris very well, but I'm quite certain the man is infatuated with you."

Georgiana stumbled and nearly fell face-first onto the ground, but Sylvia's arm shot out to steady her. A shout went up behind them as the protection officers trailing them rushed over.

"Surely it can't be *that* surprising to you," Sylvia said before letting out a nervous laugh.

"I'm fine," Georgiana snapped and waved everyone away. "I just missed a step."

Sylvia eyed her with concern before she glanced back. "Perhaps we should return. I'm feeling a bit lightheaded myself."

She suddenly looked so dreadfully pale under the golden sunlight that guilt tore through Georgiana. She shouldn't have upset her. But before Georgiana could agree, Sylvia turned around and walked toward the hotel. A cold pit of dread struck low in her belly. Georgiana hadn't noticed it earlier, but from this angle she could see that Sylvia, who had always been petite, was slimmer. And she hadn't eaten much earlier. Georgiana would have assumed she was with child if not for Sylvia's expressed disinterest in motherhood. And as far as she knew, that hadn't changed.

But something was clearly wrong with her friend. Something more than mere travel fatigue. Georgiana forced herself to move, willing her thoughts to remain positive. Sylvia was young and healthy. Even if she was ill, it was nothing serious. Because it couldn't be. Because Georgiana simply could not bear it.

* * *

To Henry's annoyance, dinner was absolutely sublime. He had been prepared to make his excuses and leave after the first course, but the food was simply too good to resist. As each course was presented, he promised himself this would be the last until a new plate was placed before him. It was incredibly disconcerting to learn just how weak his will had become. For a man who had long prided himself on his control, this little trip was proving to be his undoing. And it had all begun with her.

His gaze met Lady Arlington's across the table, and he took a generous sip of wine. She looked delectable as usual, in a low-cut evening gown nearly the color of the Bordeaux. Matching blood-red garnets shimmered along her décolletage and at her ears. No doubt gifts from the viscount. Gifts she could never expect from a man like Henry. But that was unfair. Though it would be far easier to continue to paint her with a shallow brush, he could not. Not after all he had learned about her. Henry would just have to accept that she was a multifaceted person. And, dammit if he didn't want to uncover them all. That was the real problem.

Her sapphire eyes looked a shade darker in the gaslight. Mysterious. Like rare jewels Henry ached to possess. What would it take to have her always look upon him like this?

A time machine, for one. Like in that story by Mr. Wells. *And what would that have mattered?*

He would still be the same poor lieutenant looking for a wealthy wife, and she still hunting for a title. But perhaps...perhaps they both could have been a little more honest with each other. It wouldn't have changed the outcome, but it might have made these last years easier. Just as Henry began to taste the bitterness of regret, someone loudly cleared their throat, shattering the moment. He turned to the head of the table, where Rafe was raising an eyebrow at him. They had been quite obviously staring at each other. And based on Rafe's annoyed expression, Henry guessed for some time. He cut a glance back at Lady Arlington, but she was now looking down at her place setting.

This was becoming ridiculous.

"As I was trying to say," Rafe said with a pointed glance in Henry's direction, "shall we return to our suite for some after-dinner entertainment?

"Will you play for us, Georgiana?" Sylvia asked.

"Oh yes," Rafe added. "Surely you've seen my mother's Bösendorfer. I daresay it's never been touched."

"It certainly *has*," the countess protested. "Why Mahmood even arranged for me to have lessons, didn't you?"

The man gave a very diplomatic nod before taking a generous sip of wine.

"Well *I've* never heard you play," Rafe said, fighting to hold back a smile.

The countess lifted her chin. "It's very hard to learn as an adult." Then she addressed Georgiana. "I've heard you are quite talented."

She paused before answering. "I'm a bit out of practice playing for an audience."

"That won't matter," Sylvia quickly put in. "Georgiana is being modest. Remember how well she played in Scotland?" This comment was addressed to Rafe.

He gave her an indulgent smile and reached for her hand. "How could I forget?"

Henry shifted his gaze away just as Rafe brought Sylvia's hand to his lips.

The man seemed physically incapable of going more than a few minutes without touching his wife. It was becoming quite tiresome.

Jealous.

Henry bristled at the ridiculous thought. If he ever found himself in love, he would have the good sense to keep it private. As he reached for his wineglass again, he noticed Georgiana watching him, her lush mouth curved upward in the slightest smile. Henry returned it, certain she knew exactly what he had been thinking of. The restaurant's low light illuminated the delicate curves of her face while casting others in shadow, an alluring mix that drew his eye like a moth to a flame. The chatter around them faded into a dull buzz. It was far past time for him to turn away, and yet he couldn't find the will. Her breathing visibly quickened under his inspection, and his cock thickened. It wasn't until everyone else at the table began to rise that his attention was torn away, back to the moment. He reached for his cane and stood as well, but their mutual delay had not gone unnoticed, and he pointedly ignored the interested looks both Sylvia and Rafe were casting down the table.

As their companions paired off, Henry belatedly realized that he would have to escort Georgiana upstairs. He offered her his free arm, which she took without looking at him. Whatever had passed between them moments ago was not to be repeated, then. It was just as well, he reasoned, even as his growing erection began to press against the fabric of his trousers. Even as the very feel of her presence at his side was achingly familiar. Her warmth, her scent, her inviting softness. The featherlight brush of her lusciously curved hip against his own. His fingers itched to touch her again, to revel in the sensation of her moving beneath him.

And yet, he did not speak. Did not turn his head one fraction of an inch toward her. And she did the same. Together they politely ignored each other as they moved across the lobby, into the private lift, and down the hall to the countess's apartments, the silence growing tighter and tighter with every step, until they had reached the front door and he stopped to let her pass the threshold. Then and only then did they both turn to each other. The heated look in her eyes shot straight through him.

Henry opened his mouth, entirely unsure of what he could possibly say that wasn't the height of impropriety. But before he could make an utter fool of himself, Sylvia saved him.

"Come here, Georgiana! We've found some music for you to play."

Lady Arlington turned to her friend, then glanced back at Henry. He gave her a subtle nod. He had to get out of here. The protection officers were stationed below at the entrance to the private lift. There was no reason for him to stay any longer.

But just as he prepared to say his goodbyes, Rafe came forward. "I'm afraid you can't escape that easily, Captain."

Henry longed to tell him to go to hell, but that would only lead to more questions he didn't want to answer. "Very well," he said through gritted teeth.

"Come in, then," Rafe said with a broad smile. He was enjoying this, the bastard.

Henry shuffled inside and followed him to the large parlor. Georgiana was already seated at the impressive black lacquered piano while Sylvia fussed with some sheet music. The countess's butler was pouring glasses of port, while a maid wheeled in a cart bearing desserts and a steaming pot of tea.

"Would you care for port or mint tea, Captain?" the countess asked as she moved toward the cart.

"Tea, please." Given the state of his nerves, it seemed the far safer choice.

"It's a Moroccan custom Mahmood introduced me to," she explained while pouring him a cup of the fragrant brew into an elegantly decorated glass cup. "Mint tea after a meal. I find it most calming."

Henry took a sip. "Very refreshing."

Georgiana began tapping out the first few chords with obvious skill. Even Henry, who had dutifully taken lessons for a time as a boy to please his mother but otherwise had no real ear for music, thought it sounded dreadfully complicated. "Could someone turn for me?" she said distractedly as her eyes scanned the page.

The tea must have had absolutely no effect on his nerves because Henry was already moving toward her. Already offering his help. "I can do it."

Her gaze shot to his with undisguised surprise. "Oh. Thank you," she murmured and moved aside on the bench. As Henry sat down, her skirts practically embraced his legs. They were wonderfully, terribly close.

He glanced at the sheet music. "Chopin?"

"Mr. Previn's favorite composer," she explained, her gaze still on the notes. "But rather advanced for a beginner. No wonder the countess gave up."

A sympathetic smile touched her lips, and she looked up at him. Her cheeks were appealingly flushed. It must be from the wine, Henry reasoned. It couldn't possibly be anything else. Like, say, him. But just as Henry leaned a little toward her, she abruptly turned back to the music. His mind screamed to pull back, to feign illness, anything to hasten his withdrawal, but the warnings were effectively silenced as soon as she pressed her fingers to the keys.

She was even better than he had remembered. Better than he could have ever imagined. But it wasn't simply the music pouring forth from her nimble fingers dancing over the keys. It was the way she seemed wholly possessed by her performance. She was a woman who usually moved with a delicate grace that appeared effortless. Who kept her feelings tucked away behind a gilded mask. But here all her pretenses fell away. A charged tension seemed to run through her body, while her normally smooth brow furrowed in intense concentration as her arms flexed and stretched, hammering at the notes. Here she was powerful. Full of life. Of heat. Of passion.

Henry was so distracted he missed his cue. It wasn't until she gave him a sharp glance that he remembered what he was here for.

"Sorry," he mumbled as he turned the page, and the music continued.

He made sure to keep his gaze fixed firmly on the page this time. It was the safer choice anyway. If he watched her any longer, he would be unable to hide the effect she was having on him. It had been so much easier for him to labor under the illusion that he disliked her when she was busy playing the viscountess. But in these moments, when the mask was abandoned, he found it nearly impossible. Because he had fallen in love with that girl once, and would do so again quite easily.

As if you haven't already.

Henry growled so loudly at the unwelcome thought that Georgiana actually stumbled over a few notes. He winced and apologized again, but she only smiled, eyes still fixed to the music.

"You're a terrible assistant," she whispered. "I thought you would have improved over the years."

Henry was struck dumb for a moment. How awkward he had felt during those afternoons back then, sitting next to such a lovely creature, wondering why she was paying him any attention. Not so very different from now.

"I'm afraid I'm out of practice," he whispered back, actually *flirting* with the woman who had rejected him. Twice now. Surely the lack of sleep must be interfering with his reason.

"Excuses, excuses," she teased, and even Henry could not explain away the warmth that pumped through his heart at her words.

Her hands continued to move deftly across the keyboard. Henry imagined them stroking down his chest in smooth, unhurried movements. Then taking hold of his cock with the same surety and purpose. Damn. That was a mistake. He subtly shifted his body away from her.

Only a few more pages of music and this self-inflicted torture could end. Then he could retreat to the safety of his bedroom and find sweet relief.

It won't be enough.

Henry gritted his teeth. No, it certainly would not. But he had long ago grown used to making do with far, far less than he desired.

CHAPTER THIRTEEN

Georgiana allowed herself to be cajoled into playing another piece by Mahmood, who was positively delighted by her performance. When she opened the thick book of sheet music, Captain Harris had made a noise that sounded almost like a whimper, but dutifully attended to the pages. When the last note rang out in the room, he immediately rose to his feet and began to applaud. The others joined, but Georgiana would have sworn he was motivated by a desire to move away from her. This was particularly vexing given that *he* had chosen to sit beside her in the first place. But rather than show her irritation, Georgiana simply smiled and curtsied. While chatting with Mahmood, the countess, and Sylvia, she caught a glimpse of Rafe approaching the captain. They exchanged a few words, but Georgiana couldn't quite make them out—

"Pardon?" The countess had asked her a question. "Oh, yes. I started taking lessons when I was five."

"Sylvia says you once considered a career in music."

Georgiana cut her friend a glance. "*Very* briefly. While I was at school." When she still had the luxury of fantasizing about her future. "It was only a silly dream," she added with a shrug.

Mahmood frowned. "I wouldn't say that. There's still time, you know."

Though the man was absolutely serious, Georgiana couldn't help laughing at the outrageous idea.

"I hardly have the time to play for my own enjoyment these days. Surely you can understand that."

But he would not relent. "Being a business owner is all well and good, but I can't help but think you are wasting your talent. Unless your passion for fabrics matches your passion for music."

That unexpectedly stung. She was proud of the improvements she had made to her factories. And there was so much more she could do to make a real difference.

"Oh, don't listen to him, my dear," the countess put in. "Mahmood may appear to be a proper businessman, but he is a romantic at heart."

Mahmood looked poised to respond to this, until they were all distracted by the sound of Rafe and Henry's voices rising in a corner of the room. They both immediately stopped once they drew everyone's notice.

Henry stalked out of the room without another word. Rafe called after him, but the captain did not stop. Then he let out an exasperated sigh and pinched the bridge of his nose. Sylvia immediately went to him and ran a soothing hand along his shoulder. As Rafe stared down at his wife, he grew calmer. "I'm so sorry to have spoiled the evening," he said to everyone before addressing Georgiana specifically. "Please, don't leave because I acted like an idiot."

"No, no. It's late anyway, and I didn't sleep very well last night," she said, ignoring Sylvia's suspicious glance. "Thank you again for your hospitality."

"Come tomorrow morning, for breakfast," Sylvia said, squeezing her hand. "We still have so much to discuss."

"That sounds lovely."

Then she said her goodbyes to the rest of the party, but before she left, Rafe pulled her aside. "May I have a word?"

Georgiana followed him out into the hallway. He ran a hand through his already disheveled hair. "This is horribly awkward. And if Henry knew I was talking to you, he'd have my hide—well, more than he already wants to, anyway." He let out a short laugh then gave her a solemn look. "It's just that... I need to know you aren't going to hurt him."

Georgiana's eyes went wide. How could *she* hurt the captain? She shook her head at the very idea.

"He may put on an act," Rafe continued in the wake of her silence. "But the last two years have been incredibly difficult for him. More than he'll ever say. Even to me."

She couldn't help bristling at receiving this caution from a man Captain Harris was obviously upset with. "What were you fighting about?"

Rafe let out a breath. "We don't agree on something. I can't tell you any more than that. The rest is at Henry's discretion. But even though he is angry with me, I still care about him. You can understand that, can't you?"

Georgiana had treated Rafe in much the same way in Scotland, when she needed to protect Sylvia from his then unspoken intentions. "Of course," she murmured. "I know he and I don't get along, but I certainly have no desire to hurt the man."

He gave her a strange look before catching himself with a shake of the head. "Never mind. I've quite overstepped the bounds here. I'd appreciate it if you didn't mention this to Henry?"

"I won't," Georgiana said honestly, still not sure what exactly he was talking about.

Rafe gave her a tired smile. "Thank you. I'll see you at breakfast." Just as he turned to leave, Georgiana called him back.

"Is everything all right with Sylvia? She seemed tired today during our walk," she explained at his look of confusion.

"She said nothing to me. Should I be concerned?"

Georgiana shrugged. "She looks slimmer since I saw her last as well. But I'm sure it's nothing," she said quickly as alarm filled his dark gaze.

"I'll make sure the hotel physician comes first thing tomorrow. Thank you."

"Of course," she said weakly, feeling like she had gone behind Sylvia's back. That wasn't right. But she was relieved to know the physician would see her. Then she turned and walked down the long, empty hallway alone.

When Georgiana entered the suite, the door to the balcony was open. She paused, waiting for her eyes to adjust to the dim light of the parlor. She could just make out the captain's shadowed figure leaning against the railing.

She watched him for a long moment before ducking into her bedroom, where Bea sat by the fireplace leafing through a book.

She rose at her entrance and unsuccessfully hid a yawn, but Georgiana waved her away. "Tonight went longer than I anticipated. Go to sleep."

But Bea insisted on removing her jewels and helping her out of her evening gown.

"I can handle the rest," Georgiana said as she shrugged into a wrapper.

"Yes, my lady," Bea said, too tired to protest. And hopefully too tired to notice that Georgiana did not immediately retire. Once her maid had shut the door to her room, Georgiana tightened the sash on her wrapper and headed back to the parlor. Her heartbeat thrummed in her throat as she noticed the balcony door still ajar.

As she stepped out into the cool night air, Captain Harris glanced over. Georgiana had been prepared to feign surprise, but gave up at the last moment. She had grown so tired of pretending.

"Are you all right?" she asked.

He turned to the sea view and sighed with a heaviness Georgiana could practically feel. "I should say yes."

Georgiana paused, waiting for more, but he let his silence say what he would not. She moved beside him by the railing. The breeze felt refreshing on her face. She hadn't realized how warm the countess's suite had become.

"Sylvia and I quarreled badly when we were staying in Scotland together." It felt a little strange to mention the trip, given his own fortuitous presence mere moments after she had learned of the viscount's death.

He faced her, though he was still mostly in shadow. A shaft of lamplight from the parlor grazed his cheek. "What was it about?"

"I had made a decision once that she didn't understand. And rather than explain myself to her, I just assumed she would trust my judgment. Because I thought that was what friends did."

Captain Harris grunted. Georgiana couldn't tell if he agreed with her or not.

"But I was wrong," she continued. "And I took her concern for disapproval."

"I'm not sure what you're trying to say, my lady."

"Neither am I," she said with a short laugh. "I guess my point is that, in my experience, there are very few people in the world who genuinely care about you. So it is worth the effort to understand them as best you can. And not let disagreements, however big they may seem, get in the way of your friendship."

At that he turned fully toward her. "Is that what you think? That there aren't many people left who care about you?"

Georgiana frowned. That wasn't the point she had been trying to make at all. But before she could correct him, Captain Harris gently brushed her cheek with the pad of his thumb.

Her breath caught at this unexpected tenderness. Why was it that this man who always seemed to look upon her with such disapproval handled her as if she were made of the finest porcelain?

"I suppose this situation hasn't helped," he continued, his low voice washing over her in the darkness. "Knowing there is someone out there who wants to hurt you."

Georgiana opened her mouth to respond but found herself leaning into his touch instead. Lord, it felt good. She closed her eyes and let herself be swept away by the feel of his thumb brushing her cheek as his heat curled around her body like an embrace, lifting away the weight of the last few weeks—no, the last few years. Was this how it felt to have someone else shoulder your burdens for a little while? If so, it was heaven. Absolute heaven.

After a moment Georgiana opened her eyes on a gasp and found herself tucked up against his solid chest, one arm wrapped around her back, while his other hand gently massaged her nape. Captain Harris stared down at her, as silent as ever. But she only felt comforted. Protected. She lifted slowly onto her toes, and he immediately responded. This kiss was slower, more tentative. A searching kiss with a sweetness that somehow rattled her far more than yesterday's fevered embrace. For she had laid bare a part of her that she forgot to hide. A part of her that he had uncovered before she had even realized it.

He dragged his lips away and grazed the shell of her ear. "I can't begin this with you again only to stop," he said roughly, as if it pained him to admit this. Then he pulled back and held her face in his hands. His touch was still achingly gentle, but even the low light could not hide the stark longing in his gaze. "Do you understand?"

She pressed her palm over the back of his hand and nodded, swallowing hard. "I won't stop you this time."

I can't.

Captain Harris stared at her for another endless moment as heat filled his eyes. "Good," he growled before he bent her back and took her mouth in a ravenous, all-consuming kiss while they were bathed in moonlight and the sound of the crashing sea waves below filled her ears.

Georgiana gripped the lapels of his jacket tightly in her hands, as if the force of the kiss itself could send her flying. At some point, Captain Harris maneuvered her so her back was pressed against the balcony. One hand still firmly gripped her nape, while the other slowly skated down her chest, lingering on the underside of one breast, pushing the generous flesh up into his palm.

Georgiana had always been a touch embarrassed by her bosom, both by the usually unwanted attention it attracted and by the looks of defeat that crossed the faces of modistes inexperienced with attending to ladies of her generous shape. But the latter hadn't happened in years, not since she had met Madam Laurent, a visionary Parisian dressmaker. Given the purr currently working its way out of the captain's throat as he cupped her breast, it seemed safe to assume that he could also appreciate her curves.

As if to punctuate this thought, he tore his lips from hers at that moment. "You feel incredible," he breathed.

Georgiana was prepared to deflect the compliment by making a quip in response, but all that came out was a low moan as the captain began lightly twisting her nipple between his thumb and forefinger through the gauzy fabric of her wrapper.

She dragged a finger down the side of his strong throat and looked deeply into his eyes. "Then take me to bed, Henry."

He stilled under her touch. For the longest moment he merely stared down at her in charged silence. The moon had disappeared behind a cloud, shrouding his face in shadow. But just when Georgiana had begun to worry that she had overstepped the mark, he tugged her back inside the suite toward his room. Georgiana barely had a chance to catch her breath before he shut the door soundly behind them and pushed her down onto his bed. Her breath caught as he dragged his gaze hungrily over her body. She had never seen him look so...so...*unmoored* before. The stoic Captain Harris was reduced to pure need by a few words. The man was verging on feral. He leaned over her, tangling his hand in her hair to remove the pins until coils came loose in waves that cascaded down her back and shoulders.

"Your hair," he murmured with such reverence that Georgiana had to avert her gaze. She was feeling too much again.

Georgiana unwound from his touch. "Take your clothes off," she said, forcing a chill into her voice in a desperate bid to retain some control.

Henry paused and let out a short, puzzled laugh but stepped back to do her bidding. He slipped off his dress shoes and placed his cane by the nightstand, just as he had done last night, then removed his cuff links, necktie, and jacket, which he folded neatly across the back of a chair before standing in front of her. Georgiana hadn't been looking directly at him, but now she glanced up.

"Why did you stop?"

He flashed her a wolfish smile and began rolling the sleeve of his dress shirt up over one lean forearm before moving on to the other. Georgiana's breath hitched. He was doing this on purpose. *Teasing* her. Somehow she found the strength to tear her gaze away from the strong, sinewy flesh being revealed inch by glorious inch to raise a scandalized eyebrow at him.

"My goodness, Captain. I had no idea you had experience in the seductive arts."

He threw his head back and laughed. A real, genuine laugh. Georgiana's heart did a somersault in her chest. She should have gotten up and left at that moment. Instead, she grabbed his wrists and tugged him closer, but he resisted.

"I think we should talk before we…" His gaze skated to the pillows behind her. "About expectations."

Of course they should. So why was disappointment sinking through her like a stone? "Very sensible, Captain," she said, forcing lightness into her voice. Henry frowned down at her, looking not the least bit fooled. But before he could respond, she continued: "As you noted yesterday, there is a mutual attraction here. And this seems like the ideal place to explore it. Away from the prying eyes and ears of London society," she added, the plan coming together as she spoke.

"And your family."

She let out a dry laugh. "The most prying of all, yes."

"What about Lord Pettigrew?"

Georgiana stiffened. She had nearly forgotten about Tommy. "He has no claim on me."

Henry raised an eyebrow. "And is *he* aware of that?"

"I have made no promises to him," she replied. "If he has deluded himself otherwise, that is not my problem."

"But you intend to see him again when you return to London," Henry pressed.

"Well…yes," she admitted. "Does that matter?"

A part of her wanted the captain to be bothered by her potential involvement with Tommy Pettigrew. Jealous enough to give a damn, but not so much that he wouldn't wish to proceed with this affair.

Henry's expression remained inscrutable. "No," he finally said. "But it's yet another reason for us to prioritize discretion. Besides, it wouldn't look good for my business if word got around that I was involved with a client."

She hadn't thought of the implications for his business at all, but he was right. Especially if Reggie found out. "I won't say a word to anyone. Not even Sylvia. And once we return…"

He swallowed. "It ends."

That left them with five days. Five days to sate a desire eight years in the making. It seemed both far too much and nowhere near enough. A sudden bolt of desperation thundered through her, and she reached for him again just as Henry moved toward her. Together they fell back onto the mattress, a tangle of searching limbs and ragged kisses. Henry moved onto his side and grazed the shell of her ear with his teeth. He didn't stop until he reached the base of her throat. Georgiana arched into the shiver that pulsed through her at the sensation.

"I love that," she gasped.

Henry licked the hollow of her throat. "I know."

There was more behind those words. More he wasn't saying. But before she could follow the thought, Henry untied the sash of her wrapper and pushed up the hem of her nightgown in grasping handfuls. Then he gripped her thigh and pulled her astride him.

"Is this all right?" she asked, taking care not to put her full weight on him, though she wasn't anywhere near his injured knee.

"Yes," Henry answered, rocking his generous erection against her core for emphasis. "But this is better." He snaked his hands under her nightgown, slowly easing it off, and then pressed his palms against the bare flesh of her bottom, urging her body forward.

Georgiana frowned in confusion even as she followed his lead. "I don't understand."

"You will," he murmured as he pulled her up his torso until she was nearly straddling his face.

"Henry—"

But before she could say more, he pressed his lips to her intimate flesh. Whatever words she had been trying to say turned into a low, deep moan. At the feel of his tongue, her body went boneless. Georgiana pitched forward and pressed her arms against the pillows as pleasure as sharp as a knife's edge tore through her.

She knew people did such things, of course, but had never imagined Captain Harris was one of them. What a delightful surprise.

Once she recovered from the shock, she sat up. His hands cupped her hips, lightly squeezing her backside, and urging her to rock against his mouth while his wicked tongue continued to lap at her.

He stopped briefly to instruct her to hold on to the elaborate headboard. "That's it," he praised as she anchored her body.

He returned to the task with even greater enthusiasm than before, and Georgiana's head fell back. All she could do was hold tight as he built pleasure inside her, slowly and steadily.

His long, strong fingers skated up her chest until he could

gently massage her breasts and pluck at her nipples. Georgiana pressed down harder against his mouth in reaction before immediately jerking back. "Oh! I'm so sorry—"

Henry's only answer was to pull her right back to where she had been and hold her thighs in place. His moan reverberated against her core, and Georgiana could only gasp in response. He wanted this. Wanted *her*. And likely more than he would ever say. At this realization, her release crashed over her in wave after wave of searing pleasure. Henry held her fast as he continued to lick and suck, determined to wring every last possible sensation from her, until Georgiana was sure there was nothing left. She slumped against the headboard, panting hard as he pulled away. Her skin was lightly misted with perspiration, and her body felt lighter than she could ever remember. She closed her eyes and pressed her forehead against the wall as she waited to catch her breath. Belatedly, she heard rustling behind her.

Henry.

Georgiana immediately sat up, feeling abominably selfish. But when she turned around, he was seated in the chair still fully dressed. His bare forearms gripped the chair's handles, while his heated amber eyes brought yet another flush to her cheeks. Georgiana was suddenly highly aware of her own nakedness. She began to press her hands to her chest, then decided that that was remarkably silly given what they had just done. Instead, she picked her discarded wrapper up off the floor and pulled it on, then stood. As she moved toward him, Henry's gaze tracked her every step, never straying from her. His mouth was pressed into that familiar hard line once again, but she would not be cowed by him tonight. They had made a bargain, and Georgiana intended to see it through. For better or worse.

She placed one hand on the chair's back. "Why did you get up?"

"I wanted to enjoy the view."

A smile tugged at the corner of her mouth. Given his gruff tone and malevolent expression, one could be forgiven for assuming he was not exactly enjoying himself.

"I see." Georgiana dragged a hand through his hair and tilted his face up. "And do you plan to just *look* this evening?"

Henry met her gaze. "I think you know my preference." He was already pulling her onto his lap. His hands already tugging off her wrapper. As it fluttered to the floor once again, his eyes roamed all over her body. She never wanted to forget the hunger in them. The way it made her feel cherished. Possessed. *Loved.*

Georgiana shook away the last thought and tugged on Henry's suspenders, until he pressed against her chest. "Then show me," she whispered, her voice breathless and reedy.

He wound her hair around his hand in a thick coil and tugged it back until her neck stretched out, then lavished it with decadent, open-mouthed kisses. She squirmed on his lap as the needy ache built inside her once again, unable to stop seeking friction. "Please."

Henry guided her to her feet and backed her toward the bed, all while never breaking the kiss, his hands still caressing every inch of her exposed skin. She pulled down his suspenders and tugged open the buttons of his trousers.

Their gazes locked together and he paused, now breathing

almost as heavily as she was. It was a relief to see him come undone, just a little.

"You're sure."

It was posed as a statement, but she knew what he was asking. And while she appreciated his consideration, she very well knew her own mind.

Georgiana let out an irritated huff and pulled him on top of her, letting her actions speak for her. Loudly.

Henry grunted in surprise, but he did not stop. Instead, he cupped her face in his hands and gave her a brutal kiss that only ended when she took hold of his hard shaft. A hiss escaped his lips, and he pushed her grasping hand away.

"I believe I can manage things from here," he quipped, his dry tone just barely masking the tremble in his voice. Georgiana smiled to herself. A smile that quickly vanished on a gasp as he eased into her.

"Oh God," she breathed, and Henry immediately halted. "No," she added, pressing her hands to his backside to urge him forward. "Don't stop."

It was the height of vulgarity to act so wantonly in bed. But it had been so, *so* long. And never anything like this. Georgiana felt as if she would burst into flames if she went one second longer without him inside her. And said as much.

"Very well," Henry grunted as he resumed his movements. "As my lady commands."

Georgiana bit back a laugh. She enjoyed his talk far too much, as if he were some sort of errant knight in an erotic Walter Scott story. But all thoughts of chivalry escaped her as he pushed fully into her. Henry let out a low curse and held absolutely still for a moment. Georgiana's eyelids fluttered at the feel of his hard length filling her. She hadn't known it was possible to be sated so completely. But then he began to move. And that was even better. Her fingers dug into his shoulders, still swathed in the fabric of his shirt. He moved in slow, deliberate thrusts, taking her deeper and deeper each time. She wrapped her legs around his waist, and a strangled grunt escaped his lips. He began to move harder and faster, panting by her ear. Georgiana arched her back, taking even more of him, until it felt as if every part of her was filled with him. The sound of his growing pleasure, the scent of his skin, the feel of his warm, strong body pressing against hers all pushed her closer to the edge of her own release.

"Georgie," he growled against her ear, hard and sudden. *"Fuck."*

It felt like someone had set off fireworks inside her. Sparks soared through her body as they came together. Henry wrenched himself from her just as her pleasure began to subside and let out an aching groan. Only then did she realize he had been holding his own release at bay, waiting for her. His consideration filled her with a different kind of warmth. One she had never experienced before. With the viscount, making love had always been perfunctory. An act meant to generate a result that she had never managed to accomplish. But this was something entirely new. And entirely not in keeping with the arrangement they had agreed upon.

For she wanted so much more.

Henry collapsed beside her, still catching his breath, and Georgiana pushed to her feet. She began searching for her discarded wrapper and underclothes.

"Is something wrong?"

She looked over her shoulder, and a fierce longing shot through her. He had sat up on one elbow, peering at her with a confused expression far more open than usual.

"Of course not," she said stiffly, fighting the urge to climb back into bed with him as she slid her wrapper around her shoulders.

He raised an eyebrow in question, and Georgiana's heart clenched briefly, but then she pushed the feeling aside. "I'm just tired. Can't risk falling asleep here."

Surely he could understand that.

His jaw tightened ever so slightly, but then his expression returned to that familiar wall of stone. "Quite right." He sat all the way up, still watching her much too closely.

Georgiana forced herself not to look away. "Good night."

As he stared back at her, his dark gaze was inscrutable as ever. "Sleep well."

CHAPTER FOURTEEN

———◆———

H enry awoke just as dawn was breaking over the
Mediterranean. He hadn't bothered to change out of
his clothes last night because he hadn't wanted to part with
Georgiana's scent just yet.

In other words, he was pathetic.

He moved to the edge of the bed and stretched his leg
out tentatively, pleasantly surprised to find it didn't ache
much. Dr. Abernathy's exercises were working, then. That
was encouraging, given how determined Henry had been to
not let his knee hold him back last night. It had been a risk,
but well worth it. One he hoped very much to take again.
Heat flared through him as image after image of Georgiana
flashed through his mind. She had been so lovely and so
very reactive to his touch. In truth, Henry had been more
than a little worried that he wouldn't be able to satisfy her,
that the previous evening had been a fluke, and he would

never measure up to her late husband. But the way she had crawled onto his lap after he pleasured her with his mouth had been incredibly gratifying to his ego, especially since she was the first woman he had been intimate with since his injury—not that he had ever been much of a lothario before that. But what he lacked in quantity, he liked to think he made up for in quality.

He rubbed his face and let out a sigh. He still wasn't sure what had come over Georgiana. Henry had been about to pull her into his arms and ask her to spend the night with him, or as much of it as she dared, when she began acting as if they had just swapped business tips rather than a passionate encounter the likes of which he had certainly never experienced before.

Though Georgiana had put on an admirable show, Henry wasn't quite convinced that he was alone in feeling shaken by the emotions their coupling had dragged to the surface. Her demeanor may have been calm, but she hadn't been able to hide the trembling in her fingers or the raw vulnerability in her eyes.

But that didn't mean her dismissiveness hadn't hurt.

Still, Henry was hardly in a position to confront her about it, as there were far too many things he had no wish to reveal. In the meantime he would suffer her slings and arrows while taking whatever comfort he could find in her lush, welcoming body. She had been even more perfect than he had ever imagined—and at one time Henry Harris had done quite a bit of imagining. Now he planned to acquire as many memories as he could before this affair came to an end. And end it would.

Hopefully without destroying him in the process.

* * *

Georgiana had to force herself out of bed, wishing for all the world she hadn't promised to breakfast with Sylvia. Once again she had slept in shallow, fitful bursts, as her mind was filled with thoughts of the captain—she *refused* to think of him as Henry outside her encounters. Every time she began to drift off, she would recall another tantalizing detail and the strange mix of desire and bashfulness that followed would jerk her awake. Now she felt wrung out, like a piece of heavily laundered washing.

As she readied herself for the day (with Bea fretting yet again over her increasingly pale visage) she worried that there might be some awkwardness with Captain Harris, especially given her abrupt exit last night. But she didn't have much time to ruminate on the possibilities before she found him sitting in the suite's parlor. At her entrance, he stood and gave her a perfectly polite smile just a touch friendlier than usual.

"Good morning, Lady Arlington."

Her body coiled even tighter at his deep voice. It appeared that he, too, was limiting first names to the bedroom. And yet, somehow, the man still managed to make her courtesy title sound incredibly wanton.

"Yes. Hello."

"You're having breakfast with Mrs. Davies?"

Georgiana nodded and forced herself to move across the room toward the exit. He couldn't be too upset with her then, as the man had certainly never bothered to hide his anger or irritation. She had nearly reached the door when she felt his presence close behind her and glanced back. The heat in his gaze brought her to a full stop, and she turned to face him. Georgiana wasn't sure she could have looked away even if she wanted to.

His eyes were full of hunger. Interest. Desire.

"Where is Bea?"

"In my bedroom with some sewing," Georgiana managed to say. "Why?"

Captain Harris leaned so close she could see the flecks of gold in his irises. "I don't want her to see this," he murmured as he pressed her against the door. Then his mouth was on hers in a fierce, deep kiss that sent her knees wobbling. It was over in an instant, before she could properly enjoy it, leaving Georgiana breathless and in desperate need of a chair.

"Would you like me to escort you to the countess's apartment?" The captain looked quite pleased with himself.

Georgiana bit back a smile as she tried to compose herself. "Please."

They made the short walk in absolute silence.

The countess's ever efficient butler opened the door as soon as Captain Harris could knock.

"Won't you come in? Say hello?"

She had not forgotten his argument with Rafe, but perhaps she could assist him in making amends. The captain pursed his lips, and she could not help recalling how full and firm they had been on her mouth. Urging such things from her. Things Georgiana had not known she could even give. "Another time. I have some things to attend to this morning." For once, Georgiana did not try to hide her disappointment. "But I will see you this evening. At the casino," he added just as Georgiana began to blush.

Oh. She had forgotten about that.

"Yes," she replied, doing her best not to sound quite so breathless.

Captain Harris didn't look the least bit fooled. He gave her a short bow. "Until then, my lady." Then he turned and walked down the hallway.

My lady.

Georgiana had been referred to that way hundreds of times over the years and never had given it much thought. Now it was hard to imagine how she could hear the title without thinking of him.

She let out a little sigh and entered the apartment. "Is Mrs. Davies on the terrace?"

The butler shook his head, dour as ever. "She is still in her room, but I will let her know you arrived."

Every muscle in her body went rigid. *Sylvia's illness.* "Did the doctor come to see her?"

The butler hesitated a moment before giving a small, barely perceptible nod. Georgiana was already moving down the hall toward the bedrooms, though she didn't know which one was Sylvia's. But Georgiana would find her. Guilt spurred her forward. She had been so wrapped up in Captain Harris that she had entirely forgotten. Unforgivable. She followed the faint sound of voices coming from the end of the hall, where the door to a room stood open. She could make out Rafe, speaking in low soothing tones, and Georgiana's heart clenched, but as she drew closer, it was Sylvia's voice she heard clearly.

"I've been so busy, I didn't realize..." She let out a soft laugh. "Oh, I feel like a fool. And Georgiana was so worried yesterday."

At the mention of her name, Georgiana stopped in her tracks just outside the door.

"There's nothing to feel foolish about," Rafe said tenderly. "She'll be thrilled for you, I'm sure."

She could see the two of them in the reflection of a vanity mirror a few feet in front of her. They were sitting on the bed, and Rafe's arm was draped protectively around his wife. Sylvia looked so small and pale in his embrace. One could mistake her for an invalid, if not for the dazzling smile on her face.

"But you must keep up your strength, my darling," Rafe murmured by her ear as he drew her closer. "For both your sakes."

Georgiana stepped back from the doorway before they could spot her and pressed her back to the wall as her pulse thundered in her ears.

Sylvia wasn't ill. She was with *child*. Now it was Georgiana's turn to feel like a fool. She should have recognized the signs immediately. But instead she had assumed the very worst. Georgiana gazed up at the ceiling until she could master her breathing. This was joyous news, and yet all she could hear was the viscount's insidious voice in her ear.

I paid for an heir, and I damned well better get one from you.

She retreated as quickly and quietly as possible. She would make her excuses later. For now she couldn't let either of them see her like this.

She hurried out of the suite and immediately headed for the lift. By the time she reached the lobby she needed air. Desperately. Georgiana headed toward the hotel's back terrace. It was another beautiful day outside, and well-dressed guests were happily milling around the grounds.

She looked past them all and focused on the horizon, taking in slow breaths while she tried to gather her scattered thoughts. But the urge to leave crashed over her, and before she could reason otherwise, she swiftly descended the terrace stairs and wound her way through the perfectly manicured gardens toward the front of the hotel. She was in a veritable paradise on earth but barely noticed the orange trees, frangipani, and towering palms that surrounded her as grim determination filled her every step. She didn't want to be around anyone she knew. Didn't want to be asked how she was or what was wrong. For the first time she longed for her widow's weeds once again. To be shrouded in a black veil and left alone. So alone.

As she entered a waiting carriage and moved to close the curtains, her two protection officers came bursting out the front of the hotel, frantically looking in every direction. Georgiana rolled her eyes, snapped the curtain closed and leaned back against the plush seat. They would discover her whereabouts soon enough, but those men couldn't make her return to the hotel until she was ready. Damn well ready.

* * *

"What do you *mean* Lady Arlington is missing?"

Henry had just sat down to enjoy a relaxing breakfast in the hotel's restaurant when he was interrupted by the two protection offices assigned to Georgiana.

"She went outside to the back terrace, and we lost her in the gardens," the first man said, very conciliatory.

"We thought it was just a morning stroll," the second added, far more indignant than the first. "But she eluded us."

"I see," Henry snapped. "You were somehow outpaced by a woman in a gown and heels who can barely walk faster than I can. Fabulous." He threw down his newspaper and stood. "Do you have any idea where she went?"

"She boarded a carriage that brings guests to the casino."

"Then why the *hell* didn't you follow her?"

The men exchanged a look before the shorter of the two spoke: "With all due respect, Captain, we are only assigned to watch her when she is on hotel grounds. The rest is up to you."

Well, he had Henry there.

He gritted his teeth. "Can you at least tell Mr. Previn what happened and that I am going after her? She was supposed to have breakfast with Mrs. Davies. She's probably worried by now."

Likely a vast understatement given the anxiety pumping through him at the moment.

Henry immediately headed out to the front of the hotel and boarded a carriage after speaking with the attendant who had assisted Georgiana. She had left only fifteen minutes ago, and the carriages all dropped guests off in the same place near the casino's entrance. Hopefully she hadn't gone very far. Even still, Henry was swamped with worry as the carriage made its way down the hill toward Monte Carlo below. This wasn't like Georgiana. She would certainly skip out on him without a second thought, but never Sylvia. Unless something had happened after Henry left her. Last night she had been worried for her friend. And wasn't a doctor supposed to visit this morning?

A pit formed low in his belly. If something was wrong with Sylvia, it would destroy Rafe. Utterly. Though most thought him a callow rogue, the man was sensitive, perceptive, and deeply in love with his wife. By the time the carriage arrived, Henry was practically jumping out of his skin. He needed to find Georgiana. He spoke with another attendant who naturally remembered "the beautiful English lady" and pointed him in the direction of a nearby public garden that offered a view of the ocean.

Henry thanked him and set off.

* * *

Georgiana stared out at the brilliant sea until her eyes began to water. She vaguely noted her rumbling stomach but couldn't find the will to seek out a café just yet. Her eyes fluttered closed as she pressed a hand to her temple. She placed her other hand against the balustrade in front of her and leaned forward, seeking a little relief from the weight that seemed to have settled over her shoulders. She would need to head back soon and put on a happy face for Sylvia—no, she *was* happy for her.

To hell with the viscount. She refused to let that man and his callous words continue to invade her thoughts. The lack of sleep must be affecting her more than she realized. Goodness, she couldn't even remember the last time she had slept well. Just as she contemplated putting her head down, a pair of strong hands clamped over her shoulders and hauled her back against a hard chest. "Georgiana," a familiar voice rumbled by her ear.

She let out a sigh and sank even deeper against Captain

Harris. For just a moment she wanted to enjoy this feeling. To have someone to anchor her here. To share a bit of this weight with her. But it was over all too quickly as he turned her around.

"What's going on? Why are you here?" Captain Harris's strong hand cupped her jaw and he tilted her face up. He looked stark. Worried. "Is something wrong with Sylvia?"

"No," she said quickly, and relief filled his eyes. "She... she's with child. I overheard her talking with Rafe when I entered the suite."

"But that's wonderful news."

"I know," she snapped and stepped back until he released his hold on her.

His eyes softened. "Is that why you left?"

Georgiana looked away. "What kind of friend would I be if I did that?"

"The same one you have always been," he pronounced. "Dedicated, compassionate, and human."

She turned to him in surprise, but this time the stern set of his features was a comfort. It brooked no argument. "Let's get you something to eat," he said. "I take it you haven't had breakfast yet?"

"I'm not hungry," Georgiana insisted, even while her mouth practically salivated at the mere mention of food.

"Well, I am. Seeing how mine was interrupted by a pair of incompetent protection officers."

"Oh," Georgiana said. "And then you had to come here to fetch me."

Captain Harris gave her a brief smile. "It's all right. Part of the job."

She stiffened a little at the unwelcome reminder. He may

be seeking her confidence *and* bedding her, but this man wasn't her friend, nor the solution to any of her problems. Georgiana needed to remember that.

Captain Harris failed to notice her discomfort, as he was already looking back to the main thoroughfare. He pointed to a charming little café close by and gently gripped her elbow as he guided her to it. A table opened up just as they arrived, and, ever the gentleman, he pulled out her chair for her rather than let the waiter do it.

"How is your knee?" Georgiana asked as he sat down across from her. She didn't like the thought of him traipsing all over Monte Carlo on account of her foul mood.

"It's fine," he replied, keeping his eyes on the menu.

"Bea says you do exercises for it."

That got his full attention. He raised an eyebrow. "Does she?"

"She also thinks your cane hides a sword."

"How intriguing."

"Then it's true?"

"I can't possibly comment on that," he said with a sly smile that answered for him and set down the menu. "I see a specialist my sister's husband recommended."

"Anna?"

The corner of his mouth lifted. "Agatha," he corrected.

She nodded. "You said you stayed with them after you returned from Turkey."

But before he could answer, the waiter reappeared. Captain Harris ordered a coffee and croissant.

"I'll have the same," Georgiana said without looking at the menu. It seemed like a safe choice. The waiter went off to fetch their drinks, leaving them alone once again. But

Captain Harris did not continue. He was looking off in the direction they had come from. Toward the sea. She picked up a fork and began tapping it against the table.

"That must have been nice to spend time with them," Georgiana gently prodded.

Captain Harris glanced at her, but his gaze was wary. "It was...helpful," he said, choosing the words carefully. "Dr. Burnett, my brother-in-law, is a very knowledgeable man. But I was not at my best while I was there."

"I understand."

The tension left his shoulders as he nodded, realizing she wouldn't pry any deeper. "They have a son now. William. He's named after my father."

Georgiana smiled. "Do you enjoy being an uncle?"

"Yes. As it's a far sight easier than being a parent," he said, then turned sheepish. "I'm sorry. That was an insensitive thing to say."

"No, it's fine. Really," she insisted in response to his skeptical look. "I think I was just shocked to realize Sylvia was pregnant. Though it sounds silly saying it aloud. She's been married for over a year now. And given the way she and Rafe can barely keep their hands off one another," she said as she rolled her eyes good-naturedly. "It was bound to happen."

Henry chuckled. "You noticed that too, eh?"

"Impossible not to." Georgiana returned his smile. "But I'm happy for them," she said truthfully before taking a moment to gather her courage. "The viscount was very disappointed not to have a child. And it made things between us difficult," she added softly.

Captain Harris was quiet for a moment. "I'm sorry to hear that."

This time she welcomed the sympathy in his gaze. The viscount had only ever made her feel like a failure. He had never once considered that she might have needed his support, not his contempt. "I admit that Sylvia's news brought back some unpleasant memories, but I'm feeling better now."

"I'm glad," he said and the warmth of his words flowed through Georgiana. It felt surprisingly good to talk with him like this. For them to each understand a little more about the other.

Just then the waiter returned with their order. Georgiana focused all her attention on fixing her coffee with cream before she ripped open her steaming croissant and spread it with a thin layer of butter, then jam. When she finally dared to look up, Captain Harris was giving her a fond smile.

"What?"

"Nothing." He shook his head, still smiling. "You know exactly what you like and how you like it," he added at her questioning look.

"Hard not to when it's just a coffee and a pastry."

"It's with other things as well, I've noticed."

Why did such a benign admission cause heat to flare inside her? The man was being *paid* to watch her, for goodness' sake. Georgiana didn't know how to respond, so she tucked into her breakfast, unable to suppress the delighted moan that escaped her lips when she bit into the croissant.

"That good?"

She glanced up at his deep tone and her gaze locked with his. The fond look had been replaced with his usual grim expression. The one that she found impossible to read.

"Yes," she said, then licked at a spot of jam from the corner of her mouth.

The captain's eyes noticeably darkened, and he shifted in his seat.

Well, then. Perhaps it wasn't so impossible to read him after all. Just as the tension began to coil between them, the waiter came over to ask if they wanted more coffee.

"Please," Georgiana said without waiting for the captain. "I haven't been sleeping well," she said in answer to his smirk. "I'm sure you can deduce *why*," she added wryly, narrowing her eyes.

Captain Harris chuckled and glanced down bashfully. Georgiana's heart clenched. Goodness, he was a terribly attractive man, especially when he wasn't glowering.

"Are you ready to return to the hotel?" he asked after the waiter brought their check.

"Yes." Georgiana let out a little sigh. "I'm sorry for earlier. I didn't mean to worry anyone."

"You needn't be sorry, my lady," he said after a moment. "You should be able to go wherever you want, whenever you want."

Georgiana had to look away from his too perceptive gaze. "Have you heard anything from the inspector in London?"

"Not yet. I sent him a message this morning."

"Then let's hope for good news upon our return."

As they walked back to the casino, where they could board a carriage bound for the hotel, Captain Harris was quiet. Georgiana didn't mind. She had grown used to his silences now and had even come to enjoy them. For unlike the viscount's, they did not signal his displeasure, but his contemplation.

They didn't have to wait long for a carriage to take them back to the Hotel Luna. Mr. Previn had an arrangement with the casino that ensured his guests never had to wait longer than fifteen minutes. But just as Georgiana moved to board the carriage, Captain Harris gently gripped her elbow and held her back for a moment.

"I will get to the bottom of these threats, Georgiana," he murmured deeply by her ear, while his inviting scent and heat curled around her body. "I promise you that."

Strange how only two weeks ago the very thought of this man being involved in her life in any way had filled her with outrage. Now, though...she heard the conviction in his words. His *promise*. And it filled her to the very brim with warmth. But there was only one thing she could allow herself to accept from him. And it was not his pity, nor his understanding.

She turned around to face him, and his eyes burned into hers. If it weren't for the footman standing next to them, she would have kissed him right then. He must have been able to read her intent on her face, for his grip on her elbow tightened as his eyelids lowered. Georgiana wasted no time stepping into the carriage, and Captain Harris followed close behind her. She had just managed to draw the curtains shut when he pulled her onto his lap.

They stared at each other as the carriage lurched to a start. She took off his hat and placed it on the seat beside them, then ran her fingers through his hair. His jaw tightened as his gaze bore into her own.

"You'll have to be quiet."

"I can," she promised, already a little breathless.

His hand cupped the nape of her neck and drew her closer. "I'm going to test you on that."

Georgiana chuckled. "That doesn't even make sen—" But the rest of her reply was muffled by his mouth as he delivered a scorching, insistent kiss, coaxing her lips open with his own.

A soft moan was already working its way up her throat when his tongue pushed against her own before licking deeply. Intimately.

Goodness, the man really *was* testing her.

And she was failing miserably, as she made a sound full of aching, desperate need.

Captain Harris broke the kiss and pulled back, now clucking that deliciously agile tongue of his. "Now, now, you're supposed to be *quiet*," he teased with a cheeky grin.

Georgiana batted his arm and pressed more firmly against his chest. "You'll have to show me," she purred.

Captain Harris tilted his head back against the carriage seat and gazed at her. Georgiana loved seeing him like this: hair mussed and eyes heavy-lidded. He looked relaxed. Happy, even.

"Very well," he drawled, as one hand slid down her waist and drew up her skirts. When her stocking-clad thighs were bared to him, he urged her to straddle his lap. His erection pressed against her belly, and she quickly unbuttoned the front of his trousers. Captain Harris watched her in silence, but his breath quickened noticeably. As she drew out his hard shaft, he let out a gasp, and she raised a finger to her lips.

"Shhh. You're supposed to be quiet," she teased as she

began to gently pump him. Henry gave her a desperate look as his hand covered her own. Georgiana followed his instruction and tightened her grip before moving faster. His head fell back hard against the seat and he let out a short grunt as his hands moved to grip the edge of the bench. It was unexpectedly thrilling, watching this usually starchy man slowly unravel under her touch. She continued to work his flesh as his length grew harder and hotter. Then, suddenly, Henry's hand stilled her own. She looked up in question and the intensity of his gaze unmoored her.

"Georgiana. *Now.*"

The low, rough command tumbled from his lips. She immediately raised up on her knees and opened the slit of her drawers wider as he nudged his shaft against her entrance. Then slowly, so slowly, she sank back down, taking him inch by inch until he was fully sheathed inside her. As the carriage rocked, so did he, using the motion to push upward even deeper. Georgiana began to rock as well.

"Oh *God*," she sobbed. It was almost more than she could bear, but Henry's hands gripped her tighter.

After that the only sounds between them were their increasingly labored breaths and the occasional gasp. Georgiana could barely spare him a glance, certain that any more would push her over the edge too soon. He, too, seemed similarly afflicted as his eyes were squeezed shut. Georgiana followed suit and found the darkness only added to the sensations growing inside her. She began moving faster as her climax began to grow and Henry seemed able to sense her coming release.

He clapped a hand over her mouth just as she began to cry out before dragging her head down to take her mouth in another long, deep kiss. When she finished, Henry guided her to rest her cheek against his shoulder. He tore a handkerchief from his breast pocket and pulled out of her. Then he buried his face against her neck as his own release overtook him. Georgiana squeezed her eyes shut again as he rasped her name in a voice frayed by desperate pleasure. She focused on her pounding heart and tried to catch her breath. But as her pulse returned to normal, the happiness blooming inside her only grew. Stretched to fill every crevice, reach the very end of every limb. Her arms tightened around his broad shoulders, and Henry's fingers tangled deeper in her hair, while his palm pressed harder at the small of her back. She imagined them entwined together, like the roots of some ancient tree. As if in answer, Henry let out a heavy sigh. Georgiana couldn't tell if it was a sigh of relief or despair. Couldn't tell which one she preferred. After a moment, she straightened and blinked in the low light. She had dozed off on his shoulder. They *both* had. Now the carriage had come to a stop, and she was still straddling his lap. Georgiana let out a startled gasp and immediately pushed off of him.

Henry's eyes snapped open and they exchanged a panicked look. He lurched toward the carriage door and grabbed the handle just as one of the hotel's very efficient footmen had begun to open it.

"Just a moment!" he called out in a strangled voice that left little question as to what, exactly, had gone on behind the door.

Georgiana did her best to smooth her wrinkled skirts and fix her hair, while Henry set himself to rights.

"How do I look?" she asked as she slid the last loose pin in place.

Henry dragged his gaze down her body before meeting her eyes. "Like a woman who was just thoroughly debauched in a carriage."

She pressed her lips together briefly at his knowing tone. "That is *not* helpful."

He shot her a grin. "No, but it makes me feel damn good." Then he put on his hat and pushed the door open.

Georgiana stared after him in surprise before taking his offered hand and descending the carriage stairs. She hadn't taken more than two steps when Sylvia rushed over to them.

"There you are! Oh, I was so worried."

A number of guests were milling about, doing their best to make their eavesdropping not quite so obvious, but Sylvia immediately noticed and composed herself. Georgiana's neck prickled with awareness. She hadn't at all considered that her little escape would draw such attention and slanted a concerned look at Captain Harris, but his gaze was already firmly fixed to her.

Well, that wasn't going to help silence any talk. And yet, she couldn't ignore the swell of heat inside her. This man was making her positively insatiable. Sylvia threaded her arm through Georgiana's, and as they moved toward the entrance, Captain Harris remained by the carriage, watching her with those sharp eyes of his.

"That flush alone gives you away," Sylvia murmured as they crossed the lobby.

Georgiana brought a hand to her cheek and sighed. She was being unconscionably reckless. And yet, she regretted none of it. Once they were alone in the private lift, Sylvia turned to her.

"You know, don't you?"

"It's wonderful news," she answered honestly.

Sylvia lowered her eyes. "When the butler said you left in a hurry, I realized what had happened. What you must have heard."

Georgiana grabbed her hand. "It was a shock, I'll admit. I just thought...the last time we had spoken, you said..."

"That I wasn't interested in having children any time soon. Which was true. Then." Sylvia met her gaze.

But Georgiana of all people knew how quickly things could change in a marriage.

Sylvia turned away. "Do you know how we spent a little time in Italy before Rafe had to be in Berlin?" Georgiana nodded. "We stayed with some friends of his in Venice, Alec and Lottie Gresham. I think you might know Lottie. Her maiden name is Carlisle."

"Oh, Sir Alfred Lewis's niece? Yes, I do."

"Well, they have the most adorable little boy. Alfie." A funny little smile that Georgiana had never seen before took over Sylvia's face. She was practically glowing. "I've never spent much time around children. But Rafe just adored him. They became thick as thieves while we were there. And watching them together, it...it..."

"It provided you with new information."

Sylvia's shoulders sagged with relief. "Yes. Exactly. But I truly didn't think it would happen this soon. Rafe's been so busy with work lately that it hasn't—we haven't—" Now it was Sylvia's turn to blush. "I was just surprised. That's all."

Georgiana squeezed her hand and waited until Sylvia looked at her. "I understand. And I'm sorry I ran off. I hate that I worried you for even a moment, and that I sent Captain Harris on a wild goose chase. But it brought some old feelings to the surface. And I wasn't prepared."

"You mean, about the viscount? You know you can talk to me about it, if you wish to," Sylvia added in response to Georgiana's nod.

"I know." She let out a sigh. "I've realized I'm not sure if I ever even *wanted* children. Everyone else told me I did. That it was my purpose to be a mother. And of course the viscount expected it. That's why he married me." She bowed her head. "Is it terrible of me to admit that I'm relieved the viscount and I never had a child? I would have loved any we had, of course, but I...I was just so *tired* by the end, Sylvie. Of having my entire worth based on whether or not I conceived," she added on a whisper. "And now when I think about the possibility, I can't seem to muster the desire. Only that same old dread bubbling up again."

"It's not terrible at all. Besides, you've been mothering your siblings for most of your life," Sylvia pointed out. "One could understand why you feel exhausted."

Georgiana flashed her a small smile. "That's true. They are incredibly demanding." Then she turned serious. "Please, *please* believe that I am deliriously happy for you both. You'll make wonderful parents."

Sylvia's eyes shimmered. "Thank you for saying that."

"But be prepared for that child to be utterly spoiled by their aunt Georgiana."

Sylvia let out a laugh. "I'd expect nothing less."

CHAPTER FIFTEEN

———◆———

After parting with Lady Arlington, Henry returned to the restaurant to resume his long-abandoned breakfast. The croissant, while delicious, was not enough to fill him up, especially after their activities in the carriage.

Just as he began to tuck into a steaming plate of eggs and toast, Rafe showed up at his table and took a seat without invitation. He began to protest, but Rafe cut him off. "Careful there, Captain. We don't want you causing another scene today. It's not even noon."

Henry darted a glance around the room as guilt swamped his chest. Pulling up to the hotel with Lady Arlington had drawn a fair bit of attention—a careless oversight on his part. He was being paid a small fortune to protect the woman, not create more gossip. Their tryst in the carriage had been abominably risky, but it was unnerving just how much he wanted her. And the lengths he would go to. They were due to depart for London in three days' time, and Henry had the sinking suspicion that he would be nowhere near close to satisfying this desire for her. A dangerous development. And yet, he had no intension of stopping.

"I heard the news. Allow me to offer my congratulations," he said.

Rafe broke into a grin. "Thank you."

"How is Sylvia feeling?"

"Good, apart from some nausea and fatigue, which I'm told is perfectly normal." Then he turned serious. "I came to apologize for last night. I shouldn't have pushed you to talk about Lady Arlington. My wife tells me I need to respect your wishes, even if I don't entirely understand them."

Rafe had commented on how happy Henry looked seated beside her by the piano.

I don't think I've ever seen you look at a woman like that. Surely that must mean something.

Henry let out a sigh. "No, I apologize for storming off. I may have . . . overreacted."

It was the rightness of the comment that had rankled the most. And that his infatuation had been so plainly written all over his face.

"Just a tad." The corner of Rafe's mouth lifted. "You haven't been yourself, you know."

Henry nodded. "I do," he said quietly.

"Now that we're on speaking terms again, I don't suppose you'll tell me what's *really* going on between you and Lady Arlington?"

Henry attempted a befuddled look. "What makes you think something's going on?"

"You mean aside from the fact that last night you looked like you wanted her to use *you* as a piano bench?"

Henry nearly choked on his tea. "What a mind you have."

"Thank you." Rafe preened a little.

"It wasn't a compliment," he said as he wiped a drop from his trousers.

But it was useless trying to lie to Rafe. The man had been a world-class spy before his diplomatic career. So Henry took a different approach.

"Lady Arlington is my client, and thus she is entitled to my discretion."

"Very well," Rafe said with a wry smile. "I won't ask again. But mind you, Sylvia is speaking to her right now. And she won't be deterred so easily. She can be quite tenacious when she wants something. Believe me."

Henry made a face. "Please, spare me the details."

Rafe let out a little chuckle. "Sorry. I actually wasn't trying to insinuate anything that time."

He and Rafe hadn't been able to spend much time together, given their careers, but he had missed even his occasional visits with his old friend. Very much.

"I wish you'd come back to England," Henry surprised himself by saying. "And I think Lady Arlington would like to have Sylvia closer."

"Do you?"

"She's been lonely since the viscount's death."

"Well, you may very well get your wish," Rafe grumbled.

Henry shot him a questioning look, and Rafe let out a short, harsh breath. "I thought I could make a difference in this government. And perhaps in another age I could have. But now..." He shook his head. "The ambassador is a reasonable man, so he thinks appeasement will keep the German kaiser in check. But Wilhelm is an overgrown child. Needy. Demanding. He is determined to make his mark on the world, no matter the cost."

Henry blinked slowly as dread gathered low in his belly. "What are you saying?"

Rafe stared off toward the sea with a dark look. "That we'll be lucky to make it out of the next decade without a war. The continent is a powder keg just waiting for someone to light a match." Then his eyes snapped back to Henry's. "But it *is* coming, mind you. And I don't plan on being here when it goes off. Sylvia's news this morning cemented it."

"If that is true..." Henry began. "Then you can't run from it. None of us can."

"I suppose not. But if we're starting a family, I owe it to my children to make sure we aren't on the front lines."

Henry could not argue with that. "Where will you go?"

Rafe shrugged. "New York? I've made some contacts in Washington, too. I'll try to warn the ambassador again when I return to Berlin, but I've begun to lose hope. No one seems very interested in what I have to say. I'm afraid I've made myself something of a pariah."

"Does Sylvia know about any of this?"

Rafe shook his head. "I didn't want to worry her if it wasn't necessary. But now..."

"Tell her. You shouldn't keep all of this to yourself."

"Might I encourage you to take a little of your own advice?"

Henry bristled. "How? I'm not married."

Rafe looked unconvinced by this line of argument. "No, but walking around like a damned vault does you no good."

"I'm not a *vault*," Henry protested. "You know there's only so much I can say about Turkey." And even less he wished to share.

"You can always talk to me, you know. About any of it," Rafe added quietly.

Henry nodded. "I do." But as he said the words, Henry realized there was someone else he would consider talking to. Even more than his old friend.

* * *

Georgiana spent the rest of the day with Sylvia and the countess, who was overjoyed to learn she would become a grandmother.

"You must have the baby either here or in London," she insisted. "Not in Germany, away from your friends and family. Isn't that right, Georgiana?"

"Yes, certainly."

Sylvia flashed her a sympathetic look. "I'll speak to Rafe about it." Then she deftly changed the subject.

Eventually Georgiana retired to her room to nap before changing into eveningwear for their trip to the casino. Her gown was made of deep blue silk with a train decorated with spangles meant to mimic the night sky. She didn't see Captain Harris until she entered the suite's parlor, where he was already waiting by the unlit hearth.

Her heart did a somersault at the sight of him leaning with one arm against the mantel, dressed with sober elegance in a dark suit, the same one he had worn to the Pettigrew ball. It had only been a week ago now, and yet it seemed to belong to another age entirely. He glanced up at her entrance, and though he didn't quite smile at her, the corner of his mouth lifted and his amber eyes fixed on her as she approached. That felt far more significant than if he had given her a full-on grin.

You are growing fanciful.

Yes, she was. Georgiana smiled back at him.

"Good evening, Captain. Are you planning to clean out the casino this evening?"

"You look beautiful," he murmured, ignoring her little quip. Then, to her surprise, he took her hand and brought it to his lips. Desire shivered through her. The thought of spending the evening in his room was far more appealing than going to the casino.

Georgiana gave herself a little shake. "Thank you. As do you," she added dumbly before she caught herself.

He huffed a laugh as he ushered them toward the door. "I don't think I've ever been called beautiful before."

"Yes, well. I suppose there's a first time for everything."

Captain Harris met her eyes and gave her a very brief, very indulgent smile. "Indeed."

Georgiana practically floated down to the lobby, where they met the rest of their party. She barely heard a word anyone said as they split into two groups, as no carriage could fit all of them. The captain joined Rafe, Mahmood, and another gentleman in one carriage, while Georgiana rode with Sylvia and the countess.

"You look stunning, Georgiana," the countess said. "I don't think I've ever met a woman who could wear that shade of blue so well."

Sylvia hummed with agreement before eyeing her. "But there's something else about you."

The countess laughed. "She's *relaxed*, my dear! The Riviera has worked its magic."

"Is that it?" Sylvia smiled, but she didn't look convinced.

Georgiana's chest ached with a sudden longing to reveal everything that had transpired between her and Captain Harris.

Instead, she simply returned Sylvia's smile. "Yes, it certainly has."

And every word was true.

* * *

As Georgiana was not much of a gambler, she hadn't expected the casino to be very entertaining aside from the company. But far beyond the games of chance, it offered a veritable feast for the senses. Everywhere she looked something was demanding her attention: the spinning roulette wheels, the clack of chips being placed on the tables and then raked in by the stone-faced croupiers, groups of guests shouting with glee when their numbers hit and then cries of sorrow when their winnings were lost in the next turn. Then there was the fashion. Ladies wore some of the most outrageous gowns she had ever seen—and made London society look positively stodgy by comparison.

A very small, very old man led an incredibly tall woman decades younger than him dressed in a bright pink gown embellished with matching pink feathers away from the gaming table where he had just made a small fortune.

"She is his good-luck charm," the countess said by her ear.

Georgiana turned toward her, feeling a little embarrassed to have been caught so obviously eyeing them. "Is that so?"

"Oh yes," she said with a wave of her fan. "These men love nothing more than having a beautiful young lady on their arm for the evening. Everyone treats them with more respect. And at the end of the night, the ladies will get a cut of their winnings, if there are any."

Georgiana's gaze followed the pair as they walked toward another table. Indeed, the other guests seemed to defer to the old man as his beautiful companion fluttered her fan and simpered beside him. "Hmm. It doesn't sound very different from my marriage," she muttered, then inhaled sharply and met the countess's eyes. "I can't believe I just said that."

The countess looked similarly shocked. "I can't either."

Their gazes held for a moment before they both burst out laughing. A year ago she could barely bring herself to talk about her marriage. Joking about it would have been unthinkable. But Lord, it felt good.

The countess's eyes softened. "Sylvia told me a little about your marriage to the viscount. I am sorry it was so difficult."

"I did what I was told to do by people I loved and trusted," Georgiana began. "They thought they knew what was best for me, and because I was young, I believed them. But we were all wrong. I can see that now."

"But you paid the biggest price, my dear," the countess said gently.

Georgiana nodded. "I did. And that is why I will never allow someone else to control my future ever again."

The countess was quiet for a long moment. "People must underestimate how strong you are," she finally said.

No one had ever said such a thing to her before, but she immediately felt the truthfulness of it deep in her bones. The countess then glanced past her. "I hope you have people in your life now who can appreciate you fully."

Georgiana followed her gaze. Captain Harris was watching the table play with that familiar glower she now knew meant he was in deep concentration. He must have sensed her observation and looked up. Their eyes met and the corner of his mouth lifted again in that subtle secret smile of his.

Warmth swelled around her heart, like a kettle a breath away from boiling. "I believe I do."

Just then a seat at the table opened up and Captain Harris was obligated to tear his gaze away in order to take it. Georgiana gave him a little nod of understanding. They would meet up with the gentlemen again later, as she, Sylvia, and the countess went off to visit the music hall, where a full orchestra performed every evening. She was surprised to find the theater nearly full even in this great gambling palace. Luckily Mahmood had arranged for them to have a private box, and they passed over an hour in the convivial atmosphere before returning to the gaming saloon.

The captain was still seated at the same table, but he now possessed a far larger pile of chips than when they had left. Rafe stood just behind him, smiling with undisguised pride. He caught sight of them and made his way through the crowd that had gathered around the table during their absence. Georgiana guessed it had something to do with the captain's performance.

"How was the entertainment?" Rafe asked her.

"Better than I expected from an orchestra in the middle of a casino."

"That is high praise coming from you," he replied before

taking Sylvia's hand and kissing it. "And how are you feeling?"

"A little tired. But remember, the doctor said that was perfectly normal," she said in response to the look of concern that crossed Rafe's face.

Georgiana bit back a smile. It never failed to delight her to see the man once known as one of London's most notorious rakes as the most doting husband she had ever seen. And she had no doubt that he would be an excellent father.

"We'll leave shortly," he said, then turned to Georgiana. "You don't mind if I whisk her back to the hotel a little early, do you?"

"Not at all."

"I'll make sure Georgiana and the captain return safely," the countess added.

Rafe glanced over to the gaming table. A cheer had just gone up from the crowd around the table, and the corner of the captain's mouth was tilted up. On any other person this would be equivalent to a look of pure pleasure.

"Good. He's won a great deal of money this evening. And you know that can draw unsavory attention."

"I had no idea he was so skilled," the countess said.

"Oh, he is by far the best card player I've ever seen." Rafe pointed to his temple. "It's all thanks to that memory vault. Well, and that capital poker face of his. Who knows what he might be thinking."

Georgiana tilted her head in confusion. "What do you mean, 'memory vault'?"

"Oh, only that he has an excellent memory," Rafe said, looking sheepish, like he had said too much. "I thought you knew."

"No. But I suppose that makes sense, given his line of work," she said carefully.

Rafe visibly relaxed. "Yes. Certainly. In any case, he's nearly tripled his money since we arrived. Though I believe he plans to stop imminently, which is perhaps the true secret to his success."

"Smart man," Mahmood said. "And don't worry. We will make sure he and his winnings return to the hotel safely."

As Captain Harris stacked his chips into several neat piles, an older man with dark hair shot through with white and a stiff, commanding presence drew up beside him. Even from this distance, Georgiana could see the captain's shoulders tighten as his head snapped up to face the man, who had leaned over to say something. All traces of mirth were wiped from his expression. Georgiana had never seen him look so grim before, as if he was staring death in the face. Tension gathered low in her belly, and she had to resist the urge to storm over and demand that the man step back. Instead, she subtly tugged at Rafe's sleeve.

"Who is that man talking with Captain Harris?"

Rafe glanced over and his eyes widened. "Commodore Perry. He was the one who got Henry out of Turkey."

Georgiana's brow furrowed. "But I thought the papers said he escaped." Rafe's arm stiffened, and she met his eyes. "Ah. I see," she said softly as understanding washed over her. "That's not the real story, is it."

Rafe had the decency to look remorseful. "It is not mine to tell," he murmured. "But you should ask him. It would do him some good to talk about it with someone, I think."

Georgiana swallowed hard and looked back to the captain. "And here I thought we were being discreet."

Rafe let out a soft laugh. "You are. Mostly. But blame it on the decade of espionage, I suppose. It wasn't hard to see that something had shifted between you." Georgiana's throat thickened. She longed to interrogate him on just what exactly he had seen, at least in Henry, but this was not the time. "Tread carefully, my lady," he added.

Georgiana bristled at the warning. "I'm hardly made of glass."

Rafe gave her a kind smile. "I meant for his sake." Just as heat began to bloom across her cheeks, the captain joined them. The commodore had vanished, "I'd say drinks are on you, Henry, but I'm afraid Sylvia and I are just leaving."

"I'll join you," he replied, still grim. Then he turned to Georgiana. "Unless you'd like to stay?"

She shook her head. "No, that's fine." He held her gaze for a wordless moment, and the urge to smooth his brow was so strong that Georgiana had to make a fist to stop herself.

It was decided that the four of them would return to the hotel, and the countess and Mahmood would stay behind to play a few rounds of roulette. On the ride back, Georgiana sat beside Sylvia and talked about their plans for the next day, while Rafe and Captain Harris sat across from them speaking in low tones, no doubt about the mysterious commodore.

Once they were back at the hotel, Captain Harris's mood visibly improved, and he even cracked a smile at Rafe's teasing over his winnings. But as they rode the private lift to their floor, the sense of unease that had begun back in the casino only expanded within Georgiana and mixed with her ever present desire for him. By the time they parted ways with their friends, it felt as if an iron was pressing against her chest, filled with both the weight of her want and Rafe's subtle warning.

Tread carefully, my lady.

All this time she had been so focused on her own past heartache along with the unpleasant memories of her marriage that she had completely failed to see what was before her: a vulnerable man who had endured hardships far greater than her own, and without the resources she had come to take for granted.

Captain Harris—no, *Henry* opened the door to the suite and stood aside to let her enter first. Georgiana swept into the darkened suite and stopped just past the entryway. Bea was waiting up for her.

She then turned to face him. "Will you let me come to you?"

Henry looked surprised before his eyes softened. "Of course," he murmured with a fondness that clawed at her heart, affecting her even more than his desire.

Georgiana couldn't manage to speak—not that she had a *clue* what to say anyway—so she just nodded and disappeared into her room. She had never appreciated Bea's efficiency more than that evening, as she deftly removed the heavy Worth gown, jewelry, and the absurd number of hairpins required to transform her into the viscountess. Still, it took far longer than she could stand, and Georgiana couldn't help fidgeting in her seat. Bea must have noticed, but other than a few glances she gave no indication. When she finally finished, Georgiana slid her wrapper around her shoulders and stood.

"I think I'll go look at the moon. It's lovely tonight. No need to wait up."

"Yes, my lady," Bea replied, as discrete as ever, and disappeared into her room.

As Georgiana crossed the parlor to Captain Harris's room, the blood pounded in her ears. Given the way anticipation was whirling inside her like a Catherine wheel, one would think this was their first encounter. But then, in a way it was. For Georgiana was going to him now with her eyes open. With nothing to hide, from him or herself. And she hoped, so desperately, that he could do the same—that he would *want* to. She had not felt this giddy with excitement in many years. Not since that night in the back garden at Harrington House, when she had sneaked away to meet him once before. This man she had once thought could be her future. And perhaps still was.

* * *

After Georgiana had disappeared into her room, Henry stood in the entryway in stunned silence.

Will you let me come to you?

Something had changed. She had looked so unsure, yet hopeful. It tugged at a place deep inside him, one even his memory refused to unearth. When he finally found the will to move, the sharp pain that had surfaced at the casino bit into his knee once again. He was paying the price for neglecting his exercises during this trip. Henry looked toward his private bathroom. It boasted an enormous pink marble tub he had yet to step foot in, as the shower bath was far more efficient. And Henry wasn't the sort to laze about in a tub when there was work to do. Now, though...

He glanced toward the bedroom door. Georgiana had been trussed up even more than usual this evening. She looked breathtaking, but it would be a good half hour before she would appear. Perhaps even longer. Henry turned on the golden taps, and they hissed to life as piping-hot water rushed out of the spout. An obscene luxury, one he might not be able to enjoy again. As the tub slowly filled, Henry stripped off his clothes and then eased himself into the warm water. He let out a low groan of relief. Lord, how would he ever go back to his tiny flat after this? Just a few minutes and he would get out. He leaned his head back against the rim of the tub and closed his eyes.

Henry should have known he would run across the commodore in Monte Carlo. The man had a terrible gambling habit. But it was his greeting that had set Henry particularly on edge.

I've been looking for you, Captain. Your country needs you.

That hadn't been their agreement. Henry had promised to dutifully play the part of the hero. Let the Crown use him to wave the flag and distract the populous from its questionable overseas activities. But in exchange he would be free.

Free from all future missions. Free to live his life, whatever he chose to make of it.

It will be well worth your while.

Henry already had a sizable pile of chips in front of him. He had been ready to leave. But that irritated the hell out of him, and he played one more round just to spite the commodore. To show that he didn't need his money. Henry was doing just fine on his own. And he won yet again. But as he rose from the table, his old superior—the man who had been ready to let him rot away in that jail cell until he became a political asset—made another attempt:

If money won't tempt you, perhaps information on your viscountess will.

Henry hid his surprise behind a glare, then left without a word. But this wasn't over.

The commodore had known exactly which nerve to strike, and he wasn't the sort of man who gave up. Ever. There still had been no word from the London detective, but it seemed possible that Georgiana had ruffled feathers that went far beyond a disgruntled factory owner. If the commodore was involved, this could be political. He should have suspected as much, given how many men in Parliament owned or invested in similar enterprises. Georgiana's reforms were a direct threat.

He let out a sigh and sank deeper into the tub, trying to put it out of his mind for now. Rafe offered to make some inquiries with the connections he still had tomorrow, including his brother, who enjoyed a prominent government position. But one thing Henry could not forget was the distinct quickening of his heartbeat when the commodore had said *your viscountess.* How right that had sounded. How he ached for it to be true. But Georgiana wanted to belong to no one but herself, and he must respect that.

At the feel of a soft hand caressing his shoulder, Henry's eyes shot open. He had drifted off. The bath was still comfortably warm, so it hadn't been too long.

Georgiana smiled down at him as she perched on the rim of the tub, a dream come to life. "You look quite comfortable."

Henry stretched his arms out along the rim and noted the way her eyes slid over his wet skin. "I am." Then he flexed his knee. Much better. "I don't suppose you'd care to join me?" He gestured to the expansive tub. "There is plenty of room."

Georgiana's mouth curved. "Yes, I can see that." She pushed up the sleeve of her wrapper and skimmed the water's surface. Henry could spend a lifetime simply watching the smooth, graceful movements of her hands. She then flicked the water off her fingers and turned on the tap, adding a little more hot water. "You don't mind? I like it just short of boiling."

Henry smiled and shook his head. There were a great many things he would endure to get her into this tub. She then rose and walked over to the long marble vanity, which held various bottles and perfumed soaps. Henry hadn't bothered with any of them—a bar of Pear's suited him just fine—but Georgiana opened one and sniffed. She appeared pleased and turned back, loosening the tie of her wrapper as she approached, revealing a glimpse of the pale golden skin between her breasts.

Henry swallowed hard and fought the urge to look away, reminding himself that he had already seen her quite naked.

"You're blushing."

He met her gaze. "It's warm in here."

She smirked again and turned off the tap, then tipped the open bottle over the water. Thick, golden oil poured out, filling the humid air with a sharp citrus scent. Georgiana dipped a hand in and swirled the water as the scent grew stronger. Henry shifted in place. His cock had grown uncomfortably hard in a very short amount of time. Her wrapper crumpled around her ankles, and she stepped into the tub. Before Henry could even blink, his hands were on her waist and he was dragging her down to him. Georgiana let out a surprised yelp, then laughed as water splashed around them. Her bare chest pressed against his own, all slippery and glistening. Why the hell hadn't they done this sooner?

But before he could voice the thought, her lips pressed to his, as urgent and wanting as ever. Henry kissed her back with equal force, as if their interlude in the carriage hadn't happened earlier that very day. It wasn't enough to satisfy his need, his *greed* for her. He was a desperate, hungry man who had been admitted to a lavish banquet. And he would savor every last bite. She took his bottom lip between her teeth with a gentle nibble. There was something wild, almost feral about her during these moments. Or maybe it was simply so different from the way she carried herself in public. Henry loved that he knew this about her. This delicious secret. And not for the first time he wondered if she had shared this side of herself with the viscount. This man she seemed to still yearn for when no one was watching. He kissed her harder, fighting to rid himself of the unsettling thought. Either way, it didn't matter. The viscount was dead, while Henry was very much alive. He gripped the soft, smooth skin of her bottom and shifted his hips. Then he dragged her along his shaft as slowly as he could stand it. Georgiana let out a gasp and dug her fingertips into his shoulders. He repeated the movement, dragging her up and down his length in slow, sure strokes while the warm, scented bathwater swirled around them. Georgiana tilted her head back and closed her eyes as she let out a low moan.

Henry's control slipped and his hands tightened around her waist, pinning her entrance at the very tip of his cock.

"Open your eyes," he said roughly.

As Georgiana obeyed, something else sparked in his chest. There was an openness in her gaze that hadn't been there before. It felt as if she could see right through him. Right through to his very soul—whatever ragged bit was left. Her hand slipped down from his shoulder and came to rest on his chest. Could she feel how his heart pounded? Did she know it was all for her? She shifted her hips again, and he slowly pressed inside her. She took him more easily now, as if their flesh had been made with the other in mind.

No, Henry decided between his increasingly unsteady thrusts. It had not been like this with the viscount. Because it could only be like this between the two of them.

Now, thanks to several twists of fate, they had been given a second chance. And this time he would not let her slip away.

"*Henry*," she suddenly cried out as her intimate flesh clenched hard around his length.

The sound of his name falling from her lips in the throes of pleasure pierced his chest, and joy, hot and thick, seemed to rush through his every limb. He soon followed her over the cliff.

She sagged against him, and his arms immediately circled her. They lay just like that for some time, the bathwater lapping at their joined bodies until it grew tepid. Then Georgiana climbed out of the tub on shaky legs, nearly toppling over at one point with a heady laugh before she helped him out.

"How is your knee?" she asked with concern. "I'm so sorry, I didn't even think—"

"It's fine." He curled his hand around the nape of her neck. "Don't worry." Then he planted a soft kiss on her lips. Even six months ago such a question would have raised his hackles considerably—not that he had been engaging in such activities. Heavens no. But he most definitely hadn't been able to stomach the thought of being seen as incapable by anyone. Now, though, now Henry saw himself much differently. Yes, he was not the same man he had once been in a number of ways that went far beyond the visible. But perhaps that wasn't such a bad thing.

"I would tell you if it bothered me," he said truthfully.

"Are you all right?" Georgiana had pulled on her robe and was holding a towel out to him. Henry was still standing stark naked before her.

He gave her a grin as he took the towel. "Never better."

And that too was the truth.

CHAPTER SIXTEEN

Their encounter in the bathtub was followed by another longer interlude, this time in the bed. For though Henry maintained his knee was fine, his neck *was* a bit sore. And Georgiana admitted that her own knees ached after pressing against the rather unforgiving tub bottom.

"Yes, I do believe beds are far superior for lovemaking," Georgiana said drowsily while they lay in a tangle of limbs under the sheets.

"Noted." Henry nuzzled the top of her head and pressed a kiss against her golden curls. She still smelled like that delicious bath oil. He would need to take some with him before they left.

What for?

The idea of returning to his small gray flat with the water spot and the shared bath sank through him like a stone. He did not want to go back there. Between his Monte Carlo winnings and the bill for this assignment, he could certainly afford to move into something nicer now. A place with a decent ceiling and its own bathroom—a tub, even! But while that would be very nice, it wasn't enough.

For Georgiana still would not be there.

His shoulders immediately tensed, but Georgiana was too busy drawing lazy circles in his chest hair with the tip of her index finger to notice.

"You don't have any tattoos. I thought all navy men did."

Henry smiled against her hair. "Not the ones who have an aversion to needles. And unnecessary pain. Are you disappointed?"

She lifted her head. "Not at all! But I had wondered. Sylvia says Rafe has several."

"My God. The two of you talk about such things?"

"Sometimes." She shrugged. "Don't you?"

"Absolutely not." And especially not with *Rafe*. Henry probably wouldn't be able to sleep afterward. "Any other questions you'd like to ask?" He said it lightly, but he could see her hesitation. "Georgie, what is it?"

Her deep blue gaze flickered with uncertainty. "Who was that older man you were talking with in the casino?"

Here was his chance to change things between them. To take a new path. He hovered at the edge, puzzling out the various possibilities: lie to her, tell her part of the truth, or reveal all. But if he couldn't be honest with her now, what would be gained by waiting? Henry took a deep breath and stepped off the ledge:

"Commodore Perry. He was my superior."

"You didn't look very happy to see him."

Henry huffed a dry laugh. "I was not."

Georgiana was silent, most likely mulling this information over. He knew what she would ask next, and God help
him, he would answer as best he could.

"Does it have to do with Turkey?"

The tone of the question indicated that she already
suspected something.

"I wasn't there on leave, like the papers said," he began.
"That was just a story. The truth is that I worked for Naval
Intelligence. And Commodore Perry wanted me to scout out
a fortress outside Constantinople he suspected was being
used to store illegal weaponry. It was a pet mission for him.
Some personal rivalry with a Turkish general—I never did
find out the particulars. So I asked for it to be postponed,
as it seemed unnecessarily risky at the time. Our alliance
with the Ottomans was already tenuous at best, and there
wasn't any immediate threat. Why do anything that could
potentially jeopardize it just to find out whether or not this
general was lying about how many cannons they had?"

"That sounds very reasonable," Georgiana replied.

"Yes, well, he simply sent two others in my place.
Lieutenants Winthrop and Cassius. Both young and hungry,
like I used to be, I suppose, but woefully inexperienced.
And Winthrop in particular was far more brash than I ever
was, which isn't a desirable trait in intelligence work. The
commodore must have been desperate," he added grimly.
"By the time I found out the mission was still under way,
they were already en route."

Georgiana sat up, her eyes filled with concern. "What
did you do?"

"I went after them. When I arrived they were already
drawing too much attention, taking pictures and making

notes, all while claiming to be a pair of tourists, like I used to do. And as I'm sure they were instructed." He shook his head. "But the commodore failed to mention that if you're going to play the clueless Englishman abroad, it's better to act uninterested. Bored, even. As if everything and everyone is beneath you. Not stand around scribbling pages in a notebook."

"But they had to do that because they didn't have your memory."

"No," Henry replied softly. "They didn't."

He could still see Winthrop's face screwed up in a childish sneer when Henry had appeared.

You had your chance, old fellow. The commodore said your nerves got the better of you. This is our *mission now.*

"It wasn't long before a pair of guards happened upon us. While I was trying to smooth things over, Winthrop got nervous and bolted."

"He was the man they shot in front of you," she supplied.

Henry nodded. "They found all sorts of evidence on the lieutenants that proved they had been there to spy, so Cassius and I were arrested and became bargaining chips for the Empire."

"But your escape...saving those other prisoners—"

Henry shook his head. "I failed. After Winthrop died, Cassius got sick with a fever, and nothing was done for him. I spent days memorizing the guards' schedule, noting who was less observant, who fell asleep during their shift, and which keys they used. Then I waited. I waited for the perfect moment to distract them. But Cassius was much weaker than I realized, and we didn't make it very far before we were discovered. I was injured in the struggle.

A solid hit to the knee brought me down. We only left that jail because the Crown made it happen. But Cassius never recovered. He died on the journey back to England. The commodore then decided I could be used for propaganda, so they spun my imprisonment into something palatable to the masses, as getting caught spying on one of our supposed allies isn't very noble."

"That's awful."

He shrugged. "It's the only reason I'm alive."

"Don't say that," she whispered.

He cupped her jaw gently in his hand. "It's true, Georgie. If I hadn't been worth the trouble, then I wouldn't be here." She buried her head against his chest. "So when they promised I could be honorably discharged if I went along with their scheme, I agreed, even though I knew I did not deserve to be called a hero. I feel horrible about lying, but I could not live with myself if I continued to work for the Empire. We're raised to think of Britain's expansion as some noble enterprise designed to civilize the grateful masses, while ignoring the problems on our own shores. I hate that I contributed to that for so long. And yet..." He paused to release a breath and gather his courage to force the admission past his lips. "When I finally did decide to take a stand, two others paid the worst price. If I had just done my duty in the first place, those young men would still be alive, not manipulated into risking their one precious life by men like the commodore."

"But then *you* might not be here," she said as she hugged him closer. "It wasn't your fault, Henry. You certainly didn't force those men to take that mission, and you risked your own life more than once trying to save them. Perhaps the details aren't entirely correct, but you have no reason to doubt your bravery." Henry pressed his cheek against the top of her head and let out a sigh. She raised her head, her gaze full of challenge. "It's true. Never doubt that. Ever."

He couldn't help smiling at her demand. "Yes, my lady."

"Were you recruited by the Crown too? Like Rafe was?"

Henry raised an eyebrow. "You know he was a spy?"

"I pieced it together in Scotland, and Sylvia confirmed everything."

Then she went quiet for a moment, likely remembering when she had received the news of her husband's death during that trip to Castle Blackwood. Henry had been there too, helping Rafe sort through the twists of his final mission. Then there had been a commotion and they had run out into the hall, where Georgiana, still as beautiful as the last time he saw her, was weeping against Sylvia's shoulder with a crumpled telegram beside her. Seeing her in such anguish had been an unexpected punch to the gut. The realization that she had come to love her husband was even worse. "Naval Intelligence came for me. I had a regular card game with a few other officers, and somehow word of my skills spread. Apparently the ability to bluff and count cards is helpful when one is a spy," he added dryly.

"Rafe mentioned your memory."

He let out a sigh. "Yes. I have a knack for remembering even the most trivial of details. But it has proved valuable in certain situations. Like cards, for example."

"What an extraordinary gift," she marveled.

Henry's shoulders tightened. He didn't consider it a gift. And if given the choice, he certainly wouldn't have accepted it. "It can be cruel to remember so much." The admission slipped from his lips. "But yes," he continued briskly. "The commodore certainly saw potential in my little parlor trick. He pressured me for years to work for Naval Intelligence, but I kept begging off. Until finally I..." He faltered in the face of her steady gaze.

I didn't have the will to deny them anymore.

"It seemed like the best option at the time. And the increase in rank certainly had its benefits, especially after my mother took ill," he amended, hoping she couldn't see through him.

But Georgiana immediately frowned. "How long ago was this?"

Henry briefly considered lying to make the connection not quite so obvious. "Eight years."

She reared back a little. "After my season?"

"Yes," he said hoarsely. "I had originally come to London to find a wife. If I was a family man, then Naval Intelligence would back off. Possibly for good. But instead I..." He couldn't say the rest. Didn't need to.

Georgiana laid her head back down onto his chest. "Instead you found me. And then I married someone else."

"Yes," Henry admitted after a moment.

"Why didn't you?"

Henry cocked his head, still a little dazed to be speaking to her so plainly after all this time. "Why didn't I what?"

Georgiana looked up sharply. Her eyes were a bit wild. Haunted. He had seen her this close to desperation only once before, in the Harringtons' back garden. "Marry. Why didn't you *marry*, Henry?"

Because I didn't want anyone else.

How he ached for that to be the truth. But it wasn't.

At least, not completely. Even though he had been nursing a broken heart, he still proposed to two other women with good dowries and pleasant demeanors. But they had each turned him down. Immediately.

"No one would have me," he said with a sheepish laugh. "A rumor spread that I was a fortune hunter, which I suppose was true. But I had always intended to be a good, honorable husband. I didn't want to hurt anyone. Then my leave ended, and there was nothing left for me to do."

At the time Henry had felt a strange mixture of relief and disappointment. It was only in the intervening years that he had come to see how these rejections had led him down a path that had very nearly destroyed him. Her fingers dug into his chest and she looked away, but not before Henry caught the anguished expression on her face.

"It's all right," he cooed, threading his fingers through her unbound hair. "I've made my peace with it now. All of it. At long last."

But Georgiana only shook her head and pressed her cheek to his chest. After a moment he felt warm tears dampen his skin. As he pulled her up, she hurriedly wiped her face.

Henry's throat tightened. He could not bear to see her like this. "Why are you crying?"

"I didn't know," she whispered, refusing to meet his eyes. "I didn't know."

He held her for a long while after that, murmuring words of comfort against her silken curls as she absorbed everything he had revealed.

Just as he began to drift off to be cloaked in a warm, deep sleep, one final question came: "But what does the commodore want from you now?"

"The same thing he has always wanted from me," Henry sighed as the weight of so many years and secrets pressed against him once again. "My memory."

* * *

After Henry's breathing slowed into the steady rhythm of sleep, Georgiana slipped out of his enticing embrace and retrieved her silk wrapper from the floor. She shut the door softly behind her and stumbled toward her room. The sky was beginning to fade to purple, heralding dawn's gradual approach. But she could not sleep. Not after that.

Georgiana didn't consider herself a particularly naïve person, but Henry's story still managed to shock her. She thought back to every time someone had approached him with stars in their eyes and how uncomfortable he had always looked. Georgiana had assumed he was being modest, but that wasn't it at all. He had been forced to go along with this story, to repeat this lie again and again, in exchange for his freedom.

But worse than that was the guilt that burned in her chest.

For she had been behind those rumors about Henry. That he was a callous fortune hunter, though he did a fine job pretending otherwise. They had been spread by a girl angry at the world, at the choices taken from her, and heartbroken over him, for making her dare to think he wanted her for love, and not the money she only pretended to have.

Though he hadn't come out and said it directly, Georgiana knew that those rumors had sunk his chances of marrying during that long ago season and pushed him into intelligence work.

If I was a family man, then Naval Intelligence would back off.

But they hadn't, thanks to her.

Georgiana slipped under the covers of her bed in between the chilly sheets. Her body longed to be back in Henry's warm embrace. How solidly he held her, like she belonged there beside him. And the rightness of it had sunk so deep in her bones that Georgiana knew she was not strong enough to deny herself. She wanted him more than she had even thought possible. Whatever she had felt eight years ago was but a speck compared to the emotion ballooning inside her. All the jagged pain, the aching loneliness she had endured would be worth it if she could make this thing between them work. But how? If he knew the truth, that she had been behind those rumors, how could he *not* despise her once more? And then she would lose him forever. She was certain of that.

* * *

Henry couldn't remember the last time he had slept so well—or so *late*. Midmorning sun was streaming through the balcony doors. He turned and found the bed empty beside him. Georgiana must have left during the night, Henry reasoned through his disappointment. Of course she couldn't have stayed. They had already taken too many chances during this trip, and there would be consequences for them both if their affair was uncovered, both professional and personal.

And yet, despite the very real threat it posed to both his business and his heart, a sudden urge filled his chest. Henry wanted to know what Georgiana would do if they were found out. Desperately.

For he hadn't imagined the tears that wet his chest last night, nor the look of despair that filled her face, demanding to know why he hadn't married. Georgiana cared about him. Even more than he realized. Possibly more than she was ready to admit. But for the first time in eight years, reckless hope blazed through him, refusing to yield to his cautious whispers until Henry gave up and let his thoughts run wild.

As Henry dressed, he ran through all the ways he could covertly woo Georgiana during the last days of their stay. They still had more freedoms here than back in London, and he would take advantage of it as much as he could. To show her what she meant to him—what she had *always* meant to him. And then he would hold his breath to see if she reciprocated. But when he exited his room, his heart stopped, then sank.

Georgiana's travel trunk was in the foyer, and Bea was rushing around, gathering up odds and ends. There was no mistaking what was going on here: She was leaving.

Was she running from him?

On that thought, Georgiana breezed into the room. "Bea, I've found the second dressing gown under the—" She stopped as she caught sight of Henry, then immediately crossed to meet him, a look of regret on her face. "I've had a message from Mr. Khan early this morning. The papers were tipped off regarding the threats against me. Now the owner of the building I'm trying to buy is pushing up the signing. I think he's worried I'll *die* before the deal goes through." Georgiana rolled her eyes. "So I need to leave today. I've already spoken to Mr. Previn, and he thinks we can make the afternoon train to Paris if we leave for Nice within the hour. But you can stay until our original departure date."

"Absolutely not." The idea was absurd. Offensive. *Leave* her? Why would she make such a suggestion?

Because you told her the truth, and now she wants to be rid of you, of course.

With effort, Henry dismissed the ugly thought. "Even if I wanted to, that wouldn't be appropriate," he pointed out. "I didn't exactly come here for a holiday."

Understanding flashed in her eyes and an embarrassed flush stained her cheeks. But before Henry could question her further, there was a knock on the door. "Oh, that's probably Sylvia. I asked her to come."

She stepped away to answer it and sure enough, Sylvia and Rafe entered the suite. As Georgiana explained the situation, Rafe's eyes met Henry's. His disappointment must have been clear on his face, for his friend's brow furrowed.

"You're leaving *now*?" Sylvia burst out.

"I don't have a choice," Georgiana responded, looking very grieved. "I've already told the captain he could stay—"

"Well, I certainly hope he said no," Sylvia cut in. "I know this deal is important to you, but for heaven's sake, London isn't *safe* for you right now!"

Rafe placed a hand on his wife's shoulder. "Darling, try not to upset yourself. Or Georgiana. Of course the captain is traveling with her." He flashed Henry a pleading look. "And remember that Scotland Yard has been busy investigating the threats these last few days. She is not walking into a trap."

Sylvia scowled. "I know that."

"And I'm sure her family will meet her at the station."

"Yes," Georgiana said. "I've already wired a message to my brother. I won't be alone for even a moment. Not until we uncover who has been behind these threats."

Sylvia visibly relaxed but her frown remained. "Fine. But I still don't like it," she grumbled.

Henry quite agreed with her on that point, but he kept his mouth shut. It was useless to try to dissuade Georgiana. For now all he could do was keep her safe.

"I know, dearest," Georgiana said. "Will it help if I send you a message every day until the perpetrator is caught?"

"*Twice* a day," Sylvia countered and Georgiana laughed.

"All right. You have a deal."

The two women then disappeared into Georgiana's bedroom, while Rafe followed Henry into his own. He needed to pack, and fast. Rafe shut the door quietly behind him.

"Are you going to tell her?" he asked without any preamble.

"I don't know," Henry admitted as he emptied the contents into his bag. "I thought…I thought we'd have more time here."

Rafe wrinkled his nose. "Time for what?"

Henry moved on to collect his shirts. Why had he brought so many? He gathered them in his arms.

"*Henry.*"

He didn't look up as he began to shove the shirts into the bag. "I told her the truth about Turkey last night. All of it."

Rafe was silent for so long that Henry nearly thought he had left. But when he finally looked up, his friend was still there, one dark eyebrow raised in question.

"Well? What did she say?"

Now it was time to pack his trousers. Those were in the wardrobe. Henry walked to it, but Rafe blocked his path.

"Stop. You sit while I do the rest. Watching your horrible packing is making my eye twitch."

Henry flashed him a smile and obeyed. "She was sympathetic, but I got the sense that she was holding something back."

"Well, it's a hell of a story. Perhaps she just needed time to think it over."

"Rather convenient then that she has to hurry back to London now," Henry muttered.

Rafe looked surprised. "You can't truly think she's trying to *avoid* you?"

"It feels that way," he admitted. "And we already agreed to go our separate ways once we returned."

"Is that what you still want?"

"No." The word shot out of him like a cannon.

"So tell her then. The worst she can do is reject you. And then you will be exactly where you are now. Or you can be brave and take the chance that she feels the same way as you and is also equally terrible at talking about it."

Henry let out a dry laugh. It was certainly possible. "You've grown quite wise in your married state."

Rafe chuckled. "It's a wonder what happens to a fellow when he finds his perfect match. I do wish you can have that as well," he added quietly.

Henry glanced away, but he couldn't ignore the hope still welling inside him.

Rafe folded a few more articles of clothing before tucking them away in the bag. "There. All packed up."

"Thank you," Henry said as he reached for the bag.

"Any time, my friend. Any time."

CHAPTER SEVENTEEN

———◆———

At Calais, Georgiana boarded the steamer with a knot in her stomach. Sylvia had done a fine job interrogating her back at the hotel, but she still couldn't voice her deepest desire, nor the guilt that had been plaguing her since the night before last. All Georgiana would admit was that yes, something had happened between her and the captain, but they had no plans to continue seeing each other back in London. He certainly hadn't expressed any desire to, and Georgiana was, frankly, too afraid to ask.

"Why, though?" Sylvia had pressed. "The worst thing he could say is no. And then you'll be back to where you started."

Georgiana wished that were true. That she could still be the same woman she was last week. But the last few days had filled her with a need that terrified her. Enduring her marriage to the viscount had been very painful at times, but being rejected by Captain Harris would be so much worse. She had flown too close to the sun, and the plummet back to earth would be the punishment for her indulgence. Besides, some things hadn't changed. If the papers found out about their affair, they would be merciless. And she didn't want Captain Harris's business to suffer because of her. She had already done enough.

"My lady?" Bea's voice cut through her tangled thoughts.

Georgiana turned to her maid. "Sorry, Bea. I was building castles in Spain."

"I was just asking if you needed anything from me before I retire."

Georgiana had purchased a separate berth for Bea so she could have a little privacy. It had been a long journey, and, as usual, Captain Harris had made himself scarce. But it was better for them both if he kept his distance, and she needed to get used to being alone again. "I'm fine, thank you."

Her maid gave a nod and left. Once she was alone, Georgiana let out a breath and settled on the bed. She had closed her eyes for just a moment when the sound of urgent tapping on her door woke her up. The last few nights had caught up to her.

"Coming," she said groggily as she rose to her feet and shuffled to the door. Bea must have forgotten something. But when she pulled it open, she came face-to-face with Captain Harris's scowl.

"I was about to knock down the door," he hissed as he entered the cabin before anyone saw him. "What on earth were you doing?"

"I fell asleep. I didn't mean to worry you."

"I wasn't worried," he insisted, then his face fell and he

pulled her into his arms. "All right. I *was* worried. And now I feel foolish."

Georgiana drew her arms around his lean waist and inhaled the familiar scent. "I've been recently told that it isn't foolish to worry about someone."

"Sounds like excellent advice from a very smart person," Henry said wryly, then tilted her chin up to meet his gaze. "I wanted to make sure you hadn't fallen ill again."

"No, the channel is much calmer today. I'm fine." Then she held her breath as their eyes locked together. He slid his warm palm down to the small of her back and began to rub a slow circle. "You shouldn't be here," she added, forcing the words out. But her protest was weak.

"Where is Bea?" His voice had grown noticeably rougher.

"She has her own cabin down the hall."

Henry gave her an arch look. "Well, I for one am grateful for your generosity. As I'm sure Bea is."

Before Georgiana could respond, Henry's mouth lowered to hers, capturing her lips in a deep kiss. She should pull away. Tell him that they couldn't continue this. She didn't deserve his attentions. But her words only came out as a low moan, and her hands began to stroke his chest instead of pushing him away. Henry began unbuttoning her traveling coat.

Just once more.

Georgiana pushed his hands away so she could tear the blasted thing off and toss it on the floor. If this was to be their last time together, she wanted it to last as long as possible. Henry flashed her a look of surprise before she cupped his face in her hands and pulled him back to her.

In another moment Georgiana found herself being walked backward to the narrow bed, then pulled down on Henry's lap.

"Shouldn't we talk?" Henry managed to ask in between kisses.

She shook her head and pushed Henry's coat off his solid shoulders. Lord, she would miss them. "Not yet. Please."

Disappointment flashed in his eyes, but he did not stop her, nor did he ask again. Desperation came over her as she tugged open his trousers. Henry squeezed his eyes shut and leaned his head back against the wall as she worked the heated flesh.

"Dammit, Georgiana," he cursed.

A smile crossed her lips, and she gripped him even harder. Henry cried out and stilled her hand as he cracked one eye open. "If you keep that up, you'll be disappointed."

"Impossible," Georgiana replied automatically, but the surety in her voice caught them both by surprise. Henry stared at her, wordless and panting. Then his hands gripped her waist and guided her to her knees while she opened the slit in her drawers. Their eyes met as she began to lower herself on his shaft.

"Slow down," he growled. One hand snaked up to tangle in her hair while the other nestled against her lower back and pressed her even closer to him.

"Yes, Captain," Georgiana said with an obliging smile.

Henry's answering chuckle turned into a hiss of pleasure as the broad head of his penis nudged into her entrance. Then no more intelligible words were spoken for some time.

* * *

Eventually Georgiana had to slide off his lap before she developed a cramp. They both lay side by side on the narrow cabin bed in a mostly comfortable silence as the steamer gently rocked with the waves.

"I can't fall asleep here," Henry finally mumbled against her hair, but he made no attempt to get up.

Georgiana threaded her fingers through his and drew his arm snug around her waist.

"Stay just a little while." She would have to say something before they reached London, but there was still time for that, and she certainly wasn't in any hurry.

Well, then. This was a pleasant distraction. Perhaps we'll see each other around town.

It was easier than voicing the truth.

At some point in the night Georgiana awoke alone with a blanket drawn over her. Henry had left without waking her. She huddled deeper into the covers and found the spot where his head had rested. It still smelled of him. She inhaled his warm, familiar scent and soon enough drifted off to sleep again.

Once the steamer reached Dover the next morning, they headed for the train station. She and Henry had exchanged nothing more than basic pleasantries in front of Bea, but just as they entered the station, he covertly caught her hand in the crowd and gave it a brief squeeze. The tenderness of the unexpected gesture turned her brain promptly to mush. As they waited in line at the ticket office Georgiana impulsively decided to buy Bea a different ticket in first class.

"You don't mind, do you Bea? I didn't sleep well last night and could use the privacy," she explained.

"Of course not, my lady."

Georgiana then met Henry's gaze. His amber eyes glowed with understanding. But any thought of how they might spend that time together promptly fled her mind at the sight of her brother pacing the length of the first-class lounge. "Reggie!" He looked up and frowned in her direction. She rushed over as alarm gripped her. "Is everything all right? Is it Franny? Or did something happen to Ollie?"

"What? No, Franny is fine. They're *all* fine." Then he narrowed his eyes. "I spoke to Mr. Khan yesterday. He told me the signing was moved up and that you would likely be leaving earlier than expected, so I took the next train down to Dover."

"Whatever for?"

"It's you. The *both* of you," he hissed before addressing Henry directly. "You've got a hell of a lot of nerve, Captain. I'm not paying you a small fortune to sleep with my sister."

Georgiana gasped while Henry remained silent in the face of her brother's accusations—but then, could they still be accusations if they were true?

Reggie cut her a glance before stepping closer to Henry. "I expected more from a man like you. I told you she was being reckless, and you took advantage."

Well, now that was really too much. Georgiana uttered a noise of protest, but Henry shot her a pleading look and raised his hand. "I apologize for acting unprofessionally. You can be angry with me about that, but you do a great discredit to your sister by calling her reckless. She is one of the most competent people I've ever met. What happened between us was consensual, if perhaps...inconvenient."

Georgiana blinked. That last bit stung, but it seemed

to calm Reggie. "What are you doing here?" she managed to ask.

"I heard some rumors about the two of you. I worried about what would happen if you then returned to London together."

Georgiana tilted her head. "You didn't come all this way because of *rumors*, Reggie."

"Fine," he said with a huff. "I received word that you were...were...involved."

Henry narrowed his eyes. "From *whom*?"

"Someone I trust," he snapped. "Which is a damn sight more than I can say for either of you at the moment."

Georgiana looked away. Reggie's anger was masking his hurt. She should have been honest with him about her conflicted feelings about the captain from the beginning, but it had been some horribly misguided attempt to protect her pride. She couldn't even make sense of her reasoning now.

Reggie continued to address Henry. "I think it's best if you let us return to London separately. And once there, you keep your distance. At least until the talk dies down. I've already hired someone else to watch over her."

Outraged, Georgiana was just about to tell her brother to sod off when Henry nodded. "That makes sense."

Her mouth fell open as she stared between them. Henry was the first to notice her anger.

"Georgiana—"

"No, please continue discussing what to do with me as if I'm not even *here*. I'll be waiting for my orders."

Then she turned on her heel and stalked away from them. Reggie called after her, but she was far too angry to stop. She needed to calm down before she said something she couldn't take back. But as Georgiana turned a corner, she stepped right in the path of a vaguely familiar older gentleman, who swiftly doffed his hat.

"Lady Arlington, I've not had the pleasure."

Georgiana stopped short. It was the commodore. Had he been *following* them? The thought was unsettling. He gave her a smile that she was too shocked to return and glanced past her. "Tell Captain Harris that I asked after him. And that I would like to have a chat. It will be in both of your interests."

Though his tone remained friendly, a chill ran down her spine.

"What do you want?"

"I made a proposition to the captain back in Monte Carlo, but he turned me down. I would be much obliged if you could convince him to accept it."

Though Georgiana was still angry with Henry, a protective instinct surged through her. "No," she said with a glower. "I have absolutely no interest in helping *you*."

But the commodore didn't appear the least bit offended and instead shot her a pitying look. "That's a shame. I had hoped we could be useful to one another." Georgiana swiftly turned around, but the commodore called out to her. "A piece of advice, my lady?" Despite her better judgment, she couldn't help glancing back.

His dark eyes narrowed. "I wouldn't sign those papers. You don't know what you're up against. And I'm sure you wouldn't want those you love being targeted next. Especially our mutual friend."

Before Georgiana could respond, the man faded back into the crowd. Their exchange had not lasted more than a moment. She heard footsteps behind her, accompanied by the familiar tap of a cane.

Georgiana squeezed her eyes shut and took a deep breath before straightening her spine and resuming the graceful countenance of Lady Arlington. When she turned around, Henry was giving her a remorseful look.

"Georgiana, I'm sorry. I was completely out of line."

She shook her head and forced the words out, her mind still turning over the commodore's warning. "No. You were right. Reggie, too. I'll go with him. I can't afford the scandal, especially now. And neither can you," she added at his look of surprise before he assumed that all too familiar shuttered expression. How she hated it. "I'll talk with Reggie once he calms down and make sure you are still paid."

Henry glowered down at her. "You think I give a *damn* about that?"

"Be reasonable, Captain. You didn't take this case for altruistic purposes."

He opened his mouth and then closed it, staring at her as if she was a stranger.

It was for the best, she stubbornly reminded her aching heart. For them both. Georgiana willed herself to go to her brother, who was watching them from a short distance with a wary expression.

"Take care," she said softly, and turned before he could respond.

* * *

The trip back to London was a series of long awkward silences. Georgiana was too distracted to make much conversation, and Reggie was still irritated with her. She didn't have the energy to deal with her brother's mood, as she was lost in her own thoughts, recalling everything that had transpired since that morning in Captain Harris's office. Two weeks felt like a lifetime ago. When Louisa met them at Victoria Station, she and Reggie had barely exchanged more than a handful of words.

"Aren't you two a sight for sore eyes."

Georgiana managed a weak smile, while Reggie grunted.

Louisa frowned at their brother. "What are you so grumpy about? No one ruined *your* holiday."

Reggie's mouth dropped open. "I beg your pardon?"

"Well, you shan't have it," Louisa shot back as she tucked her arm through Georgiana's and led her through the crowd while Reggie sputtered behind them.

"Has he been an absolute beast?" she asked softly.

"We haven't spoken much," Georgiana admitted. "Though I can't say I blame him."

Louisa let out a derisive snort. "Don't you dare try to take the blame for Reggie getting his knickers in a twist. He had no right to ambush you in Dover. I told him as much."

"Did you?"

"Try not to look so shocked, Georgie," Louisa said as they approached Reggie's waiting carriage. "I'm on your side. Always." Then she turned to glare at Reggie. "*You*, on the other hand..."

"What did I do?"

Georgiana let out a sigh. "If we're going to have it out, may we at least do it inside the carriage? We're starting to attract attention."

Her siblings exchanged sheepish looks and mumbled apologies.

"Yes."

"Sorry, Georgie."

Georgiana managed to resist the urge to roll her eyes as she let the footman hand her into the carriage. Once they were all seated, she cleared her throat.

"Now, then. It appears we have some things that need to be discussed. Who would like to go first?"

Just as Reggie began to speak, Louisa cut him off. "I'm not listening to a word from you until you apologize to Georgiana. You had no right to interfere, Reg. She's a grown woman. And if she wants to have a bit of fun with a handsome man, who are you to stop her?"

"For God's sake, I'm trying to protect her reputation!"

"Why?" Louisa countered. "Because you're afraid Tommy Pettigrew won't have her otherwise?"

"Yes," Reggie said testily. "As a matter of fact, that is exactly what I'm worried about."

"Enough."

Both her siblings immediately fell silent at the single word, spoken in the same imperious tone she had used when they were still children.

"I appreciate your concern—both of yours—but I need to speak for myself." She addressed Reggie first. "I am not going to marry Tommy Pettigrew. I know that is disappointing to hear, but you must trust me to do what I think is best."

"But Georgie—"

"No," she said firmly. "If my reputation is ruined, then I'll just have to bear it. But I will not marry again for anyone else's benefit except my own."

Reggie blanched at this. "What do you mean?"

"Oh, come now, Reg," Louisa huffed. "Did you think she married that horrible man because she was in *love* with him?"

Reggie, bewildered, looked between them. It was painfully clear that he had never thought about it at all. "I...I—"

Louisa cut him off. "Tell us the truth, Georgie. I *know* there is more to it."

Georgiana stared into her younger sister's pleading eyes. For eight years she had carried this burden alone, and it had cost her even more than she had realized. But no more.

"Father came to me during my season," she began. "Not long after you all came to visit. He had debts that were being unexpectedly called in after an investment did not work out as planned. He would have lost the house in Kent if he did not come up with the money quickly. And someone offered to help, but it came at a price."

Louisa's face fell. "Oh, don't tell me."

Her throat began to tighten at the sympathy in her sister's voice. "I never thought of myself as the romantic type, but I suppose that was because I hadn't ever been given the chance to decide. I had known from a young age that I would need to marry well. And I came to London to do just that. But then I...I..." She couldn't make herself say the words. Just thinking them was painful enough.

"You met someone else," Reggie supplied, as understanding dawned on his face. "Captain Harris."

Georgiana had to turn away. She nodded. "When I learned of Father's debts, I knew I couldn't possibly accept him. Not without ruining things for the rest of you."

"And Father simply agreed to this beastly proposition?" Reggie was more irate than she could ever remember seeing him.

"He didn't have much of a choice. He needed to pay off the debts as fast as possible so as not to damage his reputation in financial circles. And it worked. He was able to pay back the viscount the next year." But by then it was too late for Georgiana and Henry. "I have sometimes wondered if the viscount was the one who bought Father's debts in the first place, so that I would be pressured into accepting him," she added, voicing the theory she had been considering for many years now. "It was the same approach he used in his own business dealings."

"My God," Reggie murmured. "That's diabolical."

"And I certainly would never have married him under normal circumstances," she continued, still piecing things together. "But he must have known how I felt about Captain Harris. And that he was running out of time…" Her brow furrowed as she thought back to those few hazy weeks. There was something she was missing. Something just out of reach.

"Georgie." Her sister's voice pulled her back to the present. She had asked a question.

"Hmm?"

"The captain. What will happen now?"

Georgiana attempted a casual shrug. "Nothing."

"But you've both waited all this time."

"And we have both changed a great deal since then," she said gently. "Though we have developed a friendship of sorts."

Georgiana couldn't say more, and Henry's secrets were certainly not hers to reveal.

She turned away from Louisa's disappointed face and locked eyes with her brother. Reggie was giving her a skeptical look, but this time he kept his mouth shut.

Louisa had an errand to run in Piccadilly, so she was dropped off on the way to Pimlico. When the carriage finally reached Georgiana's house, all she could think of was the long, lonely night that awaited her.

"You're meeting with the solicitors tomorrow?" Reggie asked, breaking the heavy silence that had descended over the carriage since Louisa's exit.

"Yes. But I'm thinking of canceling the expansion. Perhaps it isn't the right time."

The commodore's grim warning flashed through her mind. *You wouldn't want those you love being targeted next.*

Henry had already suffered enough thanks to her. She couldn't stomach putting him at risk once more.

Reggie watched her for a long moment. "If that is what you think is best," he finally said.

She gave him a nod and moved toward the door. Then he continued. "But if it is because of the threats, then I hope you'll reconsider."

"You do?" Georgiana could not hide her surprise.

Reggie gave her a considering look. "I trust you, Georgiana. I'm sorry I haven't always listened to you. It was a misguided attempt to protect you. But you have my full support, whatever you decide to do."

A slow smile spread across her face. "Thank you. That means a great deal to me."

"There is something else," he called out as she stepped onto the pavement. "I'll admit I may be dense in many respects, but I know what I saw in that train station in Dover."

He then raised an eyebrow. "And it was most certainly not a pair of *friends*. At least, not any that I've ever had."

"Reg, please—"

He held up a hand. "I'm taking Louisa's advice and won't pry. It's none of my business. And like before, you have my full support."

Georgiana relaxed. "Well, good."

"But whatever you decide, this time I hope it is truly what *you* want. Not anyone else. You deserve to be happy, Georgie. Possibly more than anyone I know."

As Georgiana stood there in stunned silence, Reggie tipped his hat and pulled the carriage door shut.

CHAPTER EIGHTEEN

———◆———

M y word, you look awful," Delia said. "If you don't
mind me saying so, Captain."

"I do, actually," Henry grumbled as he took the morning's post from her.

He had only arrived back in London yesterday, but the separation from Georgiana was already unbearable. It showed in the circles beneath his eyes, the pronounced lines in his face, and the slight tremble in his fingers, as if his very limbs were searching for her phantom embrace. Her dismissal in Dover had hurt, but he must accept it. They had made no promise to one another. Had said nothing of continuing their affair in London. *Affair.* That word was so far removed from what Henry wanted that it was rendered meaningless. But he simply tightened his jaw, headed for his desk, and got to work.

Luckily, the morning was particularly busy, with people

streaming in and out of the office for hours. Henry met with a jilted wife who wanted the identity of her estranged husband's mistress, a father seeking information on his daughter's shifty fiancé, and a man convinced his landlady was trying to poison him. Henry recommended the last gentleman contact Scotland Yard. But the other cases he took on, as distasteful as they were, because that was what he did: wallow through the muck of people's private lives searching for the truth. But he couldn't remember the last time his information had made a client feel better. Mostly, he just confirmed their worst suspicions about people they had once trusted. And Henry was growing tired of it. He recalled the look of determination on Georgiana's face as she talked about her plans for her business and of the fierce loyalty she inspired in people like Mr. Khan. He had once thought her foolish for not immediately heeding the threats against her, as that was by far the easiest solution. But now Henry understood. She had discovered her purpose, and that was worth fighting for.

Just before lunch he collapsed in his chair and began riffling through the post. There wasn't much. A courier had dropped off a check from Reggie Fox that morning, even though a part of Henry had still expected the man to refuse to pay him despite Georgiana's assertions. And he would have deserved nothing less. But now the bills were all paid in full, and money had been sent to various family members. Reggie may not always be the most supportive brother, but he was an honorable man. Certainly more so than Henry felt at the moment. Then his hands stilled as he came upon a small envelope with an all-too-familiar red wax seal. He shot out of his seat and flung the door open.

"Who sent this?" he barked at Delia's back. She paused in her typing and gave him an incredulous look. "There's no return address."

"I'm not sure, sir," Delia explained, wide-eyed at his demand. "It came with the rest of the mail this morning."

Henry growled and shut the door. Then he tore open the envelope. As he read, his pulse sped up.

Commodore Perry was requesting his presence at White-hall this afternoon. Henry snorted. They both knew this "request" was actually an order. A pity Henry didn't take those anymore. He crumpled the letter in his hand and threw it in the wastebin. Then he grabbed his cane and flung the door open again. Delia jumped in her seat and glared at him over her shoulder.

"I'm going out," Henry said as he tore his coat off the coatrack.

"I liked you better when you were in Monte Carlo," Delia sighed.

"So did I," he muttered and headed for the door, then turned back. Henry pulled a few banknotes from his billfold and handed them to a bewildered Delia. "Here. Why don't you close up early and take Maude somewhere nice."

Delia raised an eyebrow. "Is everything all right, Captain?"

Henry ignored the question. "Apologies for my mood." Then he left before she could ask anything more.

* * *

Henry spent the rest of the day walking along the river, feeding the birds, and doing his best not to think about Georgiana—and failing quite miserably. When the sky began to darken, Henry returned home. He hung up his coat and moved through the tiny flat, then paused in the doorway of the sorry excuse for a kitchen.

"Have you been waiting this whole time?"

The commodore rose from the room's lone chair. "So, you *did* get my message."

"Yes." Henry lit a small table lamp, which cast the older man's frown in an orange-tinted glow.

"Is that all you have to say for yourself?"

"I don't owe you an explanation, Commodore," Henry snapped. "In case you forgot, I have paid my dues in full. You got your hero to parade about, and I can tell you no for the rest of my life."

"But that is why I'm *here*," the commodore replied, his dark eyes glimmering with purpose. Henry was quite familiar with that look. His stomach was already turning. "Your reputation is necessary to the success of this mission, which is a matter of great national importance. The Germans are—"

Henry held up a hand. "If you are so damned concerned about the Germans, then I suggest you talk to your ambassador. I know for a fact that his attaché has been trying to raise the alarm for some time, but no one will listen."

The commodore narrowed his eyes. "You mean Rafe Davies?"

Henry nodded and hoped to God he wasn't getting his friend wrapped up in something nefarious.

Commodore Perry leaned back and rubbed his clean-shaven chin. "He doesn't have the best reputation within the government. Not everyone takes kindly to having their secrets exposed."

He was referring to Rafe's actions when he had uncovered a blackmail operation that targeted a number of officials and members of Parliament. The extent was largely covered up, but a few names were fed to the papers "for the greater good."

"He had nothing to do with that," Henry pointed out.

"That doesn't matter to those men. They need someone else to blame for their indiscretions."

"And you?" Henry immediately regretted the bold question as the commodore folded his arms and eyed him. Many a sailor had broken under that glare.

"I'm not some nob who's spent his life having his arse wiped by a servant," he spat. "I will answer for all my sins when I reach the gates of heaven and be judged by none but Saint Peter himself."

Well, then.

"I thought you'd be itching to return to the game," the commodore continued. "It's been two years now. Sometimes a fellow needs a break, I understand that. And you needed to recover from your injury. But you looked very well in Monte Carlo, and I've heard great things about your little business."

Henry shifted in his seat. "A man has to make a living, Commodore. The naval pension isn't enough. You know that."

"If you work for me, I'll make sure you're taken care of."

That was likely an empty promise. But rather than reject the offer outright, Henry decided to let the commodore dangle on the line a little and see if he could get some information out of him. "Who told you I was in Monte Carlo?"

If the commodore was surprised by the question, he didn't show it. "Someone who is quite desperate for money and owed me a debt. They offered some information about you that I might be interested in. Turned out he was correct. But not to worry. Lady Arlington is no longer in danger, as long as she agrees to give up her plans for expansion."

A chill ran through Henry. "She won't do it. She came back specifically to sign the papers."

The commodore merely shrugged. "Then one of you has a difficult decision to make. You can come work for me, and I'll tell you everything I know."

Henry huffed a bitter laugh. "You'd give up your source that easily?"

"If that's what it takes. You are a valuable asset, Henry. I never should have let you leave. Or you can keep chasing philandering husbands while your viscountess is forced to sacrifice her expansion. But perhaps that is for the best. Then she can settle into a nice life with Lord Pettigrew. Have I got that right?"

Henry narrowed his gaze. The commodore knew just which buttons to push, but Henry kept silent. He would not be manipulated by this man.

"You have twenty-four hours, Captain," the commodore said as he stood and pulled on his gloves. Then he shot him a dark look. "And not a minute longer this time."

* * *

The next morning, Georgiana was met at her office by an enthusiastic Mr. Khan.

"Good day, my lady. You are looking refreshed."

Georgiana let out a short laugh. Despite Reggie's encouragement, she had been up half the night with the commodore's warning echoing in her ears. "I doubt that, Mr. Khan, but thank you for saying so."

Her secretary gave her a shy smile and cleared his throat. "The lawyers will be arriving shortly with the paperwork. I've had the conference room prepared."

"Excellent. I will be down in a moment."

Just as Mr. Khan turned to leave, Georgiana called him back. She hesitated as she stared at his open, expectant expression, then took a breath and got on with it. "I've been having some second thoughts. About the expansion. That perhaps . . . perhaps now isn't the right time."

A distinct flicker of emotion passed over his face before he mastered it. "My lady," he began, choosing his words carefully. "While I understand the last few weeks have been difficult, I admit this is distressing to hear."

Georgiana swallowed hard and glanced down at the desk. "I know," she said. "It is not what I wanted, but I'm not sure I have much of a choice."

Mr. Khan was silent for a long moment. "If that is what you think is best," he finally said, then closed the door softly behind him.

The disappointment in his words cut her more deeply than the commodore's threats. She hated this. Hated how he must think that she was a flighty aristocrat, making promises she didn't intend to keep. Georgiana balled her hand into a fist and pressed it against the wood of her desk. As frightened as she had been lately, it was still nothing compared to the horrors some of her workers had endured. Georgiana had started this expansion in the first place so that men like the commodore couldn't hold so much power. She needed to find a way to see it through. It was too important to too many people. But she would have to warn Henry that he might be targeted next by whoever was trying to stop her.

And yet you won't be honest with him about why *he would be targeted.*

Her heart clenched painfully. She had been an utter coward on the steamer. Selfish for one last night with him when she should have told him the truth. Henry deserved that from her.

She let out a sigh and straightened. "All right, then. Time for the viscountess to get to work."

Half an hour later, Georgiana strode into the conference room, and as the men in their dark suits and barely veiled expressions of distaste rose at her entrance, she knew she had made the right decision. She caught Mr. Khan's eye and flashed him a smile.

"Good morning, gentlemen," she said with a dramatic sweep of her skirts before lowering herself into her chair. "Shall we sign some paperwork?"

* * *

After the final paper was initialed and the last lawyer was tucked into his carriage, Georgiana collapsed into her chair. The feeling of triumph that had been powering her for hours began to fade. She was now officially the owner of another factory—but achieving this goal had done nothing for the ache in her chest.

"I don't suppose I can tempt you to come to my

house for dinner this evening? An impromptu celebration, perhaps?"

Georgiana glanced up to find Mr. Khan standing in front of her desk. Her mind had wandered. She wasn't even sure for how long. "Can we another time? I'm still fatigued from traveling."

"Of course, my lady."

"Please give my best to Mrs. Khan."

He gave a short bow and turned to leave before pausing in the doorway. "You've done a brave thing today," he said to her over his shoulder. "Do something kind for yourself."

Georgiana ducked her head. She didn't feel particularly brave. "If you insist."

Mr. Khan smiled. "I do. Good night." He then shut the door softly behind him, leaving her alone once again. Georgiana stayed in her office for another hour, mindlessly shuffling papers, before she found the will to leave.

As she climbed into her waiting carriage, she glanced around the deserted street. Reggie had assured her that the man he hired to monitor her would be discreet, but she hadn't seen him at all—not that she was complaining. That was what she had wanted from the beginning. To be left alone. Completely.

Back home she took Mr. Khan's advice by having a bath drawn and a dinner tray brought to her room. But while she sat alone in her tub, her thoughts turned to Henry, for how could they not? Reggie's words came to her once more: *This time I hope it is truly what* you *want.*

What *did* she want? She had been so sure just one week ago. How much had changed since then. How *she* had changed.

Georgiana stayed in the tub until the water grew tepid, then retired to her bed. Barnaby immediately curled up beside her, and she stroked his fur while listening to his soft snores. Though the bath had relaxed her aching muscles, her thoughts would not cease. Eventually she fell into a fitful sleep, only to wake with the dawn as a single thought echoed in her mind:

Go to him.

Perhaps Henry would slam the door in her face once he learned what she had done all those years ago. Perhaps she would never see him again afterward. But for once Georgiana would say everything she wanted. Aloud. And especially to him.

As she had no need to play the part of the viscountess today, she let Bea sleep and dressed quickly in the near darkness in a simple day gown before fixing her hair in a Psyche knot. As Georgiana descended the front stairs, she briefly considered taking the carriage. The walk to Henry's office from here would take some time, as she didn't know where he lived, but it was lovely out, and she needed time to collect her thoughts.

"My lady?" Mossdown appeared in the darkened hall, her faithful butler always at the ready.

"I'm going out for a walk," Georgiana said as she tied the ribbon of a plain straw hat beneath her chin. "Tell Cook I won't need breakfast."

A brief look of concern crossed the older man's face before he gave a short bow. "Yes, my lady."

Georgiana then exited her house and headed down the street. There was no one else about this early in her neighborhood, but she appreciated the quiet. She had just begun to practice what she would say to Henry when someone stepped right in her path.

"Tobias!" She clutched a hand to her chest as her heart thundered in her ears. "Goodness, you *scared* me."

But as she met his gaze, her breath caught. It wasn't entirely out of the ordinary for Tobias Harrington to still be awake at dawn after a night of carousing, but his clothes were uncharacteristically rumpled and torn, like he had been in a tussle. But it was the vacant look in his eyes that most unsettled her. Like a man with nothing left to lose.

"Tobias," she said softly as the hairs on her nape began to prickle.

He took her arm without preamble and pulled her to a carriage waiting a few feet away. "Come with me."

"No," she said calmly, still fighting against the instinct screaming inside her. "You must let me go. Reggie hired someone to watch over me. He'll be here any moment." Georgiana twisted her neck, looking around for the man. Where *was* he?

"No one is coming," Tobias said in a flat voice that turned her stomach. "I told your idiot brother I would handle the arrangements, and he believed me, as usual."

Georgiana's mouth fell open. No. It couldn't have been *him*. Not shallow, indolent Tobias. The son of her own godmother. Georgiana's feet scrabbled against the smooth pavement as her brain cried out in warning. *Do not get into that carriage with him.*

"Tobias, please," she whimpered. "Please let me go."

His jaw tightened, and he flashed her a dark look. "You stupid girl," he growled. "You've left me no choice." Then he shoved her into the darkened carriage and slammed the door shut.

* * *

Henry paced the floor of his tiny office and completely ignored the work on his desk while the commodore's proposition echoed in his thoughts.

You can come work for me, and I'll tell you everything I know.

If Henry gave up the vow he had made two years before, he could ensure Georgiana's safety and that no one interfered with her plans.

Then she can settle into a nice life with Lord Pettigrew.

He held back a grimace. The commodore had likely been trying to bait him, but as Henry searched his heart, he found it didn't matter. Even if it was true, even if Georgiana did intend to marry Pettigrew, he would still do this for her. Because he believed in what she was trying to do. He believed in her.

Henry threw open his office door, and Delia's typing came to an abrupt halt as she sent him a wary glance.

"I need to you send a message—"

But before he could say the rest, the front door burst open. It was Reggie and Inspector Crenshaw. Henry's heart stopped as he took in the grim look on both their faces.

"What's happened?" he demanded as he stepped toward them. "Where is she?"

Reggie hesitated, likely because Henry must have looked like a madman, and in that brief moment he grabbed the younger man's lapels and gave him a shake. "Say it."

"She's missing," Reggie sputtered. "Mossdown saw Tobias pull her into a carriage this morning."

Everything else fell away, and Henry became aware of a distinct ringing in his ears. This was all his fault. He never should have let her return to London. Never let her out of his damned sight. It was another moment before Henry felt a hand on his arm. It was Delia. He released Reggie Fox and stepped back.

He took a shaky breath and looked at the two men. "Tell me everything."

Not ten minutes later Henry was in a carriage with a nervous Reggie and the inspector. A man named Jasper Pickins, who fit the description of Georgiana's stalker, had been arrested last night for public brawling. Under questioning he admitted to being hired by Tobias Harrington to follow Georgiana and intimidate her, including throwing the brick through her carriage window. He had met with Tobias in a pub yesterday to discuss plans to abduct her, but he refused unless Tobias paid him first. Apparently he was still owed money. That had led to a scuffle outside the pub. Pickins had gotten a few hits in before he was pulled off, and Tobias snuck off just before a passing constable arrested him.

The man didn't know what Tobias wanted with Georgiana, only that he had become increasingly desperate once he learned she was still going ahead with the expansion. He claimed that Tobias had discussed bringing her to the abandoned factory she had just purchased, and as it was the only lead they had, they were on the way.

"I can't let you enter the factory alone, Captain," Inspector Crenshaw said as he subtly glanced at Henry's cane.

"Well, I'm not waiting for backup," Henry said, straightening his shoulders. "If Harrington is desperate enough to kidnap Lady Arlington off the street, there's no telling what else he might do. I will try to convince him to release her, but he may respond better if he thinks I'm alone."

Crenshaw gave him a resigned nod. "Fine. I'll cover you as best I can until my men arrive."

It wasn't exactly a foolproof plan, but Henry's only focus was getting Georgiana away from Tobias as quickly as possible.

Reggie let out a moan and dabbed a handkerchief across his brow.

"She'll be all right, Reggie," Henry said. "I promise."

The man gave him remorseful look. "Please accept my apologies, Captain. I was an ass in Dover. I thought you were a bounder, but Georgie set me straight yesterday." Henry cut a glance to the detective. As much as he wanted to hear this, it was hardly the place. But Reggie didn't seem to notice. "And my God, my father! Forcing her to give you up to save the family! It's positively medieval."

At that Henry stilled. "What?" he asked quietly.

"All this time I thought she had chosen him," Reggie continued, shaking his head. "That she *wanted* to be a viscountess. What a fool I was."

"Reggie," Henry said roughly. "Explain yourself."

That finally got through to him, and his sapphire gaze snapped to Henry's from across the carriage. "Father was up to his ears in debt, and the viscount offered to pay it off in exchange for her hand. I wish I had known. Georgie's always kept so much to herself, but I should have asked. I suppose that's why Father made sure she inherited those factories after the viscount finally had the decency to die, but it doesn't really make up for essentially selling her off into a loveless marriage, does it?"

It took Henry a moment to realize Reggie was waiting for his reply. "Then…she didn't love the viscount?" he asked dumbly. It felt like his head was full of sand.

Reggie gave him a pitying look. "Never."

Henry turned toward the window as he sorted through the wave of disparate emotions crashing over him. "I knew when she married him that it wasn't for love, but then I saw her." His voice sounded hollow and wooden to his own ears. "Just after she had learned of his death in Scotland. She was on the floor, sobbing."

Reggie was silent for a long moment. "I imagine those were tears of relief," he finally said in a tone that left no room for doubt.

Then he had been wrong. All this time. How much they had both lost. It nearly made him ill to think of it.

"I thought…" Henry sighed. "I had *hoped* she was happy. If only for a little while."

It wasn't until the admission left him that he realized the truth of it, even when he had been swamped with jealousy. Henry cast a tentative glance at Reggie and found the man was practically beaming at him.

"Oh, Captain," he said. "That is just what I wanted to hear."

CHAPTER NINETEEN

———◆———

Georgiana stood in the corner of a large, empty room on the ground floor of the deserted factory she now owned, watching as Tobias appeared to unravel a little more with each passing minute. Strange to think the boy she had once happily built sandcastles with during shared summer holidays was the same haggard man now standing before her.

"Are you waiting for someone?" she asked after he checked his pocket watch yet again.

He gave a brief nod, but did not look at her. "And it appears they aren't going to come. So I'll just have to do this myself," he muttered.

Georgiana's throat tightened as she tried to swallow. "Do what?" she forced herself to ask as he turned to face her. For one brief moment something like regret flashed across his face, but then his jaw hardened once more.

"You should have listened. Then none of this would have had to happen."

"Tobias—"

"No," he said firmly. "I tried to warn you, but now it's done. You knew what you were risking when you signed those papers. It's your own fault."

Georgiana inhaled a shaky breath as he approached. "You sound like you're trying desperately to absolve yourself of something."

"I don't have a choice," he insisted as he stalked toward her.

She shrank back. "Of course you do," she said, her voice unnaturally high. "You always have a choice."

But Tobias only shook his head as he reached into his coat. Amid the fear thrumming through her blood came the crush of regret as she thought of Henry and all that she never got to say. All that he would never know.

Then she made a fist and tensed her arm. There weren't a great many benefits to having brothers. They were quite messy and badly behaved and often thoughtless. But Georgiana had learned how to throw a punch and had broken up more fights than she could count. She wasn't going to simply stand there and let a man like Tobias Harrington murder her.

Just as she saw a flash of gunmetal, Georgiana kicked him hard in the knee. He let out a cry and bent forward. Then Georgiana soundly socked him in the jaw, just like Ollie had taught her, and ran.

Tobias let out a loud curse behind her, but she did not stop as she moved though the building toward the entrance as fast as she could. But just as it came in sight, someone stepped into the doorway, and her heart froze. She had forgotten about the coachman. Georgiana stopped short and ducked down a hallway, only to discover it was a dead end. She let out a frustrated cry and slapped her hand against the brick wall. Then her ears pricked up as she heard the man's footsteps coming closer, followed by the familiar click of a cane. She whirled around as Henry came storming up to her, a scowl on his face.

"For God's sake, Georgiana, I—"

But before he could say another word, she threw herself into his arms. "Oh, I'm so glad it's you," she gasped.

Henry's body automatically relaxed against hers, and his hand came around her waist. "Are you all right?" he asked gently.

"It was Tobias," she murmured against his chest.

"I know."

"He's still here, and he has a gun."

Henry's grip tightened. "Where is he?"

"At the other end of the building. I punched him and ran away."

Henry looked impressed then grew serious. "Let's get you out of here."

Together they moved back down the hallway as quietly as possible, then looked around. The building was eerily silent, but the entrance was clear. "You go ahead of me," Henry said and drew her in front of him, acting as her shield. She didn't like that, but there wasn't time to argue. Georgiana gripped his hand as she headed for the entrance.

As they reached the door, a shot rang out and Henry immediately froze. Georgiana glanced back to find him as white as a sheet, his eyes focused on the spot where the bullet struck the wall just above their heads. Thank God Tobias was a terrible shot.

"Come," she said urgently as she tugged on his hand.

But in that brief pause, Tobias appeared with the gun trained on them. His jaw was already purpling where she had struck him.

Some of the color returned to Henry's face as he glared at him. "It's over, Tobias," he said with a slight tremble in his deep voice. "Now tell me what's going on. I want to help."

Surprise flickered in the man's gaze before it turned to anger. "I will not be pitied by the likes of *you*." Then he pointed the gun at Georgiana. "All she had to do was give up the expansion. Then my debt would be paid."

"It seems like you owe a number of people debts," Henry said as his eyes lit with understanding. "You were the one who told the commodore about us."

Georgiana looked between the two men. "But how did you know?"

Tobias lifted his chin. "Let's call it a lucky guess. I saw the two of you in my mother's back garden all those years ago. That wasn't very noble of you, Captain," he sneered. "She was furious when I told her."

Georgiana's stomach turned as the missing piece clicked into place. "My God," she muttered. "Aunt Paloma knew the entire time."

"She saved you from making a fool of yourself," Tobias snapped. "Did you really think she was going to step aside and watch you marry a damned *naval* officer when you could have been a viscountess? She had made a promise to your mother to see you safely wed, so she did what was necessary."

"And the viscount was part of it," Georgiana choked out.

Tobias nodded. "He bought your father's debts on Mother's advice. You might have made a foolish choice on your own, but she knew you would never let your family suffer for it. A pity you weren't a little more selfish."

"And yet you still let me assume the absolute worst about Henry when you knew the truth."

"Don't blame me for that," he countered. "You could have gone and talked to the man instead of skulking outside the Wrenhews' card room."

Henry turned to her in surprise. "You were there that night?"

"Yes," she admitted as Henry blanched. "I overheard everything."

He winced. "I didn't mean any of it. When Tobias told me you were engaged, I was upset—"

Georgiana shot an accusing look at Tobias. "*He* told you?"

Henry nodded. "And then I acted like an ass. But if I had any idea—"

Tobias cut him off with an ugly laugh. "A bit late for that, Harris. Georgiana did her duty and married the viscount, like an obedient little daughter. When I saw you both at the opera and again at the Pettigrews' ball, I thought the commodore might find that information valuable. And I was able to settle another debt."

The last shred of Georgiana's control finally snapped, and outrage burst through her. "Are you saying that all of this has been over your *gambling debts*?"

"Well, what else would it be?" Tobias had the audacity to look affronted. "I don't have the money. Peregrine's been an absolute beast lately and is refusing to give me my allowance until my creditors are paid. Lord knows how long that will take. And Mother would have my hide if she knew about the gambling, so I offered what I did have: information and influence."

"You promised you could convince me to give up the expansion."

"Yes," he said testily. "And if that damned brother of yours hadn't gone and hired the captain, this could have been over weeks ago. Now this is the only way. With you dead. A pity you never did marry again. Now there will be no one to carry on your little legacy. But the better for me." He raised the gun again.

"Tell me who is behind this," Henry barked. "I'll make sure you are protected."

"I considered that," he said calmly. "But I don't plan to see the inside of a cell. And I still have a better chance with them than I do with Scotland Yard. I've been promised passage to the continent, and I have a train to catch."

Before Tobias could cock the gun, Henry lunged at it and they both fell to the ground.

"Run, Georgie!" Henry cried as he wrestled for the weapon.

"Like hell I will," she muttered as she reached for Henry's discarded cane.

As soon as she picked it up, she knew Bea's suspicions had been right. Henry pinned Tobias flat on his back and met Georgiana's gaze. His eyes widened and he gave her an encouraging nod. But in that brief moment of distraction Tobias punched Henry in the face and knocked him over. As the two men scrabbled on the floor, Georgiana turned the cane's handle until she heard a click and unsheathed the sword. It was really more of a dagger, but Georgiana would take it. She looked up just as Tobias delivered another hard punch to Henry and dragged himself to his feet. As Tobias retrieved the gun, Henry lay motionless on the ground. But Tobias committed a grave error: He kept his back to Georgiana. She gripped the dagger's handle and charged forward just as he began to aim. Ladies could do a number of things: run factories, embroider tea towels, and stab an awful man in the back of the leg.

Tobias cried out in pain and dropped the gun. Then Georgiana pushed him hard and grabbed the weapon. Her hands were shaking uncontrollably as she pointed it at Tobias, a man she had known her entire life.

He was breathing heavily as blood ran down his leg. "You won't shoot," he rasped.

"No, but I will."

Georgiana looked up to see a young man in a gray suit approach them with his gun drawn, followed by several constables. "Lady Arlington, I presume?" he asked as he touched the brim of his hat. "I'm Inspector Crenshaw. We can take things from here."

Georgiana lowered the weapon. "Oh, thank God. I haven't a clue how to use this."

The inspector took the gun, and she rushed over to Henry as the constables surrounded Tobias. She pulled his head onto her lap and ran her fingers through his hair. There was a cut on his cheek where Tobias had punched him, and his body was heavy against hers.

"Henry," she choked out. "Wake up, darling. Please."

After the longest minute of her life, his eyelids fluttered open. Warmth filled his amber gaze as he took her in. "Georgie," he whispered as the corner of his mouth curved.

Georgiana gasped in relief. She had never been so happy to see that half smile. "Are you badly hurt? Scotland Yard arrived after Tobias knocked you out."

"Took them long enough," he said with a grimace as he slowly sat up. "I'll live, but I'll never forgive myself for letting that coward land a punch."

Georgiana let out a surprised laugh. "I think you may have hit your head."

Henry leaned closer. "Well then, I'm afraid you'll have to nurse me back to health," he murmured as he brushed his thumb along her jaw and tilted her chin up.

But just as his lips were about to touch her own, someone loudly cleared their throat. It was the inspector. And his cheeks were blazing.

"Apologies for the interruption, but we'd like to take you both back to the Yard for questioning. That is, if you're well enough, Captain."

"Of course," Henry said smoothly, as if they hadn't just been moments away from kissing each other in full view of the entire room.

Georgiana helped him up and wrapped his arm around her shoulders as they followed the inspector.

"And here I thought you disapproved of public displays of affection," she whispered.

"I was wrong," he said as he turned to her, his bruised face warm with affection. "About a great many things, it turns out."

Georgiana patted his hand. "As was I. But now we will fix them. Together."

Henry's arm tightened as he pulled her even closer. "Yes, my lady."

* * *

While under questioning at Scotland Yard, Tobias admitted that he had struck a deal with Mr. Rigby, the competitor who had refused to meet with Henry, to intimidate Georgiana. It turned out that Mr. Rigby was as bad a gambler as Tobias and owed a considerable amount of money. As more and more workers left his factory for Georgiana's and production rates plummeted, he grew increasingly desperate to have her expansion shut down. Desperate enough to turn to murder.

After they had each made their statements, Henry escorted Georgiana home, where she insisted on dressing his injuries.

"As much as I hate to admit it, he made a good point, you know," she said as she dabbed his cheek with a wet cloth.

They were tucked away in her study with a blazing fire and a tea cart laden with all kinds of treats. Cook had gone overboard once she learned that the injured Captain Harris was recuperating under their roof. Henry was laid out on Georgiana's sofa with a blanket over his legs and Barnaby dozing at his feet. Despite his initial protests, he looked quite comfortable.

"Who?"

"Tobias," she replied, still focusing on his cut. "I should have talked to you that night at the Wrenhews' ball instead of running off. I made such a terrible mistake when I married the viscount. Not only because I hurt you, but I hurt myself as well. What my father asked of me was wrong. I see that now. But if I had simply stood up to him in the first place and told you the truth, then—"

Henry stilled her hand. "Georgie. Don't. You can't take

the blame for everything that happened. And I can certainly understand why you didn't speak to me that night. I was devastated when Tobias told me about your engagement, but it's not an excuse for the things I said. I should have handled my disappointment better and not simply assumed the absolute worst of you."

She set down the cloth and met his eyes. "There is something I still need to tell you. I was on my way to your office to do it this morning, but I confess, I am quite terrified to do it."

He cupped her cheek. "You can tell me anything."

"I was the one who spread those rumors about you years ago. That you were nothing but a fortune hunter. So it *is* my fault, you see," she whispered as she bowed her head. "If I hadn't done that, you could have married. You wouldn't have had to spy, and then Turkey would never have happened."

He was silent for a long moment before he took her face in both his hands. "You must listen to me, Georgiana," he began, his voice low and urgent. "I know that you are used to taking care of everyone around you, but you absolutely *cannot* take responsibility for what happened to me. Darling, you don't have that much power," he added tenderly.

Georgiana's nose began to sting. "But I ruined your chance to avoid Naval Intelligence. You said so yourself in Monte Carlo that they wouldn't have taken you if you had married."

"No," he said firmly. "You are not responsible for my choices. You did what you thought was right based on the information you had at the time. And besides, you weren't wrong," he continued. "I *was* a fortune hunter, and

I did propose to those two other women like an absolute scoundrel. Though I doubt I would have gone through with it anyway..."

She sniffled and looked up at him. "Why not?"

Henry began to slowly brush his thumb against her cheek. "Because it is one thing to marry for mutual convenience when both parties are unattached, but quite another when one has fallen irrevocably in love with someone else."

Love.

It felt as if Georgiana's heart was about to burst, yet she still managed to raise a teasing eyebrow. "Irrevocably?"

"It appears that way, seeing as I've now fallen in love with you on two distinct, highly inconvenient occasions," he said with a smile before his gaze grew concerned. "Is that why you didn't want to talk on the steamer?"

She looked away and nodded. "I was so certain you would hate me if you knew what I had done. And I just couldn't bear it. But I was being a coward."

"I had worried it was because of what I told you about Turkey," he admitted. "That you wouldn't want to be with me once you had learned the truth. Because I wasn't the hero you thought I was."

Georgiana's mouth dropped. "Absolutely not. You're certainly my hero," she added.

"Seeing as how you saved *me* not too long ago, I think it's the other way around."

She gave him a watery smile. "All right. But I'm so sorry you thought that for even a moment."

"Well, I forgive you," he said simply. "I lost you once before, and it was hell. I had to convince myself that the girl I fell in love with had never existed. Because that was the only way I could stop myself from loving you. But my heart has always been yours. I was a fool to think I could ever resist you."

"My goodness. The things you say." She let out a soft sigh and pressed her forehead to his. "I've loved only you, Henry. No one else has ever come close. Even when I thought you utterly despised me. It was quite vexing," she added.

He let out a short laugh. "A dilemma I can relate to all too well, my dear." She grinned at him, and he took in a stuttering breath. "But can you forgive *me*?"

"Of course." The idea that she wouldn't was so repulsive, she understood his position with perfect clarity. It was an act of love to offer forgiveness.

"Then we understand each other," he said. "At long last."

She smiled against his shoulder as relief swelled inside her. "It only took several near-death experiences."

He let out a laugh then winced. "Yes, and I'm still a bit sore from this one."

"Oh, sorry," she said as she pulled back. "I'll have Mossdown bring the hot water bottle."

"Then I'll truly feel like someone's grandmama."

"Well, you certainly don't look like one."

"And thank heavens for that," he said as he wrapped his arm around her and drew her against him once again. "Do you think this will scar?" he asked, pointing to his cut.

"If it does, you'll only be more dashing, I'm afraid."

Henry looked delighted. "I've never been told I was dashing before."

"Oh, have I not said that yet? My apologies. You are *extremely* dashing, Captain. Especially in your tan suit."

"Is that so?" He arched an eyebrow and Georgiana's pulse

raced. "I'm afraid you'll need to do a little more penance this time. A man must have some standards, you know."

"Very well," she said as she tugged his face toward hers. "If a man doesn't have standards, he doesn't have anything."

After that only a few choice words were exchanged for some time until Mossdown was finally called upon to bring the water bottle.

"And see that the guest room is prepared," Georgiana said. "The captain is in no state to leave, isn't that right?" She met Henry's eyes, and he smiled.

"Yes, my lady."

EPILOGUE

Eight months later
London, England

"S he looks just like you, Sylvie," Georgiana said. "She has your eyes."

"The countess insists she is the mirror image of Rafe when he was a baby," Sylvia replied as she placed her infant daughter in Georgiana's waiting arms. "But I've seen the pictures and he was *much* chubbier. Like a little cherub."

"I ought to burn those photos," Rafe grumbled from his position behind his wife's chair.

"Hello there, you absolute darling," Georgiana cooed to baby Cecily, who stared up into her face with a questioning look in her large gray eyes before breaking into a gummy smile. "We're going to be great friends, I can tell already."

Sylvia beamed at them before turning to Henry, who was seated beside Georgiana on the sofa. "Would you like to hold her next, Captain?"

He shook his head as he leaned over to have a closer look. "No, thank you."

"Oh, come now, Henry," Rafe said. "You don't want to hold my baby?"

"I am perfectly happy to observe her from here." Then he gave the baby's hand a polite pat. She immediately wrapped her tiny, perfect fingers around his thumb and let out a friendly gurgle.

"See? She *wants* you to hold her," Rafe teased.

Henry's cheeks reddened as he continued to stare into the baby's inquisitive face. "I will when she's larger. Much larger," he amended.

"Rafe, leave him alone," Sylvia said. "Not everyone is as interested in babies as you are."

He looked appalled by the suggestion. "I'll have you know that I wasn't interested in babies myself until we had one."

"Well, there you have it," Sylvia grinned. "I know, why don't you show Henry your new motor car?"

Rafe immediately brightened. "Oh, good idea." Then he turned to Henry. "Sylvia's grown quite bored with hearing me talk about it. She doesn't even pretend to listen anymore."

"Lead the way," Henry replied.

"I'm so glad you decided to return to London," Georgiana said once the gentlemen left the room. "It will be lovely having the three of you close by."

"Yes," Sylvia agreed. "And Rafe is much happier with his new position in the Home Office, though he won't say much about it."

"It's always some cloak and dagger business with him, isn't it?"

"I suppose," Sylvia said with a shrug. "But then he's spent nearly half his life that way. I would imagine it's hard to give up completely."

"And you support his decision?" Georgiana asked cautiously. Rafe's government work had once been a source of contention between them.

"Yes. Absolutely," Sylvia said with a vigorous nod. "I trust him to follow his conscience. And Lord knows this government could use more men like him."

"I heartily agree with that."

"And how is Henry adjusting to his new position?"

After the new Fox and Sons factory opened to great success, Georgiana decided to start a foundation to assist women and children. Henry closed his business in order to help run it, with Delia Swanson acting as his very efficient assistant. Henry hadn't heard from the commodore again, but Georgiana suspected Rafe and his new position had something to do with it.

"He says he's found his true calling. The man seems to know practically every corner of London and where assistance is needed most. He even wants to start a specific program for sailor's wives, which I think is a fabulous idea."

"Look at the pair of you," Sylvia said proudly. "You'll transform this city for the better in no time."

Georgiana returned her smile. "I certainly hope so."

"You haven't gotten any more letters from Lady Harrington, have you?"

"No, just the one. Though I did tell Mossdown to return any others unopened. Perhaps she finally got the message."

When Aunt Paloma learned of Tobias's arrest, she had actually made the journey to Georgiana's home to demand she retract her statement. Georgiana explained that it would make no difference, given that Tobias himself had confessed, but Aunt Paloma refused to accept that her golden child had done anything wrong and insisted that it was all Georgiana's fault. She had continued to hurl baseless accusations at Georgiana until Henry appeared in the parlor with a proper glower on his face, still sporting the bruises from her son's own hands.

Sylvia gave her a sly smile. "Or maybe she doesn't want the captain showing up at her doorstep to give her another dressing-down."

Georgiana chuckled. "I don't think she had heard the unvarnished truth about herself in some time."

"And to hear it delivered from him! You could have sold tickets."

Indeed, watching as Henry listed in exacting detail all of Aunt Paloma's duplicitous actions while the color drained from her face had been most satisfying. Greater still was the interlude after the older woman had flounced from the room, when Georgiana showed Henry just how much his defense of her had meant, but that was a private moment shared only between them. A few less than flattering gossip items about them had appeared in some of the more seedy papers afterward, but Tobias Harrington's fall was the far bigger story. Even his brother had publicly denounced him while commending both Georgiana and the captain.

An outpouring of support from her rivals quickly followed, as no one wanted to be seen as supporting a blackguard like Rigby, who was also serving a lengthy prison sentence.

Georgiana used the opportunity to secure promises of wage reform from each of her competitors. And if they reneged, she assured them she would use all the tools at her disposal, including Captain Harris, who was now more popular than ever. The papers had spun the story so that it had been Henry who heroically stabbed Tobias with the sword cane to save his lady love, as no editor could believe Georgiana had done it. But she didn't mind. They knew the truth.

When Cecily began to grow fussy and Sylvia failed to hide yet another yawn behind her hand, Georgiana decided it was time to leave so the new family could get some much-needed sleep. She returned her godchild to her adoring parents, and she and Henry headed back home to Pimlico.

"I don't think I've ever seen Rafe so exhausted," Henry said as they settled into the seat of their carriage and he drew his arm around her. "And we've greeted the dawn together after a long night out on more than one occasion."

Georgiana laughed. "They both did look tired," she conceded, and snuggled closer to Henry. "But happy."

He nuzzled his cheek against the top of her head. "You know, I wasn't sure how you would feel after seeing the baby. If it would bring back any memories."

Georgiana let out a thoughtful sigh. She had told Henry all about her marriage to the viscount, along with her ambivalence over having children. "I won't deny that I loved holding her," she admitted. "But all I felt was happiness for them both. And it doesn't change anything. I love our life together. Truly."

"Well, that's a relief. Barnaby's demanding enough for me at the moment," Henry said with a chuckle. "But if you ever did change your mind..."

"I know. You are happy with whatever I decide."

"As my lady wishes."

Georgiana rolled her eyes good-naturedly. "You know very well I am Mrs. Harris now, and have been for many months."

They had wed as soon as Henry's bruises healed, though, to his disappointment, he remained unscarred. It couldn't have been more different from Georgiana's first wedding, or more perfect. The ceremony was held in the small stone church of the Kentish village where she had grown up, with only their siblings in attendance. She wore a muslin and lace day gown with daisies in her hair, while Henry wore his tan suit at her request. They both had tears in their eyes as they recited their vows, and when he slipped the simple gold band over her finger, it was as if a missing piece of herself had finally been snapped into place. This was followed by a long, lazy supper filled with laugher and stories and far too much wine in the back garden of their family home. The one Georgiana had given up so much to keep. But as she had stared up at the three-story home that held so many memories, both joyful and crushing, a feeling of contentment settled over her. The twisted path her life had taken had been worth the journey in the end, for it had led her back to him.

"Of course," Henry said. "I was there when we married." Then his fingers slipped under her chin to gently tilt her face up. "But I'm afraid you'll always be my lady to me," he murmured.

She gave her husband an indulgent smile. "I suppose I can endure a lifetime of your gallantry."

"It is but a paltry trade for the pleasure of your company."

Henry's amber gaze then lingered on her mouth as his eyes filled with heat. "Shall I ask Jack to take the long way home?"

Georgiana pulled him closer until their lips nearly touched. "Yes, Captain. Please do."

GO BACK TO THE
BEGINNING OF THE LEAGUE
OF SCOUNDRELS SERIES:

A ROGUE TO REMEMBER

AVAILABLE NOW

ABOUT THE AUTHOR

Emily Sullivan is an award-winning author of historical fiction set in the late Victorian period. She lives in New England with her family, where she enjoys reading about history and writing about rebellious women.

You can learn more at:
 EmilySullivanbooks.com
 Twitter: @paperbacklady
 Instagram: Paperbacklady

Fall in love with more enchanting historical romances from Forever featuring matchmaking, disguises, and second chances!

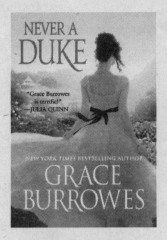

NEVER A DUKE
by Grace Burrowes

Polite society still whispers about Ned Wentworth's questionable past. Precisely because of Ned's connections in low places, Lady Rosalind Kinwood approaches him to help her find a lady's maid who has disappeared. As the investigation becomes more dangerous, Ned and Rosalind will have to risk everything—including their hearts—if they are to share the happily ever after that Mayfair's matchmakers have begrudged them both.

Follow @ReadForeverPub on Twitter and join the conversation using #ReadForever

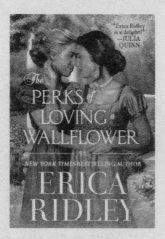

THE PERKS OF LOVING A WALLFLOWER
by Erica Ridley

As a master of disguise, Thomasina Wynchester can be a polite young lady—or a bawdy old man. Anything to solve the case—which this time requires masquerading as a charming baron. But Tommy's beautiful new client turns out to be the reserved, high-born bluestocking Miss Philippa York. with whom she's secretly smitten. As they decode clues and begin to fall for each other in the process, the mission—as well as their hearts—will be at stake…

THE HELLION AND THE HERO
by Emily Sullivan

Lady Georgiana Arlington has always done what was best for her family—even marrying a man she didn't love. Her husband's death has left her bolder—a hellion, some would say. When a mysterious enemy jeopardizes her livelihood, only one person can help: the man she left heartbroken years before. Once a penniless fortune hunter, Captain Henry Harris is now a decorated hero who could have his choice of women. Fate has given Georgie a second chance, but is it too late to finally follow her heart?

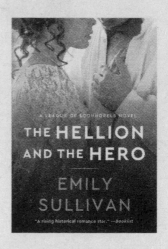

Discover bonus content and more on read-forever.com

DUKES DO IT BETTER
by Bethany Bennett

Lady Emma Hardwick has been living a lie—one that allows her to keep her son and give him the loving home she'd never had. But now her journal, the one place she'd indulged in the truth, has been stolen. Whoever has it holds the power to bring the life she's carefully built crumbling down. With her past threatening everything she holds dear, the only person she can trust is the dangerously handsome, tattooed navy captain with whom she dared to spend one carefree night.

HOW TO DECEIVE A DUKE
by Samara Parish

Engineer Fiona McTavish has come to London under the guise of Finley McTavish for one purpose—to find a distributor for her new invention. But when her plans go awry and she's arrested at a protest, the only person who can help is her ex-lover, Edward, Duke of Wildeforde. Only bailing "Finley" out of jail comes at a cost: She must live under his roof. The sparks from their passionate affair many years before are quick to rekindle. But when Finley becomes wanted for treason, will Edward protect her—or his heart?

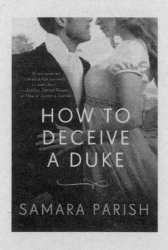

SAY YOU'LL BE MY LADY
by Kate Pembrooke

Lady Serena Wynter doesn't mind flirting with a bit of scandal—she's determined to ignore Society's strictures and live life on her own terms. But there is one man who stirs her deepest emotions, one who's irresistibly handsome, and too honorable for his own good…Charles Townshend isn't immune to the attraction between them, but a shocking family secret prevents him from acting on his desires. Only Lady Serena doesn't intend to let his propriety stand in the way of a mutually satisfying dalliance.

SEVEN NIGHTS IN A ROGUE'S BED
by Anna Campbell

Desperate to protect her only family, Sidonie Forsythe has agreed to pay her sister's debt to the notorious, scarred scoundrel dwelling within Castle Craven. But without any wealth, she's prepared to compensate him however possible—even if it means seduction. Yet instead of a monster, Sidonie encounters a man with a vulnerable soul, one that could be destroyed by the dark secret Sidonie carries. When dangerous enemies gather at the gates, can the fragile love blooming between the beauty and the beast survive?